AXE OF GOD

ROBERT N. CHAN

PublishAmerica
Baltimore

All of the characters in this book are fictitious and any resemblance to actual persons, living or dead, is purely coincidental.

First printing

ISBN: 1-4137-3931-8
PUBLISHED BY PUBLISHAMERICA, LLLP
www.publishamerica.com
Baltimore

Printed in the United States of America

To my eight-year-old son, Adam, whose imagination inspires me.

I

Only eleven percent of those recently polled correctly identified the birthplace of the president of the United States, but more than sixty-five percent responded that Saul Stein hailed from Tarsus, Turkey, and was the child of freelance terrorists. Yet, in actual fact, neither he nor his parents ever set foot in the Middle East. His self-propagated myth captured the public's imagination far more than the mundane truth that he was born in Hamtramck, Michigan, and was christened Paul Stenoski. His most cherished childhood wish had been to fit in. Neither he nor anyone around him ever dreamed that the *New York Post* would run a banner headline referring to him as "The Axe of God" while, on the same day, *The Daily News*' front page would consist of only its masthead, "The Invisible MANiac" in seventy-two-point type and a photo emphasizing his Mona Lisa smile and Charlie Manson eyes.

Saul's father, Jozef, was an atheist and a card-carrying member of Mensa. He'd been a CPA and a lawyer. Shortly before Saul was born, however, he'd lost both licenses on account of a conviction for resisting arrest after he'd offered to give a plainclothes cop a blow job in the men's room of the Youngstown, Ohio, bus station. From then on he could get employment only by lying about his past. Sooner or later the truth would ooze out, and then, yet more bitter, he would move his family to another town and try again. He never hit his son, but, worse perhaps, he was distant and uncommunicative, slow with a compliment and quick with a cutting remark. He frequently said he hadn't wanted kids and had had them just to please his wife. In one of the last conversations he had with his dad, Saul asked him if he was happy he had kids. He shrugged. "Julie was kind of dear. I miss her sometimes, but with you the jury's still out."

Saul's mother, the former Mary Poniatowski, was a statuesque peroxide blonde who talked to saints in Polish and heard them talking back. They never said a damn thing that was useful—much of it had to do with laundry detergents. She liked to clean things. She worked from time to time as a legal secretary, but in those pre-sexual-harassment days, she had a tendency to get fired when her boss's wife discovered that she was having an affair with her boss. She was a loving mother, but all her energy went to Saul's younger sister, Julie, who suffered from Down's syndrome. Julie died when Saul was fifteen, sending his mom into a depression from which she never emerged.

By the time he'd turned seventeen, Saul had lived in Hamtramck and Saginaw, Michigan; Toledo, Youngstown and Canton, Ohio; Council Bluffs, Iowa; and Nashville, Tennessee. He was an obsessive child with an intermittent spiritual bent. He was an altar boy and even felt a calling to enter the priesthood, but there were also years when he prided himself on being a pagan—a follower of his own version of various arcane forms of the ancient Greek religion. He loved magic and earned spending money entertaining at birthday parties.

His family moved to Nashville when he was nine. The neighborhood, traditionally Irish, was about half black, and race relations were spotty. It didn't help that he was one of the smaller children in his class, having skipped a grade. In addition, he enrolled mid-year—after cliques and friendships had already formed.

As he walked home from school at the end of his first week, a boy about three years older than himself grabbed his shoulder. "We need someone for our soccer game."

Saul bounced on his toes with excitement. As luck would have it, soccer was his best game—he was too small for football or hoops and didn't have the hand-eye coordination baseball required. Two teams were arrayed on the dusty field. It seemed that he should play on the Irish team, but the black team was short a man. It didn't matter to him. He'd play where needed. "Should I go over there?"

"He thinks he's a coon," the biggest white boy on the field shouted. Several of the boys doubled over and rolled in the dirt, theatrically overreacting.

Saul's gut told him to run, but he just stood there grinning like a good sport. He was dragged toward the middle of the field. He squirmed to break free but to no effect.

A whistle blew. A head rammed into the small of his back.

Then the kicking started. Saul could do little more than cover his head and face. As anyone who has ever attended an English football game knows, competitive sports tend to unite opponents in friendship.

Cleat-clad feet struck his arms, legs, torso and head. Finally, he was forced into one of the netted goals, and the game ended. Final score: a broken nose, a black eye and a bruise that seemed to cover every part of him but the soles of his feet. His testicles were swollen to the size of peaches.

When he got home, his mother was with Julie in the hospital, routine visit.

His father came home angry. There'd been an incident at work. He had a cut under his left eye.

"It wasn't my fault," Saul said before his dad had the chance to react.

"You've got to learn to accept responsibility for your own screw-ups," his father said, his self-loathing blocking affection or sympathy. "Otherwise you'll turn out like me."

"What happened?" his mother asked, when she came home.

"I don't want to go back to that school."

"You think it's hard to be a kid?" his father said, arms crossed. "Just wait until you have to earn a living,"

While Saul's understanding of irony hadn't yet developed, he suspected that his father wasn't ever completely serious and always had some unspoken agenda. Years later, when Saul would claim that his dad had been a terrorist posing as an insurance adjuster, he believed he was telling the emotional truth, if not the factual one.

"Oh, honey, come on," his mother said, before Saul had the chance to comment that even his dad rarely came home from work with broken bones. "What your father was trying to say is we're newcomers here." She stroked Saul's battered cheek. "Hard as it may be for you, it's better not to rock the boat."

"There's always something of an initiation in a new school," his father said, the corners of his mouth turning up.

"I may have provoked them," Saul stuttered. He was starting to cry, and he didn't want them to know he was crying because they'd, yet again, bitterly disappointed him. He vowed that he would never allow them to understand him, and since then he'd made it a point of honor to be mysterious—as inexplicable as his dad.

Prior to that incident, some at school had been cautiously welcoming; afterwards, they recognized that it wouldn't be in their interest to be seen as Saul's comrade.

Their house had a crawl space that he could just barely enter standing. He thought it was the only place in the world where he fit, and he began spending more and more time there. It took him weeks of hiding out there before he built up the courage to open the sealed cartons, belonging to his father, that had accompanied them on each move. The first had law books, *Black's Law Dictionary* and the like. Reading them was even more boring than doing nothing. The second contained books about hypnosis, which he taught himself with the zeal that would later come to characterize his adult endeavors.

They'd moved to Toledo by the time he'd worked his way to the third carton. It was crammed with books about ancient Greek culture and religion, which curiously, like hypnosis, were among the few subjects on which his father—an expert on everything from nuclear physics to pop culture—never opined. Saul picked one at random and began reading it just to confirm that his father was a total dork. But no. It was sort of interesting how stupid the ancients were with their silly fairy tales. He read for hours. When his mother called him for dinner, he scurried up from the basement, where the boxes were now stored, so she wouldn't learn of his secret hideout.

From time to time he read more. He liked the moldy odor and the quiet of the unfinished cellar, and didn't mind reading about the Greeks, so childlike compared to us. When he came to a volume without a cover or title page, he felt a strange compulsion to read it aloud:

> Rage—Goddess, sing the rage of Peleus' son Achilles, murderous, doomed, that cost the Achaeans countless losses, hurling down to the House of Death so many sturdy souls, great fighters' souls, but made their bodies carrion, feasts for the dogs and birds, and the will of Zeus was moving toward its end....

He shivered with excitement. It appealed to him that the gods of ancient Greece intervened in the lives of people and set their fates, but that seemed to be an insufficient reason for the thrill the passage gave him. He read it again, and a notion struck his impressionable mind like a thunderbolt from Mount Olympus. Perhaps his fate had already been fixed, and if the gods had had a hand in it, then didn't it make sense that his suffering was for a purpose, maybe even a glorious one?

His studies of the Greeks earned him eyestrain, headaches and nightmares, so when they moved to Council Bluffs, he gave them up.

However, when he was expelled from Gerald W. Kirn Junior High School for hypnotizing an elderly social studies teacher into streaking the cafeteria on Valentine's Day, he went back to the books. The discovery of a tome on ancient mystery cults turned his escapist interest into a full-blown obsession. It appealed to him that "mystery" derived from the ancient Greek word *mysteria*, meaning clandestine initiation rites.

"The Greeks had private secret religions. I'm thinking about starting one of my own," he said one night to impress his parents.

His mother dropped her fork, shot his father a dirty look, then rushed into the kitchen as if she smelled a grease fire.

His father shook his head. "Paul." He put his hand on Saul's arm, one of the few affectionate gestures that would stick in his memory. "You need to fight your unusual urges. The most important thing is to fit in."

Saul, hoping he was joking, smiled. Then he saw his father leaning back, his eyes wide and his skin stretched taut. "Dad, you look frightened," he said, his own voice shaking with fear.

His father went into the kitchen. If he didn't know him as well as he did, Saul would have thought he'd done so to comfort his wife, rather than to hide some unknowable shame.

Unlike budding psychopaths, who tend to torture animals, Saul loved them and was affectionate toward children younger than himself. His best and only friend in Saginaw, where his family had moved after Council Bluffs, was Mary Ellen Dolan, or Med, as everyone called her. His next-door neighbor, she was tall, blonde and gawky. They set up an animal hospital in her basement and were so conscientious that there were actually instances where they helped their patients. Her friendship made him feel normal, which at that stage of his life was among the best feelings he could imagine. He abandoned his Greek studies and resumed accompanying his mother to church on Sundays.

The next year, an incident involving a hypnotized school janitor filling a classroom with trash gave his mother the ammunition to persuade his fervently atheistic father that Saul needed the love, discipline and guilt of Catholic education. He didn't so much give in to her as realize that he didn't give a shit. He wished Saul luck, but hell, he had his own problems and wasn't doing well enough with them to advise anyone else. So Saul was enrolled in Shrine High School, where Med attended. She'd become distant since making the freshman cheerleading squad, but by studying her patterns, he managed to run into her frequently. Sometimes she would even treat him to her signature triple wave and mega-smile.

One afternoon, to Saul's surprise, she invited him up to her bedroom when both her parents were out. John Lennon had been assassinated four days earlier, and Saul was still grieving. An entire wall of Med's room was dedicated to John: posters, album covers, the works. Saul knew then that, even though they hadn't had an extended conversation for months, they were still kindred spirits. He loved the real music: Beatles, Rolling Stones, and Led Zeppelin, and was totally sick of the new garbage: Michael Jackson, Kool and the Gang and Queen.

Her bed was just covered with stuffed monkeys and snakes. Med sat on the corner of her bed and crossed her long legs, enticingly set off by her way-shorter-than-regulation kilt.

"Paul-o," she said. That she called him that was an undeniable sign of deep affection. She bent her head, about to confess a private fear. "I just can't seem to get trig, that sines and cosines stuff is like really a cosmic bummer. Don't you think?"

"It's easy." He hadn't felt this happy since before she'd drifted away from him, and it was an effort not to giggle. "I mean it's hard until you get the secret, then it's easy. Do you have…" He looked around the room. There were no books anywhere. "If you give me your textbook."

She took a spiral notebook out of her backpack. "It's sort of heavy, and, duh." She hit her forehead with her palm. "I left it in my locker, but here's my homework." She handed the notebook to him.

He knocked off her trigonometry, followed by her history and English, while she played *Revolver* then the *White Album* and lay on her bed chatting with her girlfriends on the phone. He'd look over, and she'd smile, maybe turn to her side. The curve from her hips to her tiny waist was mind-blowing.

When her mother came home, Med snuck Saul out and bent forward and kissed him on the forehead. "Thanks so much. God, I bet you're the smartest kid in the whole school."

Over the next month, he did her homework two or three days a week and the rest of the time fantasized about her. In his daydreams, they walked around holding hands while the other students ogled jealously. He didn't think about hardcore sex. Indeed, his understanding of the mechanics was somewhat murky and off-putting.

By January, they were again friends, and, during breaks from doing her homework, their conversation was becoming increasingly intimate.

"I hide it well, but really I'm just *such* an idiot. I like don't even know where to begin on this English paper," she confided, handing him her assignment.

"You're not an idiot. Anyway you're popular. Would you rather be a complete untouchable like me?" He'd never before mentioned his social problems to anyone, pretending instead to be unconcerned with what other people thought, and immediately regretted having done so to her.

"Once we get to college, out in the world, it will be cool to be a genius, and you'll be famous," she assured him.

Her response made him so lightheaded that he said, "I'm going to tell you a huge secret."

She sat up straight, smiling welcomingly.

"When I was a kid, I went through this sort of phase when I studied these secret religions of the ancient Greeks, and, it's complicated and I'm still a Catholic and all, but I kinda believe that my fate has been set by their gods, and—"

"I'm really, really flattered you told me that, Paul, but I don't think you should tell anyone else. It should be our secret."

She touched the tip of his nose with her forefinger, while the corners of her mouth turned up before settling into a sexy pout; Saul couldn't help falling for her.

Valentine's Day approached; it was time they went out on a date. Saul knew she'd been waiting for him to ask her out, but he, stupidly ill-at-ease as usual, kept getting tongue-tied when the chance arose. He had to act soon, because she'd begun to hang around with a group of popular jerks and, even worse, appeared to be pairing off with Jake Wilson, a football player and complete dickhead.

Knowing no Catholic ceremony that led to success with girls, Saul devoted an entire night to fasting and meditation in the fashion of the rituals of the Delphic mystery cult.

"Apollo, god of the silver bow who strides the walls of Chryse and Cilla sacrosanct. Bless my quest," he whispered as he strode through the crowd of Med's admirers. Reaching her, he said, "It's time we had a real date. Saturday night." His voice, too high pitched and loud, was beyond his control. "Let's go see *Escape from New York*."

Jake and the others, smirking, turned to stare.

Med's face reddened as she turned from Saul to Jake and then to the crowd. "I don't date pagans," she said.

That provoked wild laughter from the gathering multitude.

Jake screamed, "Pagan Paul is stoned. He's flipping out. Someone get the hall monitor. Quick!"

Finally realizing that he'd been used, Saul stuck his face close to hers. "You have no right to laugh at me," he yelled, his voice cracking. "You said you'd keep my secret." Some of his saliva landed on her cheek. He reached out to wipe it off.

She angrily knocked his hand away. She looked at the spectators, and, turning back to him, spat. She flipped her hair and sauntered off with plenty of hip sway, while the guys in the group gave each other high fives, and the girls shot him dagger eyes.

The spit burned into his right cheek. He couldn't make his feet move. Soon he was crying, much to the delight of the now-huge throng. Younger kids, freshmen, were calling him crybaby. Someone threw a teddy bear at him. Finally, a nun scolded him for making himself the center of attention—the sin of pride.

For the balance of the year, he slept twelve to fifteen hours a night and talked to as few people as possible. He prayed that things would be different in college. The conviction returned that he was marked for a special, unique and heroic destiny. If not, he was suffering without purpose, life had no reason and he should kill himself. That the idea of taking his own life repulsed him to the core of his being confirmed that a glorious fate awaited him. He wasn't a loser like his father. His life, starting terribly but ending fabulously, would be the mirror image of his dad's. If only he could make it through high school.

His freshman year at University of Michigan, he lived in East Quad. He kept to himself and took as many classes as the rules permitted. Although his intellectual tastes were eclectic, he decided that he wanted to teach the Greek classics. Yet it bothered him that teaching didn't quite seem to be a great destiny.

Friendships forming around him made him jealous, and the girls inspired lust, but the Med catastrophe had turned him off of romance. He believed himself to be too scrawny and unattractive to inspire lust in the opposite, and totally mystifying, gender. He again toyed with the idea of entering the priesthood, mostly because the vow of chastity seemed to be an elegant solution to his problems. But his studies kept him busy, and when busy he was contented enough. He spent most of his time studying and watching girls at the Ugly, the Undergraduate Library.

His roommate, Camel, was an affable long-haired dude from New Jersey, who claimed his nickname was bestowed on him in recognition of his extraordinary humping ability. Camel did wheelies on his Norton 750 over the fabled M in the center of the Diag, and he wore a heavy brass chain around the ankle of his right cowboy boot. He was the coolest guy Saul had ever met, and he seemed to like Saul. He even confided in him that his nickname actually arose out of an incident where he'd screamed, "West Quadies suck dead camels," just as a dean was taking a group of fancy alumni on a tour.

One evening, toward the end of his first year, Saul returned to his dorm room hours earlier than usual. Camel had a pound of marijuana spread out on a newspaper and, understanding that units of measurement were but another bourgeois convention for the hip to transcend, was dividing it into twenty-four one-ounce bags. Saul had never tried drugs, and his experience to date had taught him to keep a low profile. He swallowed hard. "Uh, Camel, I, uh, don't care about what you do on your own, but this could get us both into a shit-load of trouble."

"Hey, lighten up, man, it's just weed. No one gives a crap about weed. Be cool. I'll give you a lid."

"Maybe if you just didn't sell it out of our room?"

"Hey, yeah. I could rent an office." Camel's red-tinged eyes were wide with excitement. "No, like open up a store."

Saul was in a quandary. He liked Camel and didn't want to upset their pleasant relationship. Pathetic though it was, Camel was his best friend, although he doubted that Camel considered him anything more than an acquaintance. Drugs scared Saul, and it bothered him to break the law.

"Why do you do it?" Saul asked. "You don't seem to need the money." Camel's dad was one of the most distinguished dentists in all of Trenton.

Camel rubbed his chin. "Interesting question, dude. Hang around tonight. We'll discuss it in the morning."

Camel went about his business, and Saul fell asleep in the top bunk. He awoke a couple of hours later as his fantasy woman came by to procure one of Camel's skimpy ounces. Tall, thin, blonde—it seemed Saul had a definite type—and completely self-possessed, Anne Wadsworth was the star of his Statistics in Economics class. He'd been secretly lusting after her for months.

"Wanna taste some? You know, just to be sure," Camel asked her.

"Sure," she said. "But." She tilted her head toward Saul.

After a dismissive wave of his arm, Camel said, "The guy can sleep through an atomic fucking bomb or even a Clash concert or something."

Saul, taking his clue, closed his eyes and began breathing rhythmically. Anne and Camel smoked a joint. About halfway through, Camel said, "We need to conserve smoke." He took a toke, then, while holding his breath, said, "Here, put your mouth on mine, and we'll breathe it back and forth."

Saul came to understand that selling weed was an idea on a par with the wheel, movable type and the electric guitar. If only he had the guts.

At the end of the school year, Saul, Anne and Camel rented the top floor of a tumbledown house on Kinsley Street, west of campus. Listening to the two of them making love and yearning for her became the focus of Saul's social life. He simultaneously looked forward to hearing them and dreaded it. Sometimes while she and Camel were behind closed doors, he'd caress and smell the shoes she'd left in the hallway, but he abandoned the practice because the mortification outweighed the turn-on, however slightly.

Saul and Anne had several picnics in the Arboretum, and, one blissful afternoon, they went canoeing on the Huron River, known on campus as the Urine. He came to the realization that if only he could marry her all the past agonies would disappear. But if he failed—and she never gave him the slightest hint that she considered their relationship to be anything but platonic—he'd end up even more bitter and alienated than his father. At least his father was married.

For her twentieth birthday, Camel was going to make her dinner, but instead he dropped acid with a group of hippies on their way to a northern California commune and didn't make it back to the house for a couple of days.

Saul made his special organic rice and vegetables, and he and Anne shared a bottle of wine and a joint.

"You're the strangest person I ever met," she said to Saul, smiling.

"I think I'm painfully ordinary."

"You're that too," she laughed, coughing up marijuana smoke.

"I'm not used to getting high." A nervous giggle formed in the back of Saul's throat, but he managed to suppress it. "I'm going to ask you something that I'd never ask straight." Watching as if he were standing outside himself, he was appalled by how deadly serious he sounded. "Why do you put up with all this shit from a fuck-up like Camel? I mean, this isn't the first time he's just disappeared when you were counting on him. It's your goddamn birthday. You're the most beautiful, smartest—"

She put up a hand. "Please, Paul, you're embarrassing me."

"Sorry." He took the joint. "But, I need to understand."

"You need? Like, food and water?"

He nodded.

She had some wine, then shrugged. "It's just play with him."

"Oh, play. How does one get into that game? What are the rules?"

"I already know who I'm going to marry." She looked at her glass. Her face reddened. "I shouldn't've.... Now I'm really embarrassed."

"Embarrassed in front of me? No one has ever been embarrassed with me. This is the greatest day of my life. I feel like I just won the Preakness, Belmont and the Kentucky Derby."

She laughed again. "As a bettor or a jockey?"

"On foot, beating all the horses."

Laughing so hard she could hardly get the words out, she said, "I never realized how funny you are."

"It's the dope." Saul refilled her glass. "So, confide."

"You'll laugh."

"I like to laugh."

"Okay, but don't laugh too hard." She blinked a few times. "When I was home over Christmas, I got stoned out of my mind. I really don't smoke much. Anyway, I got into this made-for-TV movie, and had like this epiphany." She shook her head. "It's way too stupid."

"It's been statistically proven that made-for-TV movies bring on more religious experiences than drugs, prayer or meditation."

She giggled. "Either you should get high more often, or I should do it less." She studied the joint with elaborate seriousness, then took a toke. "I'm going to go to law school, Stanford."

"Your father's like some hotshot alum? Built a building, fucked a dean or something?"

"I'm going to meet an unreligious Jew there, and we'll get married." She hung her head. "Told you it was ridiculous, but I'm sure it's true. You know I'm not the mystic type." She tilted her head as if she'd just had an unsettling thought. "You are, though. Really, I could picture you wandering around the desert in sandals and flowing robes. Or going to the top of Burton Tower and squeezing off a few rounds." She chuckled as if she were joking.

Saul had a flash of brilliance. An epiphany? Perhaps. "Now I have a confession." He looked at the tip of his big toe poking out of a hole in his right sneaker.

Her eyes became wide with curiosity.

"Paul Stenoski isn't my real name."

"What?"

"It's the name I use, but not my given name."

"Come on."

"No. Really. I'm Saul, uh, Stein. I was born Jewish, but…I don't know. I flirted with Catholicism for a while and took this Polish name, because…it sounded Catholic, but, I mean, I'm not Catholic. So, just the other day, as a matter of fact, I decided to go back to my original name." He held out his hand. "Hi. I'm Saul Stein. Nice to meet you. I've been admiring you from afar."

After looking at it for a few seconds, she took his hand. "Anne Wadsworth." Her brow furrowed. "You are kidding, aren't you?"

Saul shook his head. It was the first outright lie he'd told in years, and it felt damn good. But as she stared at him and the silence built to an uncomfortable level, sweat pinpricked his forehead and dampened his armpits.

"You know you do sort of look Jewish." She pulled at his kinky black hair. "I always thought your complexion was too dark for a Polack." She smiled, Saul thought, to show that her remark wasn't intended as a slur. "You know who you look like?"

Saul braced himself.

"Omar Sharif."

He struggled to keep his smile confined to the boundaries of his face. "Is he Jewish?" Then he dissolved into giggles.

After he stopped, she said, "You're a good-looking guy."

"Maybe in a scrawny, hunch-shouldered sort of way."

She shrugged. "Work out. And practice walking with your shoulders back." She stood, balanced a book on her head and demonstrated, until she dissolved into giggles too, and the book crashed to the floor.

"I've been thinking about Stanford Law too."

"I thought you wanted to teach?"

"Nah, not anymore. Law will be my path to greatness."

II

Saul hung around Anne as much as she'd tolerate throughout law school. After they graduated, she got a job working in New York for Milbank & Cahill, and Saul got one with Stewart Sterling & Swain. Both were among the largest and most prestigious in the country. By the end of their first year in the city, he succeeded in wearing down her resistance. She'd later joke that he'd hypnotized her. There was no truth in that, but he did have a cabaret act based on hypnosis that ran for several months in an East Village dive, and that seemed to charm her. It was Bohemian without being too far out—"Jewish" in the best sense of the word. Also, it didn't hurt that her father loathed him, referring to him as "Pharaoh's revenge."

By the time they announced their engagement, Saul's mother had sunk so deeply into depression that the only one she ever spoke to was Saint Stanislaus. His father's response, in what would turn out to be his last conversation with his son, was "You'll regret it if you marry her, but you'll also regret it if you don't, so, I guess, you might as well."

Saul didn't have the passion for Anne that he'd had for Med, but, then again, Anne would never spit in his face. No longer a kid, thank God, he'd convinced himself that true passion could only be experienced by adolescents. He enjoyed being with her, was certainly attracted to her, and she represented the ultimate prize—acceptance. Every guy in school had wanted her, and she'd dated plenty of them, but ultimately Saul's persistence won the day. Although now a Jew who attended the occasional High Holiday service, he came to believe that she was the great destiny that his suffering had earned him. A rabbi he'd met at a party told him that such a belief was not inconsistent with Reform Judaism's non-judgmental belief system.

Her father insisted on a draconian pre-nuptial agreement, which provided that he would get nothing in the event of divorce. That didn't faze Saul. They weren't going to divorce, and, with his brilliant law career ahead of him, he had no designs on her money.

On their honeymoon in the Greek Islands, they rented a kayak to explore the area around Mykinos harbor. The rippled sand bottom was visible through twenty-five feet of placid aquamarine water. So much for Homer's wine-dark sea. They left the town behind. Solitary cedars, jagged hills and rock outcroppings. The bluest of skies accented the all-white houses. "At the next beach, let's stop for a skinny dip," the usually staid Anne suggested.

"Spectacular idea."

A flock of birds whizzed by overhead. "They're in quite a rush," she said.

Saul laughed without knowing why. "I didn't think I could ever be this happy."

The hair on Saul's arms tingled. A dull hum filled his ears. It was followed by an aggressive silence. He smelled ozone. Anne's eyes widened. Saul wanted to put her at ease, but the stillness had robbed him of the ability to speak. He rested his hand on hers.

The wind hit them with the force of a charging bull. The sky turned black. An explosion of thunder shook the boat. With each burst of lightning, the island shrank and the sea grew.

"We've got to get to shore," Anne yelled, her long, wet hair pasted to her body.

They both paddled as hard as they could, although neither had any idea which direction would take them to land.

A wave broke over them. Saul grabbed Anne's arm, then threw his weight to his right, stopping the boat from capsizing. The next wave, bigger yet, took his paddle. In an instant it was too far from them for there to be any hope of its retrieval. Another breaker tore Anne's paddle out of her hands.

"Grab the sides and hang on," Saul shouted.

Here was the rage of Poseidon so inadequately described in *The Odyssey*. It wasn't a storm but retribution of the gods. A thunderbolt crashed so close that the water sizzled as if the fires of Hades were rising to the surface.

Anne began screaming. Saul was terrified by how far away she sounded. He wrapped his legs around her waist, then pulled her back so she was lying on top of him. He wrapped her hands around the gunnels and then his arms around her. "We'll just have to wait it out," he yelled, his mouth but inches from her ear. "I love you." He felt her shaking with cold and fear.

When the tempest finally passed over them, the warm sun was setting on *aqua incognita*. Paddling with their hands, they arrived at a deserted beach surrounded by sheer cliffs. One of their paddles floated to shore. They spent the night under more stars than either of them had ever seen—each constellation as visible to them as to the ancients.

That night Saul had a dream. In it he awoke before dawn. Anne was still sleeping soundly. He could hardly believe his luck in marrying her. After watching her in the moonlight for a while, he felt an otherworldly compulsion to approach, then to climb the cliffs, although he hadn't climbed anything since he'd been a kid. He was naked, and, by the time he reached the top, he was dripping with blood and sweat. With the first rays of the rising sun illuminating his face, he was standing in the ruins of an ancient shrine. It was just a few broken columns in a semi-circle and tiles that had been part of a mosaic floor, but it offered an incredible view of the Aegean, not a boat or sign of human habitation anywhere.

He heard a disembodied voice. "So, it's Saul Stein now?"

Then he saw a vision backlit by the sun. Even without his studies of Greek mythology, he would have known it to be Apollo. "I have chosen you for a great and glorious destiny, to transform the world by your good deeds," Apollo said. "But first, you must kill your wife."

Saul's knees buckled. "When men talk to gods, it means they're devout, but when they hear gods speaking to them, they're schizophrenic."

Apollo's smile burned Saul's cornea.

He told himself that Apollo's words were just a test, like Yahweh's command to Abraham that he sacrifice Isaac.

"True gods don't test or equivocate," Apollo said. "You'll do our bidding when you come to find your life with her to be unbearable."

Saul woke. His eyes hurt as if he'd been staring into the sun. Anne was leaning over him. "What happened? Your knees, your stomach, they're all cut up."

He looked. Some of the cuts had yet to scab over. "I must have rubbed against the sand in my sleep, or maybe cut myself during the storm."

* * *

As a wedding present, Anne's father bought Anne a fabulous apartment overlooking Central Park. Married to her, working in a prestigious firm, and living like a young prince, Saul had left his youthful humiliation behind.

Over time the grind of big firm law practice became tedious for Saul, but not for Anne, who was thriving. As a young associate, he was assigned all the scut work, and he spent weeks on end in dreary file rooms reviewing tens of thousands of documents with no purpose but to add to the firm's billable hours.

He was at the firm for three years before he got the chance to write his first brief. It was for Milt Jameson, a charming inventor manqué constantly enmeshed in patent litigation and creditor avoidance. The partner in charge, the redoubtable Harrison Schmidt, saw the case as a loser—a "steaming turd" in firm parlance. He'd given it to Saul so he could gain experience on Milt's dime. Well, tens of thousands of his dimes.

Saul's brief got the entire case against Milt dismissed, costing the firm significant future billings. Milt took Saul to Firebird for lunch to celebrate—caviar interspersed with shots of vodka.

"So you like working for SS&S?" Milt asked.

"Sure. It's one of the best firms in the country." Saul was taken with the restaurant's opulent czarist atmosphere. His forebears might have served a Cossack lord in a place resembling this.

"I'd be bored out of my gourd."

"Well." Saul smiled. "There's some of that."

"Can't be very edifying being Schmidt's dogsbody." Milt downed a shot of vodka, waiting, it seemed, for Saul to respond.

Saul put a minute amount of caviar on a piece of black bread.

"I've got a regular stream of litigation—"

"I know," Saul said. "The firm really values—"

"Sure they do. Their assigning you to my case proves it."

Saul's face grew hot.

Milt handed him a shot of vodka. Saul chugged it. It burned his esophagus and made him cough. All in all, chugging straight vodka didn't seem to him to be quite the pleasurable experience that it apparently was for Milt.

"What are your dreams?" Milt asked.

"I..." Saul realized that he no longer had any and that he missed them. "I'm pretty content as is. I suppose I'd like to be a partner."

"Pretty exciting, that. You know there are litigation partners at SS&S, most of them in fact, who've never tried a case? Spend their whole careers carrying bags for the big guys and giving shit to those below them."

"And you?" Saul shifted uncomfortably. "Your dreams?"

"I'm working on something that will change the world."

"Talk around the office is that you've been doing that forever; when one idea fails, or gets you sued, you go on to the next. Same optimism." Saul regretted the words as soon as they'd slipped from his mouth. He wouldn't have said them if he wasn't half in the bag. He gulped down some water.

"Hope is the key to life. It's not achievement that yields pleasure, it's the pursuit of happiness." Milt spooned almost half an ounce of one-hundred-and-eighty-buck-an-ounce caviar onto a tiny piece of black bread and stuffed it into his mouth.

Was Saul happier now than when he was so fervently pursuing Anne? His brain was too fogged for him to know for sure, but it wasn't a clear yes. What the hell were his dreams?

"So, what's the office scuttlebutt about my romantic life?" Milt asked, caviar dotting his tongue.

Saul turned his palms up and shrugged.

"Please, Saul. Just for this lunch, let's assume I'm not an idiot."

"Well, someone compared your love life to the *Picture of Dorian Gray*. As you get older, they get younger, blonder and bustier."

Milt laughed. "Set up your own practice. I'll keep you busy half time, cover your entire overhead, plus a hundred and fifty grand a year. Plus bonuses based on results."

Saul laughed. Milt didn't join in.

"I guess it depends on two things." Milt brushed errant fish eggs from the sides of his mouth. "If you have an entrepreneurial spirit, and if you believe in yourself. What I'm proposing has to be even more fun than eating Harrison Schmidt's shit. And you'll have half your time free to build a practice and make your reputation."

"I'm flattered." To say the least. He couldn't wait to call Anne. "But, I mean we've both been drinking."

"Hey, I knew you wouldn't go for it sober." He handed him about seventy bucks' worth of caviar perilously perched on a piece of black bread.

"I suppose if it doesn't work out, I could always go back to SS&S." Saul hadn't meant to speak out loud.

"I hope you'll grow out of that kind of chickenshit thinking."

"I'll consider it. Not growing out of it, but, you know, what you propose. So graciously propose. Of course I'll need to discuss it with my wife." And she would definitely nix it as too chancy.

"Great." Milt beamed. "Take all the time you need." He looked at his watch. "It's now one thirty. Let's say you get back to me by three."

Saul laughed.

Milt stuck out his hand. Saul shook it.

He called Anne as soon as he got back to the office, and she told him to go for it. "You'll succeed at anything you put your mind to."

After getting off the phone with her, he took the elevator from thirteen to twenty-four, then climbed the Stairway to Heaven, the spiral staircase that led to offices of the high poobahs of the partnership. Like the pigs in *Animal Farm*, some partners were more equal than others. He told Harrison Schmidt's secretary that he'd like to see him.

"About?" She looked at Saul as if he were something the cleaning staff had neglected to remove from the carpet.

"Personal."

She shook her head. "Try again."

"I just had lunch with Mr. Jameson, and he proposed…Well, I need to report it to Mr. Schmidt right away."

She squinted at Mr. Schmidt's appointments diary. "He's booked all week, but he can squeeze you in at six Thursday next. If you don't mind talking to him while he changes into his tuxedo. He's got another one of those awards dinners." She apparently didn't approve of awards dinners.

Saul stood, not quite sure of what to do next.

Schmidt emerged from his office and, ignoring Saul, gave his secretary a mark-up of a letter and relayed a series of instructions about calls she was to make for him and how to deal with expected callers. Then he noticed Saul. He furrowed his brow. "Steve, uh, Saul. What do you want?" He strode away, taking long fast steps. "Walk me to the men's room," he commanded.

Saul realized that coming to speak to his august majesty drunk was a mistake, but inertia carried him forward. "Well, sir, uh, Milt Jameson took me out to lunch and proposed that I go out on my own representing him part time, and I was wondering. I mean, I just wanted to tell you. You know, complete the circle of communication." Saul heard how fast he was speaking but couldn't slow down. "Obviously, I'm not really thinking about doing it. I mean not really. But it did sound like something that I needed at least to consider. I mean subject to your—"

"You're fired. Don't expect a recommendation." Schmidt paused at the door of the partners-only john. "As we told you when you joined the firm, we expect absolute loyalty. To even think about poaching a firm client…." He curled his lip in disgust.

"Sir?" Saul bowed his head.
"There's nothing more to say."
"Be careful in there. Don't get your dick caught in your zipper."

III

Saul's office had no window and barely enough room for a file cabinet, desk and chair. His legal career, in the decade since he accepted Milt's offer, could be charted by the ever-decreasing sizes of his offices. While he didn't mind having Anne pay for his clothing—with what she made she'd never miss it—it wouldn't do to ask her to support his practice. Each morning he had to go through a ritual of controlled breathing in order to avoid the three horsemen of his personal apocalypse: rage, helplessness and humiliation.

His first two years on his own had been pretty good, but then Milt ran out of money. It had now been over a year since the man had paid him anything, and, for several years before, he'd only paid a fraction of what he owed. Saul had watched his law school classmates achieve wealth and recognition; even his own wife, damn it. He was at least as capable as any of them, but inexplicably, he couldn't attract clients, and in the law business—as everyone who practiced in New York City recognized, it was no longer a profession but a cut-throat business—the sole gauge of merit was annual billings.

Anne repeatedly told him that satisfaction only comes from within, infuriating advice from someone who had so much come to her from without. Also, she had the tendency to utter banalities such as "you catch more flies with honey than you do with vinegar," and to do so with the solemnity of a newscaster announcing the death of a pop star.

Although Saul had been loath to admit it, they'd had their difficulties recently. He'd allowed his despair over his failures and his resentment over her successes to carry over into their marriage.

"So, what do you have on tap today?" Anne had asked a few mornings back after they'd made love, trapping him in a conversation he would've preferred to have avoided. Until then, he had managed to put out of his mind that, in but a few hours, he'd be attending yet another session of an interminable arbitration.

"Same as yesterday. Rivka will be whispering inane suggestions and coughing and sneezing all over me, as I try to cross-examine her former best friend and business partner," he said. "How about you?"

"Still the General Electric reorg." She smiled. "Should be a fun day. Our team is really coalescing."

Success, like everything else in her life, came so effortlessly to Anne that she believed herself to be totally unambitious. After only six years with her firm, she'd been offered a partnership—two years ahead of schedule. She rejected the offer on the ground that several of the more senior associates were more deserving. When it had been offered for the third time, and she finally accepted, the offer had been sweetened to be all the more lucrative. She flowed through life as naturally as water, except that, defying all rules of nature, she flowed uphill. Saul was becoming convinced that the gods—in whom he no longer believed—had given her success just to torture him.

"Why don't you throw that darn Rivka out of your office?" she asked. "She hasn't paid you in months."

"She keeps stringing me on with promises." He got out of bed. "You're right. I should." Easy for her to say. When she represented General Electric on multibillion-dollar deals, payment of legal fees wasn't a problem. However, for Saul Stein, stuck with piddling matters for obnoxious people, everything was a problem; even his own clients using germ warfare on him.

"You need to be more confident," she said. "You're a brilliant lawyer."

"I've got to—" He pointed toward the bathroom.

"You're too negative," she said, as if she hadn't noticed that he was standing on the bathroom floor, doorknob in hand. "You've got to learn how to project more optimism. I don't mean fake it. I mean make it part of your inner being."

"You see the world as a fundamentally fair and decent place. I don't," he said. They weren't all that different from each other, but their experiences were. As a result, she'd come to view the world through rose-colored glasses, while his were shit-colored, and, he feared, growing opaque.

"You sound like you're accusing me of something," she said.

He opened his mouth but didn't respond. What was the use? His mind operated on a bleak ironic frequency that she never heard, and good for her that she didn't. He wished he could be more like her. He planned to tune out those frequencies. He'd made several appointments with a doctor to discuss antidepressants, but he'd broken all of them claiming that he was "too depressed." Now, however, painfully aware that he was drifting away from his wife, he vowed to keep the next one.

"I've been thinking," she began.

As a small step in the right direction, Saul resisted commenting on the inherent danger in that process.

"You should consider converting," she continued, sitting up.

"What?" he said, his voice two octaves higher than normal.

"You haven't been in a synagogue for years, and you'd benefit from some religion in your life." After three beats, her shoulders slumped, in disappointment presumably, because he failed to respond. "It would be nice to be able to be with you in heaven."

It was inconceivable to Saul that the marketplace valued her services at almost a million a year. "So, God created billions of Catholics, Moslems, Hindus and Buddhists, but only like twenty million Episcopalians get through the pearly gates? What, the rest get day passes to serve as angelic grooms and valets?"

"Everything seems stupid to a nihilist."

Saul shut the bathroom door.

"You know anyone looking for a tax associate?" she asked, ignoring his attempt to cut off the conversation.

"No." Not wanting to talk through the door, he opened it.

"Ruth Morrel isn't working out." She furrowed her brow. "I'd so much rather place her somewhere than just let her go. This economy isn't the best in which to be out searching for a job."

"You really care about what might happen to a jerk-off whose incompetence made your own life harder for the last year and a half?"

"Of course I do!"

"Yeah. Of course."

"This morning was wonderful. I'm still all tingly."

"As usual," Saul said, knowing she was as deaf to irony as she was blind to the darkness in the world. "If you can wait just five minutes, we can share a cab downtown. Just let me—" He again closed the bathroom door.

He noticed the pregnancy testing kit in the trash. He took it out, turning it in his hands to examine it from every angle. Nothing Schliemann discovered in Troy was as beautiful or intriguing.

He bounded out of the bathroom and hugged her with such passion that she said, “You must’ve had one heck of a bowel movement.”

Grinning, he pointed to the box.

They embraced again. “I love you so.” Saul’s voice cracked and tears of joy ran down his cheeks. Everything was going to be great again. He would overlook Anne’s success, perfection and sunny world view. As faults went they weren’t so bad.

But, he realized sitting in his office, a few days after learning Anne was pregnant, he still needed to do something about his career. His only significant client now, Rivka Feld, hadn’t paid him in months. At least Milt Jameson lavished flowery praise on him, and his creatively presented promises *sounded* sincere. However, Saul was angry at Milt for not calling or even returning his calls for weeks. Could things have gotten so bad that even his non-paying clients were firing him? If he’d had anything better to do, he would have thrown Milt out of the office long ago, but he’d thought it important to look busy. Yet was he even looking busy if no one was there to see it?

Milt’s cases, unlike the others Saul was handling, involved interesting issues and adversaries from the largest and most prestigious law firms in the country. Saul was adept at using the big firms’ weight against them and always emerged victorious. He was charmed by Milt’s capacity to hold on to a dream in the face of reality, hope triumphing over experience. In spite of overwhelming evidence that he was a scatterbrained dreamer, Milt still continued to work on invention after invention, each of which, he appeared to believe, would turn his fortunes around, permitting him to pay Saul’s bills with a substantial bonus.

His reverie was interrupted by a FedEx delivery, a letter from Milt:

Dear Saul,

When you read this, I’ll be dead, heroin overdose. I have inoperable brain cancer. I’m fine with my decision, so please don’t let it bother you. In inadequate appreciation of your friendship and brilliant work holding off my creditors so I could pursue women and my inventions in peace, I have made you my executor and sole heir. You’ll find my affairs to be in perfect disorder. I enclose my will and a comprehensive list of assets and liabilities. There’s also a safe deposit box at Morgan

Guaranty, 526 Fifth Avenue. You probably ought to get there before the state taxing authorities put a hold on it.

Always,
Milt

Milt dead! Saul stared at the wall, surprised that he was so affected by the news. It hurt behind his eyes. It wasn't that they were so close, but he had developed an affection for the guy and his relentless optimism.

It turned out that Milt had a negative net worth. Saul went to Milt's bank with no expectations beyond the hope that leaving the confines of his office would allow him to shake his gloomy thoughts and instead concentrate on his joy over the coming child and his efforts to be a more loving husband. The safe deposit box contained two keys and a Post-It sticker with an address in Queens and the notation "Storage locker C473." Saul heaved the keys against the wall of the bank cubicle. As much as he already missed Milt, he wasn't about to get sucked into yet another one of his frolics.

Anne and her friends and clients had lost millions investing in Milt's "smart fabrics," designed to change weight and color depending on the ambient temperature, humidity and wind speed. They even sort of worked, but sort of wasn't good enough if you found yourself sitting in a sweltering subway car in a chartreuse expedition-weight outfit. No more.

* * *

Curiosity got the better of Saul, as Milt undoubtedly knew it would. He took the Number 7 Train to Hunters' Point Avenue and walked northeast, the prosperous light-manufacturing area turning into an industrial slum. When he was propositioned by two hookers so superannuated that he thought they were going to ask for directions to the Medicaid office, he knew he'd reached the neighborhood where Milt's storage facility was located.

The decrepit loft building displaying the sign: "Condemned by order of the NYPD." It didn't appear that the police had blocked the entrance. Saul tried the keys. After enough jiggling and body English to build up a sweat, one worked. The rust-encrusted door creaked open as a herd of cockroaches scurried for cover.

He stepped inside a crepuscular anteroom the size of the guest bathroom in Saul's, or rather Anne's, apartment. When his eyes adjusted, he put his face up to a screen similar in size and shape to that of his laptop. A light blinked. A few seconds later, "Place fingertips here" flashed on the screen.

Saul complied. *Ignore this high-tech build-up*, he told himself. Milt had been all style, no substance.

A previously hidden door slid open, revealing a spotless well-lit hallway lined with storage boxes, ranging in size from slightly bigger than a breadbox to that of a Mini Cooper. C473 was one of the smaller ones. Saul inserted the key that hadn't worked on the outside door, and a corpse-sized box slid out of the wall like a body on a mortuary slab.

Saul hesitated, then closed his eyes and lifted the top. He opened them a few seconds later, expecting to see Milt lying there.

Inside was a peculiarly heavy suit consisting, not just of jacket and pants, but also gloves, boots, face mask and hood. Wrapped inside it was an axe. An axe?

A note in Milt's erratic hand read:

> *Saul, my greatest invention is yours. It isn't patented, and there's no record of my creating it. This storage facility does not have your name. When you remove the contents from the box, your retinal scan and fingerprint info will automatically erase. I'm sure you'll be at least equally clever in your use of my gizmo.*

Saul tried on the suit. It fit as if it had been made for him. Some sort of biohazard outfit? It seemed to be the last of Milt's impractical jokes. He waved his arms trying to fly, but he didn't leave the ground. He slammed himself into the wall. It hurt. He ran down the hall. He did not achieve Olympian speed. He went back to the box. No instructions, of course. Sticking his hand inside one of the pockets, he discovered a switch. He hesitated but then turned it on. Nothing happened.

Then he saw his arms, or rather didn't see them. They weren't there. Neither was the rest of him. Excitement surged through him. His laughter echoed off the hard surfaces. Laughter? He hadn't laughed much lately. The room was no longer creepy, but beautiful. He was not just invisible, but also…what was it? He felt different. It took him a few minutes to realize that the doubts and insecurities, which had become so habitual that he'd come to hardly notice them, had disappeared. It was like being in a room all day with the constant hiss of a ventilation system in the background, then having it shut off and being acutely conscious of the unaccustomed silence.

He removed the suit and sat cross-legged on the floor, examining the material, a sort of dotted plastic. He placed it up against the wall then held it a foot away. To check it out in different light conditions, he put it back in the box and closed the lid until only a sliver of light shined in; then he held it up to a window.

He put it on again, and he again seemed to disappear. After some thought, he theorized that the suit was made of wafer-thin LEDs imbedded with tiny cameras that displayed ever-changing pictures of what was going on behind them. Just as the eye perceives the many flickering pixels of the TV screen as a single image, people looking at him would see a unified picture of whatever was behind him. In effect, they'd see right through him.

His boots were cushioned so they made almost no sound when he walked, and the suit featured built-in adjustable hearing aids and magnifying lenses. Pretty damn cool, but what could he do with it? He was well past the age when strolling into women's locker rooms had appeal.

The axe was also covered with the same material and had its own on-off switch. An invisible axe? Perhaps he could be an invisible fireman. The old Saul would have tested the suit in his apartment and never worn it after that, but this new energized Saul left the facility wearing the suit.

He strolled a few blocks. None of the pedestrians he passed appeared to notice him, not that there was anything unusual about that. He felt increasingly empowered, and that *was* unusual. A premonition was growing with each step that something momentous was about to happen, something even more so than his astounding transparency. Was he really invisible? Couldn't be, but if not...was this what it felt like to be insane? An objective experiment was called for.

He came to Mulligan's, a rundown Irish bar. He strolled in and sat in a booth across from a young couple. The man, weighing in at about two-fifty, had a shaved head, and his lips, chin and nose were pierced. The woman, barely a hundred pounds, had orange hair and was liberally tattooed. "Get outta here," she said.

Saul froze. He was visible. Calm down, he told himself. It's hardly unusual to be visible.

"No, you go," her companion said to her. They each turned away from the other. The woman crossed her arms. The man fixed his lips into a snarl. Neither noticed Saul.

He wouldn't have had a clue about how to handle this situation in real life, but with the suit on, he wasn't in real life. He reached his leg under the table and stroked the woman's calf, so gently that it would barely tickle and would feel to her like skin, not his plastic boot. The corners of her mouth turned up. Saul did it again, and her face lit up with pleasure. She uncrossed her arms. He then did the same to her companion, who, in response, turned to her and said, "Look, I'm sorry. Okay?"

"Yeah." She fluttered her hands as if trying to dispel a cloud of noxious fumes. "I am too."

The man kissed her.

Saul smiled. His secondary motivation in becoming a lawyer, coming after his desire to fit into Anne's fantasy, had been to help people—something he'd had precious little opportunity to do in recent years. He'd forgotten how good it felt to be of service, and to do it anonymously made it even better. He recalled the pleasure he'd had as a kid when he and Med actually succeeded in helping a suffering creature. Perhaps he'd found his calling.

Maybe being a terrific father and husband and a secret benefactor was the great destiny that he'd been promised on his honeymoon. He found it curious that that promise, seemingly from Apollo himself, popped into his mind now after lying dormant for so long. He had the sensation—more a feeling than a thought—that his suit wasn't just from Milt but had come to him via divine intervention.

Saul noticed the Budweiser clock on the wall. If he hurried, he could make Evensong at St. John the Divine, the largest Gothic cathedral in the world, almost hidden on 112th Street and Amsterdam Avenue. He thought he should have been able to come up with something more exciting to do when invisible, but since he didn't, he took the subway back to Manhattan. Although now a determinedly irreligious Jew, he'd been taking guilty pleasure in sneaking out of the office for the service. Episcopal services, having always been conducted in English, struck Saul as more authentic than the bowdlerized English-language pabulum currently served up in the Catholic churches. He liked the boys' choir. It pleased him to imagine that the participants led spiritual, serene lives, so different from the horror of his own childhood.

He sat on the subway trying to be inconspicuous, although invisible was inconspicuous by definition. Luckily the car was not crowded, so there was little danger of someone brushing into him or, worse, sitting on him. Three extra-large-sized toughs strode loose limbed through the car. They stopped at a twenty-something woman listening to an iPod. One ripped it from her. The others chuckled. They gave each other high fives and slapped fists.

The other passengers averted their eyes or concentrated intently on what they were reading.

"Give it back," Saul commanded, much to his own surprise.

The three turned in the direction of the affront, dead eyes seething. They looked at each other then back in Saul's direction. They straightened, losing some of their swagger.

"Give it back to her," Saul repeated with as much deep-voiced authority as he could muster. "Now!"

They looked perplexed, then scared.

"Now!" he said quietly. His voice was more compelling, he thought, when he spoke quietly.

The mugger returned the iPod.

"Apologize," Saul commanded.

No reaction.

"Apologize!" Saul whispered.

"I'm sorry," the mugger said. Then he and his companions rushed to the next car.

The woman mouthed "thank you" in Saul's general direction and then looked at the ceiling.

In the church, listening to the young voices of the choir and meditating on the smell of the incense and the deep blue light that shined through the stained-glass windows, Saul drifted. In his next conscious thought, he realized the service was almost over. He'd been praying, not asking God for something, not even forming words, but trying to communicate with God on the most primal of all levels. He was transported to another place, somewhere where he almost could unlive his youth. It felt as if his senses had been heightened—by the suit? The alternative was that he had achieved enlightenment, and he considered that to be the less likely explanation.

As he exited by the side door, he saw a group of boys choosing sides for a football game on the church grounds. One, the shortest and scrawniest, had his eyes closed, hands clasped, praying.

"May I at least watch?" The boy's voice cracked. "Maybe someone will get hurt or have to leave early, or something."

The biggest kid said, "Over there on the steps." He pointed. "And keep your trap shut."

The boy, head bent, shuffled over to the designated losers' area, where he began sobbing.

"Nothing's ever as good or as bad as it seems," Saul said, sitting next to the boy. If, at that moment, he could have had one wish granted, it would have been for this child to be spared the pain that he himself had suffered.

The lad didn't answer, but at least he stopped crying.

"You're just being tested for a greater glory," Saul continued.

"Yeah, right." The boy didn't turn to look at him.

"You got another five years of this. Then fifty, during which you'll be more successful, smarter and happier than any of them."

The boy looked in Saul's direction, then up, behind him and even at his feet. Confusion etched on his face, he turned back toward Saul.

"Five bad for fifty good," Saul said. "Not a bad deal."

The boy's mouth dropped open, and his eyes bugged out.

"You know who I am?" Saul asked, giving his voice a portentous bass timbre.

The boy nodded hesitantly.

"You understand that these little humiliations are just to toughen you up?"

The boy again opened his mouth, but no words came out.

"Tell them that if they don't let you play, you're going to take the ball and go home," Saul commanded.

The boy swallowed hard. Saul repeated his directive.

The boy walked over to the sidelines and, composing his face as if he were about to deliver a Shakespearean soliloquy, conveyed the message.

"You and what army?" the biggest boy asked to the delight of his easily amused companions.

"God," the little one said.

Saul strolled over to the huddle. The bully told the quarterback, "I'm gonna slant out right, then cut left." He indicated his path with his finger on his chest. "Lead me for a change, turkey breath."

Saul jogged to where the bully had said he wanted the ball to be thrown. He tripped the receiver and intercepted. Holding the ball high, he ran toward the sidelines, then passed it to his little friend, who caught it and ran like hell. By the time the others recovered sufficiently to give chase, he was long gone.

Saul liked playing God. He felt so damned good that he decided to go to the place where he always felt the most intimidated.

IV

Still invisible, Saul got off the elevator at the 40th floor lobby, walked past the receptionist and stood in the huge under-furnished reception area, where a group of Asian businessmen whispered among themselves. He admired the view, from the oversized picture windows, across midtown Manhattan, and all the way south to the Statue of Liberty. Then he descended the majestic interior staircase, taking note of the huge Lichtenstein, not one of his best—but the point was to impress, not to make an artistic statement. He sauntered down the wide hallway, stepping lightly on the antique Persian runners that graced the center of the bleached oak floors. The art, etchings and lithographs by the impressionist masters was of no better quality than the art upstairs. Wealth and power, Saul noted, rarely accompanied taste.

Anne wasn't in her office so he went in to wait. He sat on the couch, but, realizing he was making a noticeable impression, chose one of the hard client chairs. The view, over the East River, Queens, and out to LaGuardia, Kennedy, and Long Island, was the equal of the one from reception. True to Anne's pathologically understated style, her office was furnished with standard firm-issued desk, chairs and couch. The only impressive thing in it was the "glass menagerie"—delicate crystal shelves groaning with Lucite cubes, each embedded with a prospectus or "tombstone," the ad in the *Wall Street Journal* announcing a merger or new public stock or bond offering. She'd been the lead tax partner on the biggest, most challenging corporate law matters in the country. Her success was the mirror of his failure, held up to him by the gods to torment him. He'd watched her inexorable rise to the top of their profession, while he fell further and further. He must've spent well over a year in cumulative time staring at the walls of his office, hoping for the phone to ring, and all that time his office walls were literally closing in on him. Why was he a failure and most everyone he knew from his law school class, even the real dullards, relative successes? The gods.

He didn't remember any time in the preceding five years when he'd had a thought involving "the gods" intervening in his life. Yet this was the third one he'd had today. Odd.

Anne strolled in and checked her e-mail while taking her seat behind her desk and simultaneously accessing voicemail. As usual, Saul was struck by her beauty and amazed that she was his wife. She wore a navy-blue suit from Macy's and a white, man-tailored cotton shirt. Her only jewelry was a half-carat engagement ring and wedding band, and she wore virtually no makeup. Other than an occasional haircut and regular brushing, she never did anything with her hair. Someone with a high six-figure income and eight-figure net worth had no right to dress like she did and still look so infuriatingly gorgeous.

In reaching for a pen, she knocked over the simply framed photo of the two of them on their honeymoon about to embark on their fateful Mykonos kayak venture. Sitting in Anne's office under the influence of his invisible suit, Apollo's appearance didn't seem quite so farfetched to Saul. If he could be invisible, why couldn't Apollo be visible? Plato himself commented on the Ring of Gyges which rendered its wearer invisible.

To his annoyance, Anne didn't bother to right the picture. He gazed at the photographic image of himself staring up at him. Muscular and darkly handsome, with black curly hair and eyes such a dark brown that they sometimes appeared to be black, he certainly was no longer the awkward, scrawny kid Med had spat upon. He looked to be almost a proper match for Anne—her physical opposite, but in the way that makes people say that opposites attract. They were sitting, so their difference in height wasn't apparent. Neither of them had changed much in the ensuing years, except that she'd come to sparkle with the glow of success, and he'd begun to fade into the shade of failure.

His fortieth birthday, just a few months earlier, had hit him far harder than he'd expected. He'd barely noticed any deterioration in his physical prowess, but to have accomplished so little at his age galled him beyond measure, and the ever-present success of his wife only made his failure more maddening.

He was now too old to take comfort from the story, recounted by Suetonius, of Julius Caesar, in his mid-thirties and still a mid-level functionary, sobbing at the feet of a statue of Alexander the Great over his own lack of accomplishment. Worse, he'd noticed in the mirror his father's dark circles under his eyes and his father's frown lines around his mouth. Drifting into the black hole of his dad's existence was his worst nightmare. It was even worse than the all-encompassing depression of his mother. In an odd way she seemed almost happy to be depressed.

If he had killed, as Apollo had commanded, would he by now be reveling in the appreciation of a grateful populace? he asked himself, a playful intellectual exercise. Would a legitimate god have demanded that he kill as the price for the power to do good? Zeus himself demanded that Agamemnon sacrifice his daughter in exchange for fair winds to Troy, Saul recalled. Also, murdering to save men's souls had been a tenet of Christian doctrine for well over a millennium, put into effect and carried out by prelates who had spent their lives studying and meditating on the Holy Scriptures. To make an omelet one had to break eggs. So said respected theologian Vladimir Ilyich Lenin.

He shook his head. These weird thoughts were an anomaly, perhaps, brought on by the bizarre suit. His great destiny was to be a father. And his professional difficulties? His lack of business would allow him more time to stay home with his son. He'd achieve greatness by being the best father and husband that he was capable of being. His son would never have to suffer as he did. His love for Anne welled up inside him. He was damn lucky to have her, and it was about time he began showing her how much he appreciated her.

C. Everett Brewster, a litigation partner of Anne's whom Saul had met a couple of times and unaccountably loathed, knocked several times on her open door. Shave and a haircut, two bits. Saul wondered how Brewster could pull off something so uncool and still seem to be with it? He wore a charcoal-gray, pinstripe, three-piece suit, with a gold chain in the vest, white shirt and crimson and white polka-dot bow tie. The outfit would have looked silly on Saul, but it suited the tall, graceful patrician. Elder Brewster, the first Brewster on these shores, Anne had told Saul, had not been a mere passenger, but the chaplain on the *Mayflower*.

She glanced up from her computer, gave him her game-show-contestant wave and smiled a little too warmly for Saul's taste. Saul wondered if that smile had given Brewster the wrong idea about Anne. She was so naïve that she didn't understand male lust.

"G.E. has a claim against Citibank," Brewster said, taking a seat on the couch. "Growing out of a complex derivatives transaction, potentially big damages. We're conflicted out, of course, having worked for both companies. So are most of the first-rank firms. I was thinking of referring it to Saul."

Wow! Saul had had the feeling that something great would happen, but this was beyond great. This invisible suit was phenomenal. Stop! It had nothing to do with the suit. Maybe. Well, who cared? A case like that could keep him busy for years and open up connections that could, at long last, finally make his career. He grinned. Now he could be a successful lawyer, husband and father—the normal life he'd always wanted. He reminded himself that he would have to sound surprised when Anne gave him the news.

Staring at Brewster as she used to gaze at Saul, she said, "I don't know."

Saul sat bolt-upright.

She continued, "I just don't think it looks right to send a lucrative case to the spouse of a partner."

Only Anne could say something like that and truly believe it, Saul thought.

"From what you've told me, he's very competent," Brewster said. "Do I remember correctly that he was number one in your class at Stanford?"

"Oh, he's sharp as a tack."

Anne's cliché made Saul wince. And she was pulling down eight hundred fifty grand a year, while he was barely covering his office rent. Could that happen in a just or fair world?

"Well, it's your call," Brewster said, standing. Any man seeing how he was staring and smiling stupidly would have recognized his dishonorable intentions, and, Saul thought, women were yet more sensitive to that sort of thing.

She scrunched up her nose, looking all too cute. "I don't think it's a good idea, but I'll tell Saul you thought of him." Anne's smile was as close to a come-on as she ever came.

Saul's stomach clenched in rage. His face was hot. His temples throbbed.

"Okay, later then." Brewster touched her hand affectionately, and she squeezed his. As he stepped away, he threw her a kiss.

She responded in kind. From a certain kind of woman, it could have been a meaningless flirtation or playful gesture, but Anne wasn't frivolous and hadn't been playful for some time.

Saul reminded himself that just a few days ago they'd learned that Anne was pregnant. He was being paranoid. She wouldn't cheat on him now, and, in truth, would never have.

She motioned for Brewster to come closer. When he did, she yanked on his hand and began performing a vigorous and most un-Anne-like fellatio on three successive fingers. She didn't stop until Brewster moaned. Her eyes drifted to Brewster's raging hard-on. She smiled. "Later," she said.

Saul's insides burned. Pain shot into his extremities and ricocheted back. His vision blurred. He started to hyperventilate. He tried to control his breathing.

Brewster patted her still-flat tummy as a proud papa might. She leaned back thrusting her mid-section forward, offering herself to his touch.

Brewster grinned. "I got some good news this morning."

Practical considerations intruded on Saul's wrath—their prenuptial agreement. He could do without material possessions, but penury meant powerlessness and forever abandoning his dream of winning glory for his yet-undevised world-bettering achievements—the only aspiration now remaining to him.

"Yes?" Anne asked, smiling.

"I got a timetable from my lawyer." He held up four fingers.

"Years?" Anne pouted.

He smiled. "Four months until I'm free, and we, you and me, can come out of the closet." Exaggerated sigh. "But it will feel like years."

She quickly ran a fingernail along his zipper. "We'll try to make the time bearable."

"At least our baby won't be a bastard."

Anne pulled back.

"Or worse, Saul's," he said.

Anne laughed.

Saul felt the globs of Med's spit rolling down his cheek, burning like hot lava. He would never allow himself to be that vulnerable again—no matter what. He knew what he had to do. He had no choice. And he had four months at the outside. He'd eaten more than his share of shit in his life. He would eat no more.

As the Greeks knew, and the Christians naively deny, man cannot avoid his fate.

V

Saul, invisible, stood at the corner of Broadway and 80th Street. Wet with sweat, a wave of nausea buckled his knees. Would he have felt sick if he were really about to embark on the road to a glorious god-pleasing destiny? This was just a test run, he reminded himself. He took a deep breath and let it out slowly, causing a dog to turn in his direction and bark excitedly.

A cold wind blew clouds across the sliver of sky visible between the dirt-encrusted skyscrapers. The cloud-cover made the low rumble of the bus and truck traffic sound menacingly louder. A flock of pigeons dive-bombed in his direction and then veered away—surely a bad omen.

He was about to pack it in when he saw her. Tall, thin and blonde. He fell in step behind her. She stopped short at a newsstand to glance at the tabloid headlines. Saul grabbed the side of the stand to avoid slamming into her, but his axe brushed against a pile of *New York Times*. She turned in his direction. His throat clenched and a wave of dizziness washed through him. He knew then that he would never be able to pull it off.

She continued walking, and he followed out of inertia. The memory of Med's spit burned his cheek. Was he going to just accept Anne's atrocity as he had Med's? Was he a loser, cannon fodder for fate?

Crossing 78th Street, an odd adrenaline calm came over him. He realized that he'd raised his axe, but he had no recollection of doing so. Still he wasn't about to bring it down. He had no destiny but dust.

A handsome yuppie smiled at her. She returned his smile, a glint in her eyes. Then there was a break in the foot traffic. She and Saul were alone on a portion of sidewalk. Two pigeons landed near them, then one of them flew off. The clouds parted, and the traffic quieted.

He brought the axe down hard.

* * *

"She looked frightened," the witness said between staccato breaths. "As if she'd seen, uh, or heard something terrible. No one was anywhere near her. A second later, her head…it split open." He pointed a stuttering finger to the body being photographed and scrutinized by six people wearing NYPD windbreakers. "I mean, there was this noise, then it just split open. She fell to her knees." He shook his head. "Blood covered her face." He swallowed again. "What was left of it. Then she fell forward."

"Guess she was right to be scared," Detective Susan Thomas said. She sneezed, barely raising her hand in time to cover her mouth.

"Any idea who she is?" she asked the man.

"Well, uh…yes, actually." His legs buckled, but he steadied himself against a parking meter.

Oh, Christ, she thought, *don't go into shock.* If he really knew the vic, she couldn't just let him faint. She might even have to ride with him to the hospital to complete her interview. Noticing that he was staring at the pool of blood and that his skin had a greenish tint, she grabbed his chin and turned his head away from the corpse. Why couldn't he have thought to do that himself?

"Sonja Wilhelm," he said. "She lives, uh, lived in my building, 50 Riverside Drive. We'd speak occasionally in the elevator. Her husband, John, is a stockbroker with Merrill."

The fat part of his tie was over his right shoulder, twisted to show off the Hermès label. Sloppiness or studied casualness—either way, she didn't like it and didn't like him because of it. Why was money wasted on the rich?

"John took me to play golf at his club once." He looked at the body. She again turned his head away. "They have two kids, a boy and a girl," he whispered. "A nice family."

A cab, swerving to intimidate a pedestrian crossing against the light, fishtailed into a puddle, splashing a roostertail of greasy water over the corpse.

"This John—"

"No. Forget it," the witness said. "He'd never…"

Thomas wished people would stop watching *Law & Order*. It made them imagine they understood cops.

"Anyway he's out of town; annual guys' golf trip to Myrtle Beach. He says it's what the world would be like if there were no wives—all golf courses and strip clubs." Responding to her hostile look or his own internal governing mechanism, he cut off a nascent smile. "Her head just split open." His voice cracked.

Thomas handed him her card. "Give me a call if you think of anything else."

He gave her his. "Please let me know if you figure out what happened."

She looked down at it. *What the fuck is CS First Boston?* she wondered. Some sort of foreign investment bank, no doubt, trying to palm itself off as American by using the name of one of our cities.

"When," she said.

"What?"

"Not *if*"— Her Clint Eastwood squint— "*When*."

He turned to go, but then turned back and smiled self-consciously. "Are you single by any chance?"

"Depends on whether my girlfriend has had a change of heart." Men. She shook her head. A minute ago, the guy practically lost his breakfast.

"Really? You don't look.... All that feminine curly red hair, alabaster skin, pure light-blue eyes."

"Come on, with a little effort couldn't you have come up with an even more prosaic way to describe me?" Although turned off by his trite description, she turned her face to protect it from the sun's damaging rays. "No. Maybe you couldn't at that."

Her partner, Juan Santos, strode over. "Well," he said, "this is something we don't see every day."

He was breathing hard, his face flushed. Thomas thought he looked like the kind of movie cop who'd stop to swap sports anecdotes with wayward kids and take a bullet mid-film, protecting his screw-up partner. She usually mistrusted men with weight-trained bodies, dark hooded eyes, Dudley-do-right jaws, and the confident air of former high school jocks; but Santos was so unthreatening that those qualities only endeared him to her more.

Even after all these years on the job, he still made the mistake of letting the shit get to him, she noted. As if there were something he could do to make the corpses any less dead. "Yeah, I'll say," she replied. "All eyewitnesses telling the same story. That's one for the record books." Neither Thomas nor Santos, partners now for five years, bothered with cynical or sarcastic tones. "CSI people have anything useful to say for a change?" Since that ridiculous TV show, they'd become insufferable. It was as if they really thought they solved crimes.

"Just that the wound is consistent with the vic being struck hard with an axe." He mimed bringing an axe down on someone's head. "A couple of the shoppers at the—" he pointed toward the West Side Market— "saw a strip of blood lifting up out of the wound. One of them said it 'defined' an axe head." He screwed up his face as if he, too, didn't understand what he'd just said. "Like there was this three-inch-long dripping red thing passing through the air. Then it just disappeared."

"Oh, so we've caught a break."

Santos looked at her quizzically.

"We look for an invisible axe," she continued. "From it, we'll get invisible fingerprints and fibers that will lead to the invisible perp."

"You don't really believe that she was killed by an invisible—"

"Of course not, but then again, I don't believe anything." She blew her nose. "That's the key, Juan. Don't believe. You know there was a time when all of Europe actually thought that the wafer was the body of Christ and that He died for our sins."

"Lots of people still do," he snapped.

"What's gotten your ass so out of joint?"

"Did you see her?"

"Yeah, gruesome." She rolled her eyes. "If she'd just stubbed her toe, they wouldn't've brought in the homicide dicks."

He stared at his watch with open-mouthed astonishment. "Folks, it's a half hour into the shift, and this is only the first time she's referred to herself as the prime part of the male anatomy. I think we have, yes we do, a new longevity record!"

She scrutinized his eyes with the deliberation of a parent checking out a teenager after a party. "Make sure we get copies of some of the better pictures." She pointed to the photographers.

He nodded. "Sure, fatten up the file."

"I was thinking more in terms of illustrating my memoirs." She felt her face settle into its permanently angry look, like someone who was starved as a baby—according to her ex-ex-girlfriend, an Ivy League phony artist with a trust fund.

"Really?" Santos asked.

"No. Not really. It's good to hear you sounding stupid again." She hoped her smile conveyed the affection she felt for him, affection tinged with worry because the guy was so vulnerable. "You scared me the other day when you again started quoting that freakin' frog."

"Flaubert is his name, and actually it wasn't him but Barnes, the guy who wrote *Flaubert's Parrot*." Although he smiled as warmly as she had, she knew he was offended.

She'd read it but wasn't about to encourage him by talking about it. "If Internal Affairs were to hear you talking that shit, they wouldn't give a crap if it's limey shit or frog merde; it all smells the same to them."

"I really don't see where there's anything wrong with inserting a little culture into our dialogue. I actually have a dick, so I don't always need to act like I've got one." His eyes showed pain, presumably regret over his own uncharacteristically harsh comment.

She looked around to make sure that no one was within earshot. "No, nothing wrong with it, except that whenever you make a literary allusion, it means you're high."

He shielded his bloodshot eyes.

He was getting stoned more and more frequently, and there seemed to be nothing she could do about it. Yet she wasn't willing to just sit back and watch his career turn to shit. She sniffed noisily. "This fucking cold. Feels like *my* head is splitting open. Let's get the hell out of here."

VI

Saul had stared at the shattered skull, the growing pool of blood, the floating clump of effervescent blond hair and the gray goop that was once part of a functioning brain. He wouldn't have taken the life of another if he hadn't been absolutely convinced that the positive contribution he would eventually make to the world would far outweigh the deaths that made his success possible, he reminded himself. Who among us would act within the law and conventional morality if given such a special power? Could there be any doubt that he'd been given the power to be invisible for a reason? But this innocent person? He'd been through it over and over. There was no other way. He'd had to kill to survive. He'd followed a biological imperative that had been hardwired into the species long before it learned to walk upright.

As his body metabolized the adrenaline, he felt drained and downhearted. His skin was damp and clammy. He may have done what he had to do, but he sure didn't feel good about it.

For at least the tenth time that morning, he looked down to check if he was still invisible. Then he examined his suit. Perfect, no blood splatter. Drops of blood seemingly suspended in mid-air walking down the street might attract attention. Craftsmanship always pleased him. His victim was almost indistinguishable from Anne and, thus, was perfect for his plan.

He started to look at his watch, only to remember that he was invisible. He wanted to change out of his heavy suit, shower, clean his axe, which hung wet and bloody, from a loop on the inside of his cloak, but he couldn't go home until Anne had left for work. He'd told her he had an early breakfast meeting with a potentially huge client. So now he had another two hours to kill.

He walked uptown and then ambled aimlessly West on 81st Street, still willing himself to banish the image of the shattered skull and instead to bask in the afterglow of a job well done. Another woman caught his eye. She was also about five feet ten inches tall, thin, had long blonde hair, and was in her mid-thirties. Like the star of an old movie, lit more brightly than the supporting players, she appeared to be larger and brighter than life strutting across a stage set created just for her. Her piercing aqua eyes were ready to take on the world, but there was also a deep sadness in her face. Although most people would miss it thanks to her sly smile and those all-conquering eyes. What was she smiling about? Saul needed to know. She was carrying a large, flat, professionally wrapped package. What was in it? Before he realized it, he was next to her, marching in time with her on the otherwise empty sidewalk. A hint of tension appeared on her brow. He feared she could hear his quickening breath, or even his footfalls, in spite of the special cushioning on the soles of his boots. She sidestepped the decaying body of a pigeon, a gaping fly-infested hole in its gut. Saul sidestepped it as well.

A crow cawed. Saul turned, and it met his gaze.

The woman stopped at a doorway on 83rd Street that looked like it hadn't been painted since the Cuban Missile Crisis. She pushed the doorbell for Josh Carpenter, psychotherapist. This was the Upper West Side, the Therapy District, like the area around 47th Street was the Diamond District.

In response to a buzz from inside, she entered. Losing her balance momentarily on the frayed carpet, her package slipped. She let go of the doorknob to grab it, and the door flew open. Riding the crest of fortuitous events, Saul followed. This apparently was his morning for spontaneity. He again felt calm; his sadness dissolved. Following her was the right thing to do.

Not only was she a most intriguing woman, but also he'd been considering therapy. It wasn't because there was anything wrong with him; rather it would be useful to make a record with an impartial professional of certain pretended emotions just in case the police were to come nosing around.

The therapist's waiting room was furnished with two rickety chairs and a ratty couch. A ragged pile of old *New Yorker* magazines teetered on a knotty pine end table. There were three other doors. One, wide open, led to a pink-and-black-tiled bathroom, one, also open, to an unoccupied office. The third was closed. Saul thought he heard waves crashing on a beach. Then he realized the sound was coming from a small machine by the door, presumably there to make it harder for someone in the waiting room to eavesdrop on the therapist's sessions.

The woman slipped off her elegant robin's-egg-blue raincoat, revealing a slinky black cashmere sweater dress, black stockings, and gold mesh earrings, each anchored by a medium-sized emerald. He knew little about women's clothing, but he knew grace and elegance when he saw it. What was a classy girl like her doing in a dump like this? Anne had repeatedly accused him of not liking women, but his flood of affection for this stranger put that theory to rest.

A slight man in his early thirties with otherworldly slate-gray eyes, presumably Josh Carpenter, opened the door. He wore a faded-to-pink baseball cap. Saul had to squint to read the pale legend on the hat: "Jews for Jesus." *Christ,* Saul said to himself, wearing a hat inside was moronic enough, but one with a message, particularly that message, was moronic squared. Saul had nothing against religion, but he thought it gauche to advertise one's creed.

"Luriel," Josh said. A smile lit his face; this Luriel was clearly more than just a client. "Come." He ushered her in, placing a surprisingly large and scarred hand on the small of her back.

She returned his smile with something out of a toothpaste ad. Saul felt it to the center of his being, or perhaps even a little lower. The shining aura that had surrounded her on the street expanded to include Josh as well, and the two of them now called to Saul's mind not so much the stars of an old movie but the central figures in a rococo religious painting.

Saul, confident in his noise-proof boots, followed them. A small roll-top desk held a laptop, a telephone and answering machine, and, mounted on a chrome pole coming out of a marble base, a battered bronze helmet of the type worn by ancient Greek warriors. Saul smiled—he and this Josh shared an interest, but his smile soon faded. Was the deep, undoubtedly fatal cleft in the helmet a bad omen? Half-hidden by the base of the helmet was a shiny disk attached to a thin thread. Saul's smile returned. He noted that he and Josh shared another interest. Perhaps one day, he would come up with a way to use it to his advantage. Breathtaking abstract photographs, which, on inspection, turned out to be closeups of nature scenes—sand, gravel, leaves, flower pistils—graced the walls. Saul noted the absence of any diplomas, licenses, family pictures, or, for that matter, people.

The curtains on the single large window were pulled back to display a glorious sunset over the New Jersey Palisades, the gray-green Hudson and Riverside Park shimmering with newly fallen snow. It was so spectacular that it took Saul a few seconds to realize that it wasn't a window, but a cleverly framed backlit photograph.

Luriel held out her package to Josh.

He shook his head.

"Josh, you won't let me pay you; the least you can do—"

"Won't let you pay me? What do you call all this?" He waved his arm in an arc encompassing the photographs on his walls. "I must still owe you for several dozen sessions."

"Not even close." She pressed the package on him.

He grimaced, then unwrapped it. It was a large framed photograph of a rectangle cut into two almost equal triangles, one all white, the other one divided into a deep-blue triangle and a blue/green one.

"Wow! Beautiful," he said. "What is it?"

"The edge of a sail, water and sky." She smiled, unable to hide her well-justified pride.

"Photography and sailing, the two great passions of your youth. When was the last time you did either?"

Her smile disappeared. "Not since I was pregnant." She sighed. "My childhood dream was to be rich and sail in the America's Cup, then do a photographic book on it."

"Perhaps you should get back to your old loves."

She touched the tip of her nose, an impish gesture that Saul was sure conveyed some meaning. "My photos are all deceptions. They look like what they're not. Hard as I try, I can't be completely straightforward."

"Useful trait for a lawyer, but as a person you need…"

"I'm nicer, more thoughtful, more loving than most."

"I didn't realize you set such a low bar for yourself."

Her dagger eyes were as piercing as any Saul had seen in Shrine High School.

Sitting on a cracked black leather couch, she had the perfect posture of a former dancer. Josh parked himself on a simple shaker chair, and Saul reclined on the floor. From that vantage point, he had a terrific view of Luriel's legs.

"So?" Josh asked.

Saul was impressed with how Josh, in a single word, had managed to convey such extraordinary concern, warmth and affection, and he vowed to practice in a mirror until he was capable of doing the same. Was it possible, Saul wondered, that Josh actually was as compassionate as he looked? Saul's lawyerly cynicism told him that it was more likely that Josh just had an actor's ability to control his facial muscles.

"I'm doing good," Luriel said.

"But?" Josh's forward-leaning posture, wide-open eyes and raised bushy eyebrows showed interest, concern and—there it was again—compassion. Perhaps Josh actually felt compassion for her; but was it just because she was his patient or did lust figure into the mix?

She cleared her throat. "You know my paranoia that followed, uh…" She made a circular motion with one arm. "And how it disappeared a few months ago?"

Josh nodded.

"Well, on the way over here, I had this eerie feeling that someone was walking in step with me. It was as if I could almost hear him breathe. His faint footfalls were just a little off-stride from mine." She pulled her shoulders in and mimed a shiver. "It even feels like he's here with us now."

"Any return of the feelings that Allen's been cheating on you?"

"I'm not sure he wasn't," she said sharply.

A feeling of comfortable warmth embraced Saul. That she believed her husband was cheating on her was yet further confirmation that, since he'd donned the invisible suit, the gods were looking out for him. Saul had never cheated on Anne, but what he saw between her and Brewster a couple of weeks earlier certainly gave him license to do so. Although, now that he had killed, there seemed to be little point in parsing the moral issues of cheating.

"What's really bothering you?"

She broke eye contact. "I found out about you."

Josh pointed to himself with an exaggerated facial expression. Most people wouldn't have realized that he was pretending to be surprised, but Saul knew because he so frequently had to fake emotions he didn't feel. He had so few and people expected so many.

"You have no training in psychology, no degrees, no licenses whatsoever." She sounded like a prosecutor concluding a successful cross-examination. "As far as the state—and more importantly Google—is concerned, you don't exist."

Josh's face and body language betrayed no sign of guilt.

"I'm not saying…" she continued. "You've been very helpful. I couldn't've gotten through the, uh, thing with Ben without you."

"His death. It's been a year. You should be able to say that he died." Josh was compassionate but firm. "Accept it and go on. Hard as it may be, it's the only way."

"I should be able to do a lot of things." She sighed. "People say that a mother doesn't even bond with a child who dies within the first week."

"People say a lot of things, most not worth listening to." Josh seemed to be looking at Saul, and Saul thought he saw recognition in Josh's unnatural gray eyes.

"I wouldn't've changed careers without you," Luriel said.

"So, then?"

"Just want you to know I'm on to you."

Josh smiled like the canary who ate the cat. "Okay."

Saul was impressed by Josh's sangfroid. As he knew all too well, short men had to be extra tough just to get by. Yet this Josh, at around five feet six, two inches shorter than Saul, seemed perfectly at ease, so much so that Saul felt drawn to him and considered that Josh's compassion, generosity of spirit and empathy, unlike most everyone else's, might even be genuine. However Josh himself was anything but genuine, not licensed or even educated in his field.

"A little more of an explanation is in order," Luriel said.

Saul liked her forthrightness. The name Luriel reminded him of Uriel, the archangel of purity; the warrior who, when Michael stepped aside, led the armies of heaven into cataclysmic destruction in the aim of all purity. That destruction shamed even the angels, whose judgment showed no remorse.

Josh shrugged. "I want to help people." His eyes were now a different shade—darker. Or were they lighter?

Luriel crossed her legs in a blatantly seductive way, but she did so without sacrificing a scintilla of sophistication.

"What is it you're trying not to tell me?" Josh asked.

"Things with Allen…" She shook her head. "I've been…he's been…I don't know. If he'd only go back to work. I mean with his credentials, if he really tried…" She uncrossed, then recrossed her legs. "I come home, and he seems to expect me to chat about my day. Worse yet, to hear about his. Hell, that would be fine with me, if he ever did anything of interest." She squinted and pursed her lips, reflecting uncertainty and regret. "That really wasn't fair, but generally I just want to lose myself in a novel or something. Actually, what I want? There's this young lawyer who works for me. He's sexy as hell, and sometimes I feel like jumping him."

Josh's eyes darkened. "You wouldn't—"

"Of course not, but that doesn't stop me from fantasizing."

Josh's nod communicated acceptance rather than approval.

"Allen is pretty uninterested these days," she continued. "He took me to Nobu, my favorite restaurant, for my birthday, but was snoring like a hibernating bear within five minutes of our return home. When we do it, maybe once a month as a favor to me, it's always making love, a couple of prescribed positions. I want…" She broke eye contact. "Well, I want to get fucked." Her eyes opened wide with shock, as if someone else had offended her by cursing in front of her. She'd used the word for effect, but apparently it had affected her more than she'd anticipated. "Sorry," she said, seemingly more to herself than to him. "I love him, but neither of us will ever get over Ben's death." She paused, perhaps seeking recognition that she finally brought herself to say *death* without hesitation, or maybe to regain her strength after the effort of doing so. "It might be better if Allen and I move on separately. You were right about encouraging me to change jobs. Maybe I should transform my entire life."

Saul saw, in Josh's slight hesitation before answering, a struggle between professionalism and his urge to encourage her to leave her worthless nerd of a husband so he could take a shot at her. But, Saul acknowledged, that might just be his own projection.

"You can't run away from problems," Josh said. "You don't really want to leave your husband." He flicked out his fingers for emphasis. "Surely you know you don't want to have sex with this young man in your office. Although it may feel liberating to say stuff like that to me." There was something a trifle off about his pronunciation. He had the hint of an accent, too faint to narrow down. English wasn't his first language.

She bent her head one way, then the other, indicating grudging acceptance of his statement. "Maybe an affair would—"

"I've never seen one that's helped a marriage, or, more to the point, that's helped anyone get his or her life together."

Saul caught himself staring at Josh with almost the intensity with which he had been gaping at Luriel. He lingered on Josh's huge, powerful hands and their large round scars surrounded by ridges like lunar craters. Bullet holes or puncture wounds. Saul's scrotum tightened at the thought. Josh didn't get those scares working in an office, and his eyes weren't those of a man content to spend his days listening to people whine about their problems. Saul had the feeling that he didn't just wander into this office by accident, but rather their fates were intertwined. And Luriel? Their fates, too, were intertwined, but Saul was on firmer ground on that one, because he'd make it happen.

She again impishly touched the tip of her nose. "I know nothing about you. Are you married? Straight? Have children?"

Josh glanced at a photo on the wall—waves breaking over rocks. His eyelids fluttered, and a portion of his consciousness seemed to depart. He wasn't about to share his secrets—dark and useful ones, Saul was now certain—and Luriel would have to accept that.

"So, you think I should stay with Allen?" she asked.

"As do you."

She nodded. "Oh, I didn't tell you." Her smile brightened. She was indeed brighter than life, as opposed to Anne who, modest or ashamed of her beauty, always tried to meld into the crowd. "We got all our funding. I've done it!"

Josh leaned forward, then back. "Tell me."

"A couple of months ago, Peter Simonson came up for the day and—"

"The guy with the yacht?" Josh made it sound as if being a famous billionaire and living on a three-hundred-foot yacht were bad things.

"It was his idea to add sound science as one of our goals. I resisted at first, but he finally convinced me, then the money just flowed in."

"Sound science?"

"There's so much junk science in the courts," she explained. "So-called experts testify that someone killed because of a sugar rush, because of the sudden surfacing of repressed memories or due to some newly discovered psychological malady."

Josh's eyes darkened to an ineffable shade between charcoal gray and disapproving. "I thought your passion was prisoners' rights and the rights of children and the poor."

She pulled at the hem of her dress, which, Saul noticed, had risen to mid-thigh. "Sound science is a cause célèbre with corporations and conservative money men." She frowned in response to Josh's raised eyebrows. "And they're right, damn it." She slapped the couch for emphasis. "All this pseudo-science undermines our justice system."

"Oh, yeah, justice *has* always been the primary concern of conservative businessmen." The corners of Josh's mouth turned up. "That and a fair distribution of wealth."

"Our by-laws stipulate that I and I alone determine where to devote our resources." She crossed her right leg over the left, loosened her right shoe—a strappy sling-back model with long anorexic heels—and let it hang on her big toe.

"So, you've deceived right wing fanatics into funding a left wing organization?"

"I've raised money to set up a first-rate not-for-profit law firm that will promote my values. I couldn't care less how someone labels them." She touched the tip of her nose, indicating, Saul realized, that the subject was closed. "Remember my telling you I'd agreed to defend an accused serial child molester?"

Josh grimaced. "The one whose victims' repressed memories were retrieved by hypnosis?"

"An entire first-grade class of supposed victims," she said. "We presented solid scientific evidence that that simply can't happen. Severe stress interferes with the hormones that form memory. So it can't be 'retrieved' because, if the experience was too stressful to recall, the memory of it would never be formed in the first place." She paused, apparently waiting for approval that didn't come. "The hypnotist sold her memoirs to *People* and Lifetime for almost a million bucks. That's a heck of a lot of inducement to fabricate a story. Children not being molested never excites the public interest."

"Doesn't mean the guy was innocent." They glared at each other. "Do you truly believe he didn't do it?"

"If I didn't, I wouldn't've taken the case." She sounded offended by his having asked.

A smile and a lightening of his eyes accompanied Josh's nod. "And that case caused the conservative money to flow in?"

"To *flood* in, a torrent."

"So now you move on from sound science?"

"Hey, come on, take it easy on me." Her smile was openly seductive. "When I started seeing you, I was a corporate litigator. You've transformed me into a do-gooder. We should both take pride in our accomplishments."

"Pride can precede destruction."

A laugh was strangled in her throat. "But mine is tempered by humility." She fixed him with a glance. She obviously liked and respected him, but that didn't mean she'd take crap from him, or anyone else for that matter. "I grew up poor surrounded by spoiled rich kids. I so desperately wanted to be normal—meaning rich. This is a big change for me."

Saul recalled the sadness he had initially noticed in her face coupled with that sly smile, and, admittedly jumping to a conclusion, decided that she might actually come to understand him, and, most importantly, laugh with him. Had any woman ever been on his wavelength? Well, he'd seen women in movies with exquisite senses of humor, so he knew it was possible.

After Luriel left, Josh stared in the direction of the doorway for several seconds, then typed a note on his laptop and, without bothering to turn it off, darted out of his office with the unpredictable energy of an untied balloon.

Saul, who stayed behind, was struck by how little information was on Josh's computer. He didn't even have a separate file for each of his patients, just an alphabetical listing. It included an occasional short notation and, other than that, the patient's name, address, phone numbers, e-mail address, dates of their visits, and a brief description. There was no psychobabble or technical language, perhaps because the man had never received a degree in psychology. The note Josh had just typed was most intriguing: "Arrange to meet Peter Simonson. Is he the one with the sick son?"

Josh saw Luriel every Tuesday at 8 A.M. Saul intended to attend those sessions to amass information to use to seduce Luriel and shitcan her marriage. As Saul viewed it—based, he knew, on scanty evidence—her worthless husband was an old sick elk ready to be culled from the herd by the wolves. The unalterable laws of nature. It occurred to Saul that, now that he had his invisible suit, he'd come to believe in Darwinian competition, a belief he didn't harbor back when he was failing to make the grade.

He decided to make an appointment with Josh. He liked that Josh's office had no pesky security devices; it wouldn't be hard to set him up to take the rap. Someone had to. Leaving the murders unsolved wouldn't be tidy, and Saul was punctiliously neat. He could already see the tabloid headlines: Shrink Goes Berserk, Psycho Psychologist and Death Therapy For Blondes. Of course, Josh would have to die, as it wouldn't do to have him around to present his version of events. Saul already liked him, but as his parents had never ceased to remind him, this was an imperfect world.

VII

Very nice to meet you, Mr. Stein." Josh's tone conveyed almost as much concern, interest and affection as it did when he had greeted Luriel. His oversized, scarred hand ushered the now visible Saul into his office as it had previously guided her.

Saul sat and waited for Josh to ask a question. The couch was soft and mushy. No, it was too deep. Well, something about it was just not right. Saul shifted self-consciously. He wanted a cigarette, although he hadn't smoked—marijuana or tobacco—in more than a decade. Although he could conceive of no reason why he should be nervous, sweat pinpricked Saul's neck and forehead. Josh reminded Saul of a Zen sensei settling into meditation—at once very much there and somewhere else entirely.

"I haven't fully articulated even to myself why I'm here." Saul brought two fingers to his mouth as if they held a cigarette. "I guess I'm not quite as happy as, well, I might be. Truth is, I've always felt pretty alienated. I don't have a bunch of close friends, other than Anne, my wife. I'd be lost without her." After Anne was dead, Saul intended to use Josh as a witness of how much he loved her. "Actually, this is her idea. She thinks it's unhealthy for me to be so totally wrapped up in her. So, well, here I am." He held his hands out, palms up, symbolically presenting himself to Josh.

"This alienation?" Josh asked, grimacing as if Saul's discomfort pained him.

Saul shrugged, ignoring the prickly feeling in his skin. "Anyone who's not alienated in this society is truly crazy."

Josh didn't even smile. "Then why does it bring you here?"

Saul flashed his most charming smile. "I suppose it's traditional in these situations to start with my childhood." He paused, but Josh continued to play the Cheshire Cat. "It's not easy being the only son of a successful man." Saul formed his hands into a steeple, tapped his chin lightly with it, then unclasped his hands palms-up as if the balance of his sentence would drop like manna from heaven.

"What did your father do?" Josh asked.

"Suicide bomber."

In spite of Saul's letter-perfect delivery, Josh again failed to smile. "Not exactly a long-term career."

"He'd agree to do it, then euchre some poor schmuck into going in his place, making sure the bomb was sufficiently powerful to obliterate the guy. Then he'd disappear and my mother would collect the money. Between Iraq, Saudi Arabia and others, we'd clear almost a hundred thou a shot. Later, he cut a deal with the Israelis."

Saul was angry with himself. What was the point in sharing his fantasy past? Even if he did sort of believe it. He reminded himself that his problems weren't psychological. Unable to pursue his glorious destiny because he was a cuckold stuck in a soul-destroying job, he'd been forced to kill. Would therapy help him with that? Of course not. And even if it would, he certainly wouldn't choose this schlemiel with the threadbare office—cheap, frayed rug, walls faded from institutional green to a universal non-color. The creep wore a baseball hat inside. Perhaps Saul could overlook the rest but not that.

"Where were you born?" Josh asked, without even bothering to sound interested.

"A city of just over a hundred thousand on the south coast of Turkey."

"Saul of Tarsus?" Josh smiled coldly. "Maybe you can help me out with something I've been curious about."

"Sure, if I can." Saul scratched his ear, then his other one began itching.

"Why would a patient lie to a therapist?"

"Probably the same reason a therapist would lie to a patient." Confirming what Luriel had said in her therapy session, Saul had done his own research; Josh Carpenter was not only unlicensed, he didn't exist.

Their eyes locked. Neither broke eye contact.

"As Pontius Pilate famously asked Jesus, 'What is Truth?'" Saul quipped. "I suspect that we're two sides of the same counterfeit coin."

Josh grinned. "You speak very well. I like the way you put words together. Ever address groups? On TV? Write?"

A bead of sweat tickled down Saul's side. He dropped his shoulders, not wanting the dampness under his arms to reveal his discomfort. His communication skills seemed to him to be quite besides the point. Yet Josh, leaning forward, eyebrows raised, appeared more interested now than Saul had ever seen him—except when Luriel had mentioned Peter Simonson.

"This is the most uncomfortable couch," Saul said, but then realized how transparent his attempt to change the subject was.

"How did you hear of me, by the way?" Josh asked.

Saul smoothed a non-existent goatee. "David Jaskiel." Saul had learned of Jaskiel and his death from Josh's computer. "Terrible thing, his accident and all." Knowing that most liars sound too sincere and volunteer too much information, Saul waited for Josh to ask another question.

"For as long as you can remember, you've had the overpowering certainty that you are destined for greatness?"

Saul felt as if he'd just been hit with a hundred tiny high-velocity bullets. He pointed as he did when cross-examining a hostile witness, then folded his finger in, not wanting to reveal his hostility. "We just learned that Anne's pregnant." He grinned. "We're thrilled." Just this morning he'd rechecked the math, for at least the twentieth time since he'd observed Anne with Brewster. Brewster was the father.

"That's wonderful."

In spite of the many variations of blinding smile that Saul had seen Josh employ, he only now noticed Josh's teeth. They were jagged and twisted and showed signs of decay. Because of his innate warmth and the way his eyes lit up when he smiled, it didn't much detract from his appearance, but it did show that Josh hadn't grown up in a culture blessed with fluoridated water or orthodonture. Saul, realizing that his own hand was covering his mouth to conceal similar defects, rested it on his lap.

"I guess my motivation for coming here is really that I want to become the best father possible."

"Just let yourself love and show it."

"I can't wait."

"Success will elude you until you learn to become more comfortable in your own skin."

"We were talking about my impending fatherhood." He glared at him, as he would have if Anne were carrying his child and Josh were ignoring what he'd said to harp on his obsession with success. "Apparently it's you who's obsessed with success, and, quite frankly, I'm not interested in spending my money to listen to your theories on the subject. I sometimes come off as a bit nervous, but I'm just a little high-strung." Noticing that he was drumming his fingers on his knee, he folded his hands on his lap. "Truth is, I'm completely at ease—"

"You're at odds with yourself, and it's obvious to anyone who meets you. You'll never achieve your destiny unless you come to terms with yourself."

"And how do I go about achieving this state of satori?"

"Faith." Josh's delivery was deliciously deadpan. "You're not succeeding practicing law. The alternative course you've embarked upon won't get you there, either."

Alternative course? Saul didn't even recall mentioning that he was a lawyer. Saul squeezed his thigh, hoping the pain would keep him focused. "You gave me a very sage piece of advice when you told me to just let myself love my wife and new baby."

Josh sighed as if he personally bore the weight, not only of Saul's sins, but also of those of all humanity. "If only you were capable of following it."

"What the hell is that supposed to mean?" Saul snapped, his left eye twitching.

"Our fates are entwined."

"Ah, so that's the real Josh. The spiritualist mystic."

"This is my second time here. The first time, it felt like home. I knew everyone around me, and they knew me. Believe it or not, I was actually charismatic. Now, plopped down in New York City, I'm a bit off. Everything seems, well, different. I don't have the self-confidence to inspire devotion. I mean, do I seem charismatic to you?"

Was that a normal question for a shrink to pose? Saul asked himself. Was this his second time in New York, or was he claiming to be reincarnated or something similarly nutty? Something didn't quite ring true about Josh. "Actually, you almost do," Saul said. "Why did you leave here the first time?" Saul had a flash of intuition. "Trouble with the law?"

"Yes," Josh admitted.

Perfect—a criminal record would make him the perfect dupe. That Josh was a fellow felon explained why Saul felt such a comradeship with him. Saul also decided that Josh had been able to pick up on his destiny fixation because Josh had one of his own.

"All this talk about destiny is to traduce me into joining you in the same sort of illegal flimflam that got you nailed the first time you were here," Saul said.

"Yes. Nailed." Josh smiled like he wasn't merely in on the joke, but that he understood the joke behind the joke.

Saul told himself that this odd little baseball-cap-wearing pseudo shrink had nothing up his frayed and faded sleeves that Saul couldn't handle, but then why was he so uneasy? Whatever it was, he vowed that he would soon get the upper hand.

"You do intend to suck me into some sort of conspiracy, though?" Saul leaned forward like a cross-examining prosecutor.

"Absolutely." Josh leaned back his pale gray eyes fluttered.

As the silence grew to an uncomfortable length, Saul realized that Josh wouldn't tell him anymore and that he would lose face if he tried to push the issue. He didn't understand why, but he was intent that he do nothing that would demean himself before Josh.

Saul, pointing to the shiny disk on Josh's desk, said, "You use hypnosis in your practice?"

The backlit photo of the sunset flashed. Light zigzagged from the ceiling fixture. Saul turned his head, and Josh disappeared. He turned back, then Josh appeared, huge. The Greek warrior's helmet floated in midair.

Saul's skin felt prickly. "Shit, not now," he said to himself.

Attempting to stand, he staggered to his right. The muscles on that side didn't seem to work. His legs felt as if they were on fire. Josh leaned forward sympathetically.

"I'm getting a migraine." Saul took a deep breath. "Coming on very fast. Some signs this morning but ignored them." He gritted his teeth. "Bad one." He steadied himself with his left hand on Josh's chair. "Got to go."

"Lie down." Josh pointed to the couch

Saul shook his head.

"You won't make it home."

Saul sat. He took a series of scorching breaths. The trip home would be horrendous, but he had to go. It could be days before this subsided, and it would get worse soon, and then he wouldn't be able to move. "Please, Josh, help me to a cab," he said, and he began to stand again, but Josh shoved him down.

Saul's eyeballs felt as if they were being forced from their sockets. He was sinking. He couldn't move. He couldn't breathe. His body felt far away. Struggling, he managed to take a deep breath. It felt like a shot of adrenalin, but then the pain gathered on both sides of his head. He closed his eyes and curled up on the couch.

Josh put his hands on Saul's temples and pressed hard with his fingers at the center of his forehead, where Buddhists believe the enlightened ones attain a third eye. The pain centered itself under his fingers. Then much of it seemed to depart through them.

Josh began rhythmic breathing, forcefully exhaling, and Saul fell into his cadence.

"Migraines are among the many things that medical science doesn't understand," Josh said, some minutes later. "Are you well enough to move?"

"God, that was a bad one. I've never had it come on so quickly." Saul blinked three times. "Or recede so fast." A tsunami of affection for Josh almost lifted him off the couch. The only thing in his prior experience he had to compare it to was the rush that accompanied the contact of skin against skin the first time with a new woman—something he'd experienced a grand total of three times, Anne included. "I'd like to see you regularly," he said. His throat constricted as it had in his youth when he'd asked a woman on a date.

"So my job will be to help you achieve your true destiny?"

"Yes," Saul said. If only Josh knew how true that was.

VIII

Saul woke to a cool April morning. It was raining lightly. Today wouldn't be suitable for killing. The drops would cling to his invisible suit, making him all too visible. Now what? His thoughts drifted to Luriel. He stroked the inner thighs of his still sleeping wife.

Anne stretched like a cat. "What a nice way to wake up."

He put his mouth over hers to shut her up. Then he kissed her neck and ears.

"Oh, Saul," she said, "I love what you do to me."

Saul had heard her say that to Camel and knew she was saying it to Brewster. After she learned she was pregnant, her sex drive seemed to have picked up. His plummeted after seeing her with Brewster. He pushed his fantasies about Luriel into high gear. The mental gymnastics that sex with Anne now required were almost beyond his abilities.

Luriel or Anne whispered, "Oh, God, Saul. Oh, God!"

One of the many things about Anne that annoyed Saul was that she *always* had orgasms during sex. Too much of a good thing? Well, it wasn't normal.

As soon as they were finished, his skin became unpleasantly sensitive to her touch and the seeping sticky dampness. He was yet again struck by the exasperating perfection of her naked body. She hadn't worked out in years and never dieted, but there it was. Had he ever really loved her? The pain he felt when he realized that Brewster was the father of her child was too intense to be based on anything but love. He knew the pain of humiliation and the pain of love, and that was definitely the latter.

After she left, Saul checked the last number she'd called from their phone. She'd called Brewster while Saul was in the bathroom.

* * *

The next morning it was again raining, but this time he was happy about it. He directed the cab driver to stop at 84th Street and West End Avenue and gave him a twenty for a four-dollar fare.

"Please wait here," he said. "As soon as you see that door open," he pointed across the street, "start to drive. I'll hail you. Stop for me, not the woman who comes out."

Emerging from Josh's office, Luriel opened her umbrella. A gust of wind wrenched it from her hand and into traffic. She covered her head with a newspaper.

Saul yelled, "Taxi!"

The only cab in sight with its for-hire light on stopped for him. "I'm going down to Wall Street," he screamed to Luriel so he'd be heard over the deluge. "Would that help you?"

"Sure would." She smiled. "Thanks."

He held the door for her, positioning his umbrella so it sheltered her and not himself. "I'm Saul Stein," he said, as she slid across the cracked upholstery.

"Luriel," she said.

"Luriel, as in the—"

"It's a corruption of something unpronounceable in Russian. My mother was a poet who hailed from impoverished Russian nobility and... Actually, I never much liked the name."

"You a lawyer by any chance?" he asked as the cab started downtown.

"Well, yes. How did you know?" she asked politely enough, but she opened her newspaper on her lap and flattened it with repeated strokes.

"Takes one to know one." He held his head high, the way he thought someone confident and optimistic might. "I'm one of the last of the general practitioners."

She speed-read, her finger and eyes darting across the page, concentration was etched on her face. She had the gravitas that Anne lacked. He knew from attending her therapy sessions that she had a mordant and dark sense of humor not unlike his own, which, even more than her looks, attracted him to her.

"I've been working on a fascinating case," he continued. "There's this electromagnetic field litigation."

Her finger stopped, a place holder. She turned toward him.

"It's been going on for years. Appeals, reversals, new trials. Plaintiffs claim they contracted cancer from living near power lines."

Her eyes drifted to his nervously flitting fingers.

He kept them steady on his lap and continued, "So-called experts testify on their behalf, but scientifically speaking, it's complete horseshit. Pardon the language. It gets me a bit peeved."

From his research on the Internet, Saul had learned that helping the powerless and the oppressed was more important to her than pushing for sound science in the courtroom. He'd planned to launch in on an impassioned exegesis on the rights of prisoners, but her breathtaking sexuality had the effect on his confidence that leaving headlights on all day would have on a car battery, and he couldn't muster the credibility to properly deliver such a speech. So he stuck to sound science, a subject in which he believed.

"I just finished a brief on that very subject." She sounded tentative, as if she hadn't yet decided if having a conversation with him was worth giving up precious reading time. A New York minute might not be shorter than one elsewhere, Saul realized, but it sure was a hell of a lot more valuable.

The driver was screaming over his cell phone in furious Bengali.

"Are you with the Manhattan Legal Foundation by any chance?"

She raised her perfectly trimmed eyebrows. "You know us?"

"I'm a great admirer." Feeling his eye twitch, he placed his hand on that side of his head. "You almost singlehandedly revamped New York's foster care system." He shook his head at the wonder of it all. "And, wasn't it you who proved that recovered memory was a dangerous fiction?"

She nodded slightly, but smiled with her eyes. They were so pure and vibrant that someone steeped in sin could bathe in them and come out clean and pure.

"I like your dedication to the poor and the maimed and the halt and the blind." As soon as the words left his mouth, he regretted, as too obscure, his allusion to the New Testament, a book as foreign to New York intellectual life as *The Egyptian Book of the Dead*, *The Great Hymn to the Aten* or *The Upanishads*. "Could you use help? I'd be delighted to volunteer my time." His other eye began to twitch. "I happen to have an extra copy of a memo of law I'm drafting in the power-line case." He wrote his name and telephone number on the bottom, then handed it to her. "Call me, if you like my style. As I say, I'd love to help in any way I can."

She took the brief. "I will."

He understood that she was letting him down gently.

"Please just take a look at the first paragraph or so, just to see if we're on the same track."

She grimaced, but apparently decided to be polite.

Their driver, now almost apoplectic, was waving both his arms, occasionally pounding the dashboard with his fists.

A car darted in front.

The cabbie jerked the steering wheel. "You, New Jersey," he cursed at the car as his cab shot onto the curb, causing the more chickenhearted pedestrians to scatter while others stabbed at it with umbrellas, some with swashbuckling flare.

He gave the wheel another swing, and the taxi, after getting good air off the curb and hydroplaning across a large puddle, returned to the road with a tooth-jarring bump.

"If we were looking for safety, we'd've taken the subway," Luriel said to the driver. "But you only get extra points if you do that kind of thing on two wheels."

Her timing and straight-faced delivery were so perfect, and such a contrast to anything Anne would have said, that they confirmed for Saul that she had indeed been chosen for him by the gods.

Without slowing down, the driver turned fully around to them. "You see what that Jersey did?"

"Don't worry, he didn't get any points either," Luriel said.

Saul grinned. Her sense of humor was as dry and perverse as his own.

Her eyes returned to Saul's brief, her face showing focused concentration as her finger darted across the page.

Their cab screeched to a stop. The flashing police lights indicated that someone ahead of them had had the bad taste to get into an accident.

A homeless man, the rain pouring over his head, knocked on the window at Saul's side, held out his hand and mouthed, "Please."

Saul, viewing this as yet another sign that the gods were, at long last, with him, rolled down the window and gave the man his umbrella.

The man flashed a toothless smile.

Saul closed the window to avoid the stench.

Luriel said, "That was a wonderful thing to do."

He was sure that reflected light from her smile made him glow like a full moon.

"True charity, giving without seeking self-aggrandizement, is quite rare," she said.

"Give to the poor and thee shall have treasures in heaven," he said. "I find that the New Testament, in spite of its obscurity, has endless potential as a source of humor." He immediately feared that he might have offended her. Anne would have jumped all over such a remark.

"Sure, almost everything in life can be illuminated by a quote from it. It more than holds its own with the more modern members of the Western cultural canon, like *The Godfather* trilogy and *Sergeant Pepper's*." Her tone was flat and serious, but her eyes twinkled.

Saul laughed. He felt rotten about having killed and the murders that would have to come, but everything was going to work out just fine in the end.

She went back to reading. She crossed her legs. The top one mesmerized him as it moved to a secret rhythm.

She turned toward him. "You wrote this?"

"Sure, why? Any good?"

"It's dazzling." Her eyes were wide. "I've read an awful lot of legal writing, but I've never before seen any that..." She completed the sentence with a roll of her hands. "Ever write fiction, or even poetry? The way you put words together, it's amazing."

"No interest. My number's on there. Call me if I can be of some use. You have a card, by any chance?"

She handed one to him.

"I saw you hesitate for a moment there."

She blushed. "No."

"I'm happily married." He punctuated his sentence with an enthusiastic smile. "Our first child is due in September."

"Congratulations!"

"I just didn't want you to think—"

"I wouldn't..." She brushed errant strands of hair from her face and tucked them behind her ear. "Well, I might."

It occurred to him that his desire for her had a Gatsby-like quality to it. As with his headlong pursuit of Anne, he wanted what she represented, the fulfillment of the American dream. But unlike Daisy Buchanan and Anne, Luriel had substance and most importantly an ironic sense of humor.

"Actually, my wife looks a little like you." He slid Anne's picture out of his wallet, a gift from Anne. Not only did he want her to drop her guard, but, as he had in his session with Josh, he also wanted to make a record of his love for his spouse and his excitement over the coming child.

The cab approached the Woolworth Building, an early twentieth century cathedral to industry, built in the shape of a cross, and briefly the tallest building in the world. Now long past its prime and the home to grubby personal injury lawyers. The Manhattan Legal Foundation occupied four of its tower floors.

"How much time a week can you give us?" she asked.

"How 'bout if I take you to lunch tomorrow, so we can discuss what I can contribute?"

"Super."

They shook on it. Her thin-boned hand felt delicate in his, like a bird he could squeeze to death.

IX

Josh woke just before sunrise. The basement room in which he'd resided for the past year contained a small bed, a beat-up steamer trunk, a toilet, a sink, and a half-refrigerator with a hot plate on top. A rope stretched across the room served as both a closet and a clothesline. Despite cracked linoleum and chipped paint, the place was clean and neat. Rather than choose more comfortable accomodations, he preferred not to always charge for his services and to give most of what he made to the poor.

As he had every morning for as long as he could remember, except, of course, for Saturday, the Sabbath, he stood, took his tefillin in hand and placed the *shel yad* upon the bicep of his left arm, adjusting it so it rested against his heart. Before tightening the strap, he, like any other Orthodox Jew, recited the *L'ho-niach Tefillin*. Then he fastened the strap, winding the two coils over the leather extension to form the Hebrew letter *shin*. He made seven coils on his forearm, then wound the rest of the strap around his palm. He placed the *shel rosh* on his head so the knot was just above his neck, and the box containing the most ancient and holy of prayers rested on his forehead, centered midway between his eyes. He then unwound the strap in order to make three coils on his middle finger and wrapped the remainder around his palm. He recited the *Al Mitz-vas Tefillin* before adjusting it, then chanted, "*Boruch shem kiv-od malchuso l'olam vo-ed.*"

It was raining lightly when he emerged from his apartment. He pulled his baseball cap over his kippah, or skullcap, so that visual manifestation of his orthodoxy wouldn't detract from his effectiveness as a therapist—his patients suffered from such benighted prejudices. He didn't bother to lock his door because he wanted to provide refuge for the neighborhood homeless.

He'd had some problems with them when he first moved in, but now they'd learned to respect his place. Sometimes he still found empty bottles, but no more drug paraphernalia. They'd stopped using his sheets, and now took nothing but food, which he was happy to provide.

At the glatt kosher delicatessen on the corner, he still, after so many visits, couldn't take his eyes off the concentration camp numbers tattooed on the forearm of the man behind the counter. The counterman must have been just a boy when he'd been in the camps. Josh reached into his pocket to pay for his whitefish.

The counterman, as usual, shook his head. "No, Rabbi."

Josh believed that the rules of kashrut were contrivances of man, not God, but they were part of his upbringing, he thought. Actually, his childhood memories were disconcertingly vague. Just the same, he kept kosher because it helped him to be continuously aware of his obligations to God and man.

As he strolled up Second Avenue, the rain ceased. The clouds momentarily parted, sending a shaft of sunlight down on him.

He opened the plain wooden door to the basement of an old brownstone. Several of the small congregation said, "*Shalom*, Rabbi Yeshua." After counting to assure himself that there was a *miniyan*—at least ten men as required by Jewish law as the minimum number to hold a service—he took his place in front of the holy ark and led the morning service.

Afterwards, as usual, he walked the four miles to his office. It was now a gorgeous spring day. He was by nature optimistic, but today he had good reason to be so. He was finally making progress on his grand design. Having done it with reasonable success once before, he had a general outline in mind of how he intended for his plan to play out, but details still needed to fall into place. Saul, he thought, could be quite useful.

At Fifth Avenue and 36th Street he stopped, and someone smashed into him from behind. "Fucking tourist," a woman well into her sixties screamed. "Watch where I'm going."

He pointed to the red light.

"This is New York; they're just advisory." She tilted her head and narrowed her eyes. "Where the hell you from, anyway?"

A pure white dove landed on his right shoulder.

"Ugh." The woman flicked her fingers at the bird. "Pigeons, they're dirtier than rats or cockroaches," she warned. She flashed an angry look at the traffic that was blocking her way. "So, how are you enjoying your visit?" Apparently having decided that it would be a more productive use of her time to make small talk with a stranger than to do nothing until the light turned, her tone was now warm and friendly.

Seeing that she was all in black, Josh started to ask if she was in mourning but then realized that it was the fashionable color. "Is it so obvious that I'm not from here?" Josh asked.

She scurried off as soon as the light changed.

Josh had doubts about Saul, but he reminded himself that greatness hadn't often been produced by a satisfied mind. Even Jesus wasn't perfect. The Gospels contained numerous snappy rebukes to his mother: "Who is my mother?" And how about the time that he killed a fig tree out of pique because it wasn't bearing ripe fruit when he happened by? And, as for his relations with his wife, well, as the Counsel of Nicaea wisely decided, the less said the better. It would have been quite strange indeed if a Jewish man in Israel at the time was still single at thirty-three, but the Gospels never commented on his marital status even at the risk of encouraging speculation that he was gay.

If Saul could be useful, Josh had to use him, just as last time, he'd used others. Fowls neither sowed nor reaped; lilies grew without toiling or spinning; but still there was some work that had to be done.

He was about to enter Central Park when he heard a loud belch. A middle-aged man in a pinstriped suit chugged a bottle of Nyquil, then tossed the empty bottle at a passing bus, catching Sara Jessica Parker, in an ad for *Sex and the City* reruns, square on the forehead.

Josh came to a field of daffodils that a pair of youngsters were decapitating and stomping while their mothers chatted.

"It's nice to see your children enjoying themselves," he said to the mothers, "but the flowers are for everyone."

The women stepped toward him aggressively, but when he locked eyes with them, they called to their kids.

After they departed, he extended his arms over the desecrated field.

He proceeded uptown parallel to the Park Drive, watching the profusion of joggers, rollerbladers and bicyclists. Most had pained expressions, yet this was their recreation. He had almost reached 81st Street, where he would exit the park, when three young women jogging caught his eye. Their mouths and gesticulating hands were moving as fast as their feet. They happily greeted everyone they saw, and the recipients of their largess continued on smiling, passing their happiness to others. Josh wanted to teach the ability to transmit such delight.

The one closest to him, a tall, thin blonde, smiled and waved, a purely joyful gesture free of nuance or expectation of gain, and he responded in kind.

A large black cloud passed in front of the sun, sending them into shadow and dropping the temperature. Just before the cloud blew off, a beam of light spotlighted her, and Josh felt a kinship with her that he was at a loss to explain.

As he always did when he left the park for the final leg of his journey, he listed his sins: anger, pride, dejection, arrogance and distress of heart. If he defeated them, he'd achieve his goals.

* * *

"What a nice way to wake up." Luriel rolled over and melted into Allen. Rain beat upon the dark windowpanes.

He licked her neck. "It's taken me fourteen months to wake up," he said.

The apartment was filled with a faintly familiar, warmly evocative odor.

She stroked between his legs. "You seem to be well up now."

"From now on I'll be the husband you deserve."

"You've been fine." He hadn't been, but she hadn't been the wife he deserved, either.

"No." He lightly kissed her lips. "I've been depressed, selfish and obsessed with myself, but I promise that, starting a couple of hours from now, all that will change."

She squinted and pursed her lips. "And between now and then?"

"I'm going to fuck you until you scream."

He licked her neck and ears until she moaned lightly with each warm, wet contact, then he worked his way down until he was sucking on her big toe. After doing each one in turn, he started up again. Suppressing her instinct to give him pleasure in return, she lay back and let her desire build like she knew he wanted her to.

By the time he'd reached the backs of her knees she was bucking, screaming and digging her nails into him, hotter than she'd been in years.

"Please. Now. I can't wait."

He held her by the wrists, while he did amazing things to her inner thighs.

"Yes. Please."

He looked up. "Not quite yet."

He was amazingly handsome in the morning light.

He moved up, and her desire for him took over her entire being.

Later she was lying in his arms, deliciously crying. "I've missed you so much," she said.

His hand drifted along the full length of her body. "Losing Ben, seeing you so devastated, being unable to work. I just..."

"It was easier for me. I could throw myself into work." Her voice sounded as if it was coming from far away. It couldn't be that she and Allen had ever had problems. It must've been a bad dream or something. "Sometimes then I'd forget for a little while."

"But it will be better from here on in, I swear." They kissed. It was amazingly arousing for her to taste herself on his lips. "Anything pressing at work this morning?" he asked.

"Depends on what alternatives you have in mind." She smiled like the sex kitten she used to pretend to be.

* * *

The air was cool, but the bright sun was warm on their naked skin. The roof of their apartment building was the highest point for several blocks and the parapets made them invisible from all but passing helicopters. Luriel had never been up there, and certainly had never been naked up there. They were lying on a couple of old sleeping bags. The champagne, kept cool in an ice-filled garbage pail, hit the spot. The idea of drinking it out of one of her shoes at eight in the morning was exquisitely silly. The muffins, both the chocolate and the apricot, were perfect. Allen must have gotten up at 3 A.M. to bake them.

"This is the most romantic morning of my life," she said. "I love you so."

"We've got plenty better to come." He handed her a muffin.

She licked her lips, then took a bite. "Ouch!" She reached into her mouth. She pulled out a gold ring with a flawless sapphire. "Allen, this is a bit much." She couldn't stop grinning. "Above and beyond."

"If you don't want it, throw it overboard." He uncoiled an arm out to the edge of the roof, seemingly the edge of the world.

"It's beautiful." She kissed him. "But can we afford—"

"My mother's stone. I had the setting changed."

"On second thought, I think I'll keep it."

"Beautiful enough to get me laid?"

"Again?" She opened her eyes and mouth so wide that they hurt.

She had grown up in a tiny apartment over a butcher shop in the dilapidated downtown of vertiginously upscale Greenwich, Connecticut. Her dad, a disillusioned and defrocked Episcopal priest, had worked in the store.

Her mom, a published but unread poetess, had ineptly played the role of the normal mother while struggling to keep her dreams in check. Young Luriel's friends were all rich kids, and she was popular, smart and extroverted. An excellent sailor, they all wanted her to crew for them. Throughout high school and her first two years of college, she had the same boyfriend and remained a virgin. Her secret was that she—and thank God, he—became exceedingly skilled at oral sex. And now she used that talent to make Allen beg.

Later the sleeping bags were soaked through with sweat and other fluids and torn in several places, but neither of them felt like moving. Just the same, she sat up. "I should go."

"Why?"

"I've got lunch with this guy."

"This guy?" He raised his eyebrows in mock jealousy.

She shoved him playfully. "The one who let me share his cab yesterday."

"Oh, the sexy, brilliant writer who gave his umbrella to the homeless man."

"You must be confusing him with another of my admirers. This one is the brilliant writer who gave his umbrella to the homeless man."

"You said he was interesting and 'although he was perfectly nice and all, there was something not quite right about him: nervous, tense, off-putting, a little scary even.'"

She laughed, flattered by his remembering her exact words and capturing her tone almost perfectly. "I appreciate that you're a good listener, but I still don't see where the sexy came from."

"'Interesting' and 'scary' are code words," he teased. "When women use them they mean sexy, and 'nervous' and 'tense' connote passion in woman-speak. Better watch it; I've deciphered your secret language."

"Hmm. Interesting theory, if a bit scary." They kissed. "I'll be right back. I need to call him to reschedule." She pulled on her jeans and T-shirt. "You really should read his brief. You'll see why I was so impressed."

"Leave it for me."

Luriel smiled. He sounded enthusiastic for the first time in months.

"If after you do have lunch with him, you still find him sexy," Allen said. He mock flinched as she raised a fist. "Uh, I mean, 'interesting,' let's all get together for dinner sometime."

Because Ben's death haunted their old friendships, she'd been suggesting that they try to make new ones. She'd met some fascinating people through her new job, but Allen had resisted her attempts to get together with them socially. One of the reasons she fell in love with him was that he had been so sensitive. When their infant son died, his sensitivity became a negative. He turned in on himself so completely that he seemed to disappear. She feared he was having an affair, but Josh persuaded her that he was too emotionally crippled to have any human interaction, and her paranoia was a projection of her yearning for *interesting* and *scary* contact.

After she got over her initial period of deep mourning, rather then turn inward like her husband, she'd turned outward. She threw herself into the challenge of founding and building her public-interest law firm, yet she still needed more distraction. The distraction she got this morning from Allen sure hit the spot.

They spent the rest of the day sailing in a decent wind on a surprisingly responsive Hobie Cat that Allen had rented out of City Island. Later, Luriel shot five rolls of film.

"Oh, by the way, I got a job. I start next week," Allen said casually, while pouring the wine at dinner. "So you think you got some good pictures today?"

"Wait. What did you say?" She feared she hadn't heard him right.

"Jim Tarlow, one of my former students, is now managing partner at Banner Hastings. They were looking for someone to head up their New York corporate department, and—"

"Fabulous!" She touched her glass to his.

"I'm sorry it took me so damn long to get off my butt, but—"

"I don't care. I don't care about anything. Jesus, head of the Banner Hastings corporate department, wow."

He rested his hand on hers. "I know how much you wanted me to go back to work."

"I just thought it would be good for you, and for us." She had a disquieting thought. "You do want this job? I mean you're excited about it, right?"

"I really appreciate how little you did to manipulate or trick me into getting a job before I was ready."

She wasn't quite sure how to take that. "Josh too keeps commenting on my being devious, but really, I don't quite see...."

"I love you like crazy, but you are kind of Machiavellian."

She pointed to herself questioningly.

He smiled. "Like the time you cross-examined a key witness while waving around a deposition notice, making him think you had in your hand the key document in the case. He'd actually destroyed it but you got him so unnerved he admitted every damaging word of it."

She laughed. "That was when I was a corporate litigator. It was part of my job description to be underhanded."

"When we first went out you were seeing four guys for months, but each one thought he was the only one."

"Come on. That was just a phase."

"And at school when you discovered that the outgoing editor of the law review had plagiarized his big article, and you used the information to get yourself appointed—"

"You're not saying I didn't deserve—"

"I'm just saying I never want to be on your bad side."

She topped off their glasses. "You never will be." They touched glasses and each took a big gulp.

* * *

Tiny bright green leaves had, seemingly overnight, replaced the buds on the trees along 85th Street. A few of the trees were flowering, white and pink, filling the air with a fabulous fragrance so wonderfully foreign to New York City. Running was easy for Chris this morning, particularly after winter's dank darkness and then the chilling cold and freak snows of early spring.

Catching the traffic light just right at Central Park West, she entered the park without having to break stride, surely a good omen. Jennifer and Gina, her sorority sisters at Penn State—was it really possible that college was twelve years before?—were stretching, waiting for her at the Park Drive. They were going to do the full six-mile loop this morning at a sub-eight-minute pace; Gina was gearing up for the New York Marathon. Chris and Jennifer had pledged to make sure she'd be ready. The three of them planned to be running in Boston the following Patriots' Day, having just missed the sign-up date for this year's race.

On seeing her, Jennifer glowered at her watch. "Big night with Eddie?" Unable to hold her stern expression, she broke into a smile.

"What a day this is." Chris spun on her toes. "We're going to pick out a china pattern at lunch."

"Just do as well as you did on the bridesmaids' dresses and you'll be fine," Gina said.

Jennifer's turn to run in the middle position, she wore a T-shirt with an arrow pointing left, "Gina," and one pointing right, "Chris."

They started fast, downhill all the way to 77th Street.

"Suck it up," Chris yelled to a septuagenarian struggling up the hill.

He responded with a chuckle and a V-for-victory sign.

She didn't wave at strangers elsewhere in the city, but in the park, she felt as safe as she did in her own living room. Smiles, waves and shouted encouragement passed between them and approaching runners. The three friends rarely missed a morning. All three had met their boyfriends running, but still they ran together, just the girls. One day they'd run pushing baby carriages. None of them had ever put a man before their friendships with each other, and none believed they ever would.

At 80th Street, Chris felt the warmth of a shaft of sunlight, then waved to a man with sincere pale-gray eyes who, also spotlighted, was staring at her.

Flowering dogwoods and cherry trees lined the roadway. They came to a field of daffodils. "Look at those flowers," Jennifer said. "Gazillions of people have walked by and no one has picked them or anything. Isn't the city just the best?"

A burning pain ripped though Chris's shoulder.

"Damn it. Missed," a man said under his breath.

Blood squirted from her.

Gina screamed.

Chris stumbled. Jennifer put an arm around her waist. Chris tried to lift her arm. She couldn't. Pain shot through her. She felt cold.

A strip of blood headed toward her head.

X

Unnerved by seeing Josh leave the park, or rather thinking that it might have been Josh, Saul had hesitated when his chosen victim came into view. The man's presence, real or imagined, exerted a powerful pull on his psyche. Although Saul still believed Josh to be a grifter and a criminal, his unconscious had transmogrified him into a symbol of conventional morality, and even love. Weirder still, Saul caught himself yearning to please him as a child does a parent. Josh had even entered his dreams, first as a bit player but lately in the starring role. Dreams, Saul reminded himself, were not communications from the gods, as the ancient Greeks believed, but meaningless fragments of memory the brain discards to keep its files from becoming overstuffed with worthless information.

As the runner approached, Saul felt as if his invisible suit had taken over. The suit, not he, had raised the axe. It and he brought it down hard but—as they worked at cross-purposes—inaccurately, missing her head by a good six inches.

On the second try, he let the suit—or perhaps the will of the gods as manifested through the suit—do the work. The blow was perfect. He slipped the bloody axe head into a loop on the inside of his suit.

Now, he was sweating, alternatively cold and hot. He blamed it on the latex gloves and cheap long cotton underwear he wore under his suit. He'd been scrupulous about never letting his skin touch his suit. If crime scene unit investigators were to one day examine it, they'd find none of his DNA and only the fibers from Hanes' most common style of long underwear.

Next, he would do Anne. With the murder of the two previous tall, thin, attractive blondes, the police would believe her death to be the work of an invisible serial killer with a physical type. No one would think that Saul was just another guy ending his marriage with extreme prejudice. He told himself that Anne's father would bear the moral responsibility. It was he who had locked up all his money in trust and insisted on the prenup. Not that money itself held much of an attraction for Saul. It was merely a tool to achieve his destiny, and destiny meant everything. If he could have killed Anne and not others, he would have, but he couldn't think of a way to do it without him being the prime and only suspect. Particularly once the autopsy revealed that she was carrying someone else's child, and it came out that he would become a multimillionaire on his wife's death but get nothing in the event of divorce.

Looking at the shattered skull and pool of blood, he was having trouble believing that he'd been justified in killing. But still, it seemed as if the invisible suit had been a gift from the gods and the axe wasn't there so he could become an invisible woodsman.

* * *

"Christ, not now," Detective Susan Thomas said in response to the ring of the phone that woke her.

"Don't they *ever* give you any peace?" Gwen, her girlfriend-du-jour whined, then yawned.

"People get killed at the most inconvenient times."

"I didn't mean—"

"I know." Thomas stroked Gwen's cheek. "I always seem to end up with artsy lovers who don't like cops and whose time is their own." Thomas regretted the words as soon as they were out of her mouth.

"That's nice; I like being part of a long gray line."

"I didn't mean—"

"I know," her companion said, but she still hadn't responded to Thomas's touch. "Why the hell are you a cop anyway? You're not the least bit like one. Look at this place." Gwen unfurled her arms. "Books stacked from floor to ceiling, Russian icons hanging from every inch of wall space that's not covered by books." She pushed a button on the remote to play the Lucinda Williams CD they'd fallen asleep listening to.

"You should see me on the job." Thomas again stroked Gwen's cheek. This time her companion held her hand there. "You'd never be able to imagine me as anything else."

"Split personality?"

"Just complicated. Like everyone else is, I guess."

Gwen got out of bed, took a joint from a gold business-card holder in her purse and lit it. "Want some?" she asked, her voice gravelly from holding her breath to keep the smoke in.

"Please, not here."

"What's it to you?"

"I'm a cop. You're not supposed to break the law in front of a cop."

"It's a stupid law."

"I guess," Thomas said, feeling more tired than she should have this early in the morning. "I used to be quite the little peace-and-love hippy chick, back when I was at Spence."

Her companion's eyes widened. "You've got to be the only one on the force who graduated from Spence; the place was far too snotty for me to get into."

"I didn't graduate. My older brother was shot—random street crime. I sort of fell apart. When I came out of it, I was a straight-arrow in public high school dreaming of being one of New York's finest. I went to Brooklyn College at night but didn't graduate from there either."

Gwen put the joint out on her tongue, put it back in the holder. "I guess you've got good reason to be angry and bitter."

"Angry and bitter?"

She stroked Thomas's hair as one would a beloved cocker spaniel. "Not to me, but I bet when you're on the job—"

"I suppose my brother's murder changed me forever." Thomas sighed. "I seemed to have realized that ideas and literature weren't important. Am I making any sense at all?"

"Of course," Gwen said, meaning "no."

Thomas smiled. "If you'd like a drug, I've got some decent coffee."

"Okay." Gwen looked around as if seeing Thomas's apartment for the first time. "How the hell do you afford this? High ceilings, huge rooms, top floor of a loft in the West Village. This is the kind of place where cops live in the movies, and investment bankers have in real life."

"My family built the building like a hundred and seventy-five years ago." Thomas put on a bathrobe, set the water to boil and began to grind the beans. "The bottom floors housed their metal-working factory, they lived on the top two. As each generation degenerated, we sold it off piece by piece. This half-floor is all we have left."

Gwen nodded, satisfied—for perhaps six seconds. "Hey, Susan, what's the story with that partner of yours?" Gwen composed her face as if she considered it to be one of her art works. "The great-looking one you're always talking about?"

"I'm not always—"

"You sure as hell are. He gets high. He spouts off about Victor Hugo. He—"

"Flaubert," Thomas corrected.

"I don't care if it's Baudelaire. Point is you've got the hots for him."

Thomas sighed. Why did they all give her gas about exactly the same thing? "Even if I were into guys, I wouldn't choose him."

Gwen rolled her eyes.

"You know, I never even mention a book on the job," Thomas said as much to herself as to Gwen. Thomas gathered from Gwen's frown that she needed to close the door on her companion's jealous fantasies rather than change the subject. "Juan just brings out my most paternal impulses." She put the beans into a filter, then poured the boiling water through. "Speaking of which, I have to..."

Leaving Gwen's cup on the counter for her to serve herself, Thomas went down the hall and into the spacious bedroom that her father had occupied for his entire life—childhood and marriage. "Hey, Daddy." She kissed him.

He continued staring at the always-on TV and, as he was in the late stages of Parkinson's, didn't respond. As she'd done three times a night for the past year, she fed him through a tube. Then she sent an alphanumeric page to the nurse to come look after him while Thomas would be at work. It was lucky that her place was paid for, otherwise she'd have nothing left from her salary.

* * *

"She looks something like the other one," Santos said to Thomas. He sneezed, having caught her cold. Even with his red nose and glazed, watery eyes, he still looked like the high-school-jock heartthrob turned do-gooder cop.

"Maybe the *invisible* perp has a type." By her tone, Thomas communicated that she, unlike her partner, didn't believe that the killer was invisible. She put her arm around the still-sobbing Gina. Did the few extra pounds around her hips and her curly dark hair save her life? "Anything you can tell us would help."

"She was my best friend," Gina said through heaves and tears. "Everyone loved her."

Thomas was struck by the ordinariness of Gina's comment. They shouldn't issue life insurance to anyone beloved by everybody. She handed Gina a Kleenex, but it was like trying to put out a forest fire with a leaky pail.

"She was going to be married in six weeks and two days. I just bought a dress."

"Please tell us what happened."

"We'd been running about ten blocks." Gina paused to gather her strength. "I heard this thud, then Chris screamed. I turned toward her." She reached out toward Jennifer, who was talking to a unformed cop a few yards away.

The police had intended to keep the witnesses separated until they each gave a statement, but Jennifer, a skinny brunette, broke free from the cop who was holding her, dislodged Thomas's arm, and embraced her friend. Gina went into an unrestrained cry, and Jennifer shot Thomas an accusatory stare. Thomas gave them each a fresh Kleenex.

"This big…like hole opened up in her shoulder," Gina continued. "This red blur came down toward her head. Then it split open."

Jennifer nodded her agreement.

"Could it have been the shape of an axe blade?" Thomas asked.

Gina tilted her head to the side and squinted. "You sound…does this, like, happen a lot?"

"No, not a lot," Thomas said. Out of nowhere she felt like crying, too. The image of her adored brother being shot right in front of her, the life oozing out of him and she, just thirteen years old, unable to do a damn thing. Sucking it up, she took a deep breath.

"I'm starting to think that we may really be dealing with an invisible killer," Santos whispered to his partner.

"It's always a problem when you start to think," Thomas said, but then her expression softened. "There's got to be another explanation."

"Why? Weird things happen."

Thomas believed that if her partner had been born a couple of decades earlier, he would have been a flower child who became one of those Hare Krishnas giving out incense in airports. "It's like magic tricks. Does the lady really get sawed in half or is it an illusion?"

"Billions of people believe in miracles. What makes you smarter than all of them?"

* * *

Saul covered his mouth to stop from laughing. These detectives were clowns. But then his eyes strayed to the jogger's cleaved head and shoulder, and he continued to cover his mouth, but it was now to stop from gagging.

Well, he told himself, *at least I've evened the score*.

Evened the score? Where did that ridiculous rationalization come from? It struck him that, maybe because he was abused as a child, he thought of himself as a perpetual victim—particularly in his interactions with women—and being the injured party made him feel justified, even obligated, to use every weapon at his disposal to level the playing field. He could well have done without that little burst of self-knowledge. He couldn't stop staring at the mutilated meat in jogging clothes that had so recently been a living, breathing human. His gut cramped with self-loathing. The crying of her two companions was so loud it hurt his ears.

"Apollo, charioteer of the sun, great archer whose arrows never miss their targets, dispenser of severe justice who cannot be resisted. To you I swear," he whispered, "I will do all in my power to give back to humanity a multiple of what I took by this killing. By the time the Fates see fit to end my life, there will be a substantial positive balance in my accounts with man and the gods. Please accept this sacrifice before you as a symbol of my sincerity and dedication."

He again willed himself to turn away from the body. Perhaps he shouldn't have killed her, maybe he could have set up Anne's death in a different way, but what was done was done, and he had no doubt that killing Anne was necessary to fulfill his destiny—Apollo himself had told him that.

* * *

His extra-hot shower washed away all but the deepest of his doubts. By the time he emerged from the subway a couple of blocks from his office, he was, for the first time in weeks, excited about the day ahead, and it wasn't just his lunch with Luriel. He had a new client coming in with what promised to be a large case. He enjoyed the practice of law when he was busy. It was the long slow periods—and the obnoxious, hyper, self-righteous clients like Rivka Feld—that drove him crazy.

"Your client is already in the reception room," the receptionist said like a school teacher chastising a tardy pupil. She never would have used that tone with one of the lawyers in the firm, but Saul was a mere tenant filling expansion space, and shit flows downhill.

Saul opened the heavy brass bank-vault doors that an overzealous architect had installed at the entrance to the conference room. Albert Grossman, an overweight bald man, was yelling into a cell phone.

"Hi, I'm Saul Stein." Saul extended his hand, which Grossman ignored.

"Need a couple of minutes here, Saul. The fuckheads have landed." He returned to his call. "Look, asshole, if I want shit from you, I'll squeeze till your eyes turn brown."

A problem with litigation was that nice people rarely got into lawsuits, so clients tended not to be the kind of folk Saul would hang out with if he had the choice. Just the same, it would be good to have work to do. Not only would it be diverting, but also, in case the police came nosing around, it would be better if his practice appeared to be busy.

"I'll stop back."

Saul went into his tiny office to check his e-mail and voicemail.

The only message was devastating: "Hi, Saul. This is Luriel. I apologize, but something came up." It sounded as if she paused for a suppressed giggle over some private joke. "I'm available any day the rest of the week, and I'm buying to make up for this eleventh-hour cancellation."

He called back. "Lunch at Nobu, twelve thirty tomorrow," he said to her answering machine, having remembered her reference to that restaurant in one of her therapy sessions. "I'll come by at noon so you can take me on a quick tour of your office."

Then he telephoned the unemployed actor he'd hired to fake an epileptic fit as they were leaving Luriel's office building. "Sorry for the late notice, but I need to adjourn our show until tomorrow, same time and place. Please confirm that this works for you."

On Saul's return to the conference room, Grossman held up a finger indicating that he'd be off the phone in one second. Saul straightened the artwork on the walls—pretentious post-modern crap from the private collection of one of the firm's senior partners. After several minutes, it occurred to Saul that Grossman might have meant one hour. Saul pointedly looked at his watch.

Finally, Grossman placed his phone on the conference room table, just in case Saul was about to forget that he was less important than Grossman's least important call. "I hear that you're a real junkyard dog," he said.

"I pride myself on that." Not that Saul had any idea what a junkyard dog was or why anyone would want one for a lawyer. "On the phone, you said you'd bring me the contract and letters that spell out the problem."

"You're a good listener, Stein. I like that." He handed Saul a slim file folder.

As Saul looked through it, his stomach clenched into a tight fist. That all-too-familiar feeling reminded him that he had to get out of the practice of law, even if he had to kill to do it. "The way this looks, and, Al, please tell me what I'm missing, you owe two and a half million bucks on goods you resold for a healthy profit. You seem to have no defense whatsoever."

He slapped the table. "I knew I was in the right place. I've got a helluva lot more litigation for you down the pipe. This one is just the top of the iceberg."

"Sorry, I still don't quite get it. If you owe the money, what exactly is it you want me to do for you?" After seventeen years of lawyering, almost all questions Saul asked were rhetorical.

"Jerk the bastards off. Discovery motions, the works. Few years down the road, settle. Given the time value of money, I'll clear at least three quarters of a mil, net of your fees. I'll pay you as we go and toss in a kicker of ten percent of anything you save me over seven hundred and fifty thou. I want you motivated."

"I think you ought to get yourself another lawyer."

Grossman laughed. "Don't negotiate with me, Stein. That's my final offer."

"It's just not what I do. I mean, if you had some defense, but here—"

"Fuck, make something up. Be creative."

"I know it sounds naïve, but I believe people should honor the deals they make."

The corners of Grossman's mouth turned up but stopped mid-smile. "Shit, an ethical lawyer. You're a walking contradiction, you know, like an Italian war hero or a Puerto Rican—"

"Al, if you only knew." Saul stood. "I'll walk you out."

Saul yet again felt like one of the undifferentiated members of that abundant but rarely mentioned class of lawyers who ooze and slime through the mud-bottom darkness pursuing an ever-dwindling supply of plankton. He was a grubby little murderer, killing because he wasn't talented enough to make it on his own.

His lunch with Luriel tomorrow would finally start him on the path to the sunny uplands. He could hardly wait.

XI

Saul, invisible, didn't see her. Was he too late? He needed to hear about the handsome, brilliant, kind man Luriel had met in the cab after her last session.

He hoped she would recount every detail of their lunch. The chemistry between them had been literally mind altering. The hormones that flooded Saul's brain left him forever changed, and bound his future to hers; he had no doubt that she'd been similarly affected. He played the highlights film in his head. As soon as the maître d' had seated them, Luriel, already staring into Saul's eyes, put her hand almost next to his. "I'm amazed that you had the presence of mind to act so quickly when that poor man had that horrible fit."

Saul had then covered his face to hide his smile and to look as if he'd had a discomforting thought. "God, I just realized, I never even asked if you like sushi, just bulled ahead and picked my favorite place. I'm sorry. Sometimes I'm a bit rough around the edges. Is this okay?"

Her smile cured his self-loathing. "It's my favorite place too."

Not long after that, her bare knee *accidentally* brushed across his.

"I don't know if you drink at lunch," he said, "but they make a Midori martini that's unbelievable; nectar of the gods."

"I don't believe in drinking at lunch." She brought her fist down so hard on the table that the ceremonial plate bounced.

Now what could he do to recover from that faux pas? he wondered.

"But, you say it's unbelievable," she'd smiled yet again, "so, if I can't believe it, I guess a Midori martini would be fine." She blinked twice. "Or maybe two, you know, for balance, just to be on the safe side."

Saul had laughed so hard and so happily that when his hand came to rest on hers, it was practically a spontaneous gesture.

"Anyway," she'd continued, moving her hand, probably just for propriety's sake, "with you coming on board, I'll be able to spend my afternoons asleep at my desk."

A mother pushing a stroller with bawling twins along the cracked West End Avenue sidewalk brought Saul out of his reverie. Where the hell was Luriel? She was late for her therapy session.

Then she appeared. Sweat glazed her face, presumably from speed-walking to get there on time. He was struck by how tragic it was that he would have to wait a reasonable time after Anne's death before he could consummate their relationship—her husband was a low hurdle, easily vaulted. Sure, killing Anne, her baby and two others was troubling, but Luriel would help him get over it. It occurred to him that he was developing a psychopath's lack of conscience. That seemed like a particularly positive adaptation, for a murderer.

Josh opened the door at the sound of her footsteps. He must have been so eager to see her that he was incapable of waiting for her buzz. Their eyes met. He put a hand on the small of her back to guide her in. Anger erupted in Saul's gut. He was sure that Josh wanted her as much as he did.

"You look a lot less tense than the last time we met," he said after the three of them took their now-accustomed places.

She smiled almost as brightly as Saul did, but hers was visible. Chiding himself for his silly jealousy of Josh, Saul wondered whether she was going to start with their meeting or go directly to their unbelievably erotic lunch.

"Oh, really?" She licked her lips and flipped her hair, Cameron Diaz style.

Saul understood that she wouldn't play the coquette unless she was in a particularly good mood. He sure had read her right over lunch.

"Allen got a job!"

What did she say? Some sort of arcane joke? Saul's intestines cramped.

"It's changed everything. His mood…the transformation is incredible, wonderful. He's warm and loving, looking for us to make new friends." She shook her head in wonderment. "In one fell swoop, he's turned into—turned back into—the ideal husband."

Saul struggled for air as if he'd been kicked in the solar plexus. His synapses sent a burning sensation down his back. Even his hair hurt.

"We're trying to have another child." She bounced in the chair as if she were so full of energy that she'd explode if she didn't dissipate it. "It's unbelievably sexy. Like we're eighteen again. The other morning, my God!" She covered her face, theatrically emphasizing the wonder of it all.

Saul wished he'd brought some of—no, all of—Anne's morning sickness pills.

Well into the session, she was still on her everything-is-beautiful theme. "The firm is going great. We're helping so many deserving people. We're *really* making a difference."

"And it feels good. Right?"

She nodded, in thanks for his assistance in leading her on to this particular Nirvana, although it felt more to Saul like his private Calvary. "A new guy joined our staff, part-time. Really a first-rate mind, a truly extraordinary writer, too. You read his stuff and you just know you're in the presence of a genius, but he's weird, sort-of like a Martian who learned our mannerisms from watching TV. Just the same, he's going to be a great addition."

Josh sat back—his tell, Saul decided—indicating a very high level of interest. He raised his eyebrows, prompting her to continue.

"When I first met him, he gave his umbrella to a wet homeless man. It was a totally spontaneous unselfconscious act of kindness." She built up speed as she spoke. "Yesterday, we were on our way to lunch when a guy had this terrifying epileptic-like fit right in front of us. People stepped away. My first reaction was to call 911, but Saul—that's his name—jumped right in, maybe saved his life. He seems to be a wonderful person, but he's so tense and off-putting that likely most people never bother to see that side of him. Because of his personality flaws, his law practice is barely struggling along." She shrugged. "Our gain, I guess. A brilliant lawyer with time on his hands."

Josh leaned forward. "If it's not confidential, I'd love to read what this guy has written."

Why did he so want to read it? Saul wondered.

"I happen to have a copy of his brief, which I'd made for Allen. He was as impressed as I am." She reached into her briefcase. "You'll see it's poetic yet incredibly persuasive."

He glanced at it. "Saul Stein," he said more to himself than to her. He placed it on his desk, and a self-satisfied smile spread across his face.

"You know him?"

"I'm starting to." He paused. "So, tell me more about him."

She crossed and recrossed her legs. "How did we even get on this subject?"

"You brought it up."

She turned the discussion back to Allen and his amazing transformation.

* * *

Days crawled by like a geriatric garden slug. Saul hadn't been sleeping. Each time he'd see Anne, he'd be angrier about her betrayal. He'd been enjoying working with Luriel the way a masochist enjoys the lash. He desperately wanted her, and it was agonizing that Allen was standing in his way. She must have wanted him, too. Her sensual stretches, darting tongue and flipped hair betrayed her true feelings—he hoped. Yet, he knew that even if she had such desires, she thus far hadn't even admitted them to herself. What did he really know? He conceded that his understanding of women was below average, and that average was none too high. It was a scientific fact that, genetically, male chimpanzees had more in common with male homo sapiens than men did with women. This gender gap was, in Saul's view, never more treacherous to navigate than in the initial stages of a relationship. In the past, he'd managed to make the journey only when sex lubricated the process. But now that very thing was working against him. Allen had the fortuitous and unfair advantage of being married to her and being able to use sex to stimulate the flow of oxytocin—the hormone responsible for making people feel as if they're in love—to her brain. Saul had to remove that advantage.

Telling himself that he had to get to know his archrival, Allen, to learn how best to destroy him, Saul considered suggesting a dinner among the four of them. However, he was concerned about what Luriel would make of Anne. Book-smart and successful though she was, as a dinner companion she was less scintillating than the third re-read of the menu. At least that was how she'd appeared to Saul recently. Before he saw her with Brewster, he hadn't noticed how boring she was. Ultimately, he decided that he needed to bring Anne and Luriel together for Luriel's good. He knew, from watching movies Anne had dragged him to, that second wives sometimes believed themselves to be in competition with ex-wives. It was only right that Luriel meet Anne so she'd understand that she was in a class by herself.

Luriel pulled strings to get them not only a reservation at Forest Primeval, the latest apotheosis of new American cuisine, but also a corner table far from the kitchen and away from the front door.

Saul ordered for the group a beguiling white burgundy to start, not expensive enough for him to seem to be trying to impress, but of sufficiently high quality for Luriel to take note.

Allen began telling them about a "fascinating bankruptcy matter" he was handling.

Luriel beamed at him, her hand resting on his. Saul decided that she'd become inured to boredom by years of marriage,

"'Fascinating bankruptcy' is an oxymoron," Saul said, perhaps a bit too harshly. "Like a distinguished doorman."

Glowering at him, Allen was about to respond when Anne said, "Why can't we, say every five years or so, just declare emotional bankruptcy? You know, pay everyone like ten cents on every dollar's worth of our emotional debt and wipe the slate clean. Ethical and intellectual bankruptcy are already quite common." Anne took a dainty sip of water. "There the problem is the opposite; we need to find a way to limit filings to every five years."

Allen laid before them a smorgasbord of tepid scientific tidbits, which actually seemed to fascinate the women. In spite of Saul's efforts to tune them out, he couldn't help but hear, "All organisms, from worms to elephants, are allotted about a billion heartbeats. The shorter-lived they are, the faster their hearts beat."

The wine steward refilled their glasses, and Saul ordered a young but beguiling cabernet.

Allen said that moths taken into space grow in a spiral pattern because weightlessness causes them not to know which end is up.

Saul said, "Speaking about weightlessness, your endless discourse—"

Anne held her hand practically in Saul's face and leaned forward as if she had something fascinating to say. "Did you hear?" she said. "They found the bodies of the Greek gods—all but Eros—in a cave on the side of Mount Olympus. Suicides, tainted ambrosia." She leaned forward even farther. "Here's the weird thing. As best as they can tell, they all died on the date of publication of Copernicus's *De Revolutionibus*."

Even though Saul had never shared with Anne his growing belief in the Greek gods, anger surged through him. He forced a smile.

The only thing Allen said all night that Saul found amusing was, "Have you been following this story about this supposed invisible killer?"

Anne stuck a fork into her pâté with black and white truffles. "His two victims were tall, thin blondes in their thirties," she said to Luriel.

"You don't have to worry, dear," Saul said to his wife. "You won't be thin for long." He turned to their guests beaming. "We're expecting in September."

It occurred to him that Anne was more classically attractive than Luriel, but Luriel, on account of her dynamism and depth, was sexier. While Anne's face was a model of perfection, Luriel's mouth was too large and her lips, full and sensual, almost Latin, were incongruous on her otherwise Nordic face. Anne's nose was delicately molded; Luriel's nostrils flared, communicating strength and passion. Their skin was unblemished porcelain, except Luriel had crow's-feet that added gravitas. Anne's teeth would make an orthodontist proud. There was a space between Luriel's two front ones—a sign of sensuality, Camel had told him.

"Terrific," Allen said, looking at his wife, who nodded as if to indicate that she was okay. "Do you know what flavor?"

"I do, but Saul wants to be surprised," Anne said, shifting uncomfortably in her seat.

"Maybe you should cut your hair," Allen said to his wife.

"Come on," Saul said, "the odds of any given woman being murdered by a serial killer are so small as not to be worth worrying about. It's like the stupid fuss everyone is making about this new disease in China or somewhere. It killed a couple hundred people, and everyone's in this panic, canceling trips, closing airports. Thirty-five thousand people die of the flu every year in this country alone, and it's accepted as no big deal."

Ignoring him, Allen said to Luriel, "Please think about it."

Luriel shook her head in sexy defiance, her hair flying.

"So, Saul," Luriel asked, tucking some hair behind her ear, "you think there's really an invisible killer out there?"

Saul laughed. "One of the few certainties in life is that the press gets everything wrong."

"What, these women's heads are just spontaneously splitting open?" Allen asked.

"Whatever is happening, there's a perfectly rational explanation," Saul said.

"You must have a theory," Luriel said, her admiration of Saul obvious.

"Saul has a theory about everything." Anne's tone left it unclear whether she was complimenting him or putting him down.

"Maybe someone shot them from far enough away that he wasn't seen," he said. "A rooftop or something would give the right angle of impact. Probably random, just a coincidence that there are some superficial similarities between the two he, or she, happened to hit."

Allen began to roll his eyes, but stopped in response to a look from Luriel. He said, "There was no bullet, no gunshot, and the wound was consistent with an axe, not a bullet."

"What if he had a crossbow-like device with which he shot arrows with axe-head points and..." Saul had some wine. "Say the arrows were made of frozen oxygen. They'd sublimate and disappear into the atmosphere as soon as they hit."

Luriel smiled. "We're lucky you're not a serial killer."

"Saul would have nothing against killing per se, but he's too vain to make himself invisible," Anne said.

Why Allen and Luriel laughed was beyond Saul.

Seeing that Allen was about to speak, Saul readied himself to jump on it and eviscerate him.

"Viruses evolve so quickly; in a day, they can go through as much evolutionary change as we do over a million years," Anne said. "I wouldn't be surprised if they soon learn to excrete human pheromones to make their hosts irresistibly attractive in order for the germs to transmit themselves to others."

"Seriously," Allen said, as if he'd just had a death in the family, "have you read about that terrible new strain of STD? If it infects a pregnant woman, it systematically destroys her fetus."

While the others chattered away, Allen's remark percolated through Saul's unconscious. Soon he, with the assistance of the gods, had formulated a plan.

* * *

They shared a cab home. Allen and Luriel dropped Saul and Anne off at 81st Street and Central Park West and continued on. As soon as the taxi started up again, they were necking like sex-drunk teenagers.

About an hour later, they lay on a wet and messy bed. "Anne seemed completely genuine, great sense of humor," Luriel said.

"She has to, given who she's married to."

"*Allen*, it was very nice of Saul to take us to dinner. And you have to admit he's very bright."

"I guess. But so weird, tense and combative."

"He's just majorly insecure. When he's more comfortable, he's less odd and, believe it or not, really funny."

"Odd being a euphemism for rude and off-putting?"

"In the office the other day, we were all discussing a case, and he launched into this riff. Suddenly, he became, well, charismatic."

Allen laughed.

"No, really. It's a bit hard to picture, but believe me, we were all enthralled."

"You know what's wrong with you?" he asked. "You always see the best in everyone." He kissed her. "I'd be happy to get together with them again. But he's lucky he has her. He'd be insufferable without her."

"He seems to realize that. He's said as much to me."

He poured Luriel a glass of water from a pitcher by the bed, then took one for himself. She nodded a thank you for the water, and, realizing how thirsty she was, took a gulp. She delighted in the way he seemed to anticipate all of her desires these days.

"You do know he's madly in love with you?" he said.

"You're just projecting. You think everyone loves me." Allen had made her feel exquisitely lovable lately.

"You didn't notice him staring at you?"

"You've *got* to be kidding."

He shook his head. "By the way, I was serious before when I suggested that you cut your hair, just until they see what's up with these murders."

"Allen, do you have any idea how long the odds are of me being a victim of a serial killer?"

"Just think about it."

"People are funny when it comes to risk. Back when AIDS was rampant in New York, the risk of catching it from an unprotected sexual encounter between people in low-risk groups was about the same as the risk of dying if you drove your car four miles to get to that encounter. Yet you never heard people say, 'I'm sorry, but I won't sleep with you because I'm not willing to risk driving to your house.' There are more fatalities from TVs falling on people than shark bites. Yet, while people are scared to swim in the ocean, no one is afraid of being crushed by their television while watching *Jaws*." She giggled, then covered her face. "I guess I had plenty to drink tonight."

"That entire speech sounded like something Saul might say."

She laughed. "It did, didn't it?" She started teasing his nipples with her tongue. "I bet you a nickel I can get you turned on again."

"You're on."

* * *

"You're infatuated with Luriel," Anne said as she and Saul got into the elevator.

"Ridiculous."

"Ridiculous is exactly the way you looked staring at her like a love-sick teenager. At one point, Allen turned to me and rolled his eyes. We both smiled. You, of course, didn't notice."

Where does she get off being jealous? Saul wondered. "I enjoy working with her and having interesting work to do, even if I'm not being paid for it. Maybe I was just staring off into space while Allen's tongue was wagging to no effect."

"You didn't like him?" She actually sounded surprised. "I thought he was quite interesting, and certainly caring. They're a terrific couple. You can just see how deeply in love they are." She drew in her shoulders and arms as if she were suddenly cold. "I can barely imagine what they must have gone through losing a baby like they did. I don't think I could survive it."

He kissed her, closed mouthed. He needed to keep her calm until Monday morning. After that, she'd be plenty calm.

XII

Saul, invisible, stood by the 81st Street entrance to Central Park.

A pair of double-length cross-town busses lumbered through the intersection, blocking his view. When they passed, he saw Anne rushing to make the light, while a cluster of pedestrians waited on the curb. Perfect, there was no one within twenty feet of her. A twenty-something jogger caught her eye and smiled. Anne smiled back flirtatiously.

Saul raised his weapon. "Anne," he whispered, "I love you."

She turned toward him. Her face showed shock, then understanding.

A bicyclist with methedrine eyes jumped the curb, coming within inches of being decapitated by Saul's axe. Saul hopped back, losing his balance.

Anne screamed.

Several pedestrians froze. The jogger turned back toward her.

Saul steadied himself and again lifted the axe. His heart pounded so hard, he was sure it could be heard from ten feet away. He didn't want to kill her.

Anne began to run.

"Hey, you okay?" the jogger said.

She stopped. "Help me."

Not wanting her to suffer, Saul brought the axe down hard and sure.

The jogger ran over. Saul backpedaled, then he sauntered to his apartment building, where Mrs. Rubin was just finishing cleaning up after her arthritic collie. He followed her too closely and almost bumped into her when she stopped to talk to the doorman about the weather.

The security system permitted the elevator to go only to the floor set by the concierge in the lobby, so Saul got off at eight, behind the dog walker. After she entered her apartment, he went up to his floor via the firestairs, having left the door to them unlocked when he'd followed Mrs. Rubin out earlier. He hid his suit and axe in a secret compartment built into his living room couch, then climbed into bed. He was sick to his stomach, but, he thought, that might help put him in the proper frame of mind. His big scene was coming.

* * *

"Just before her head, uh, exploded, she screamed for help, terrified," the jogger told Detective Susan Thomas, his voice trembling. "If this was the Invisible Maniac, I think she knew him."

"Seems like you were looking pretty closely," Thomas said, turning so her face would be out of the sun's damaging rays.

"She smiled at me." The jogger adjusted his a-little-too-well-coiffed hair. "She was beautiful." He tried to swallow, but looked as if he were about to choke. "I'd seen her before."

Thomas raised an eyebrow.

"We never spoke," he said, responding to her unasked question, "but we had this smile and eye contact thing going." He was taking rapid short breaths. "I run every day.... I see her like maybe once a week."

Juan Santos came over to them after examining the body and interviewing some witnesses. "Her name was Anne Stein," he said, his back to the jogger. "Lived over there." He pointed. "Apparently she was on her way to work. Once again, no one saw anything except her head splitting open. You might not believe the killer is invisible, but no one seems able to see him."

"Let me get your name and a contact number," Thomas said to the jogger.

He gave her a business card from his fanny pack, then jogged away, weaving as if drunk.

"Why would someone carry business cards with him when he goes for a run?" Santos asked her.

"Same reason sharks take their teeth when they go for a swim." She looked at the card. Peterson & Feinburg Attorneys-at-Law, to distinguish themselves, presumably, from all the attorneys who weren't at-law. "She married?" she asked Santos.

"Yeah. Should we talk to the husband?"

"Sure, that's always a hoot."

* * *

They showed their shields to the cadaverously thin doorman. "We're here to speak to Anne Stein's husband."

He nodded, apparently having already heard about the murder. Detective Thomas was always amazed at how quickly such news traveled through a neighborhood.

"He in?"

"Didn't see him leave."

"What if he was invisible?" Santos asked.

"Never seen him invisible." The doorman sounded perfectly serious.

"Let's talk to him." Thomas pointed to the concierge. "Hopefully, he's the brains of the organization," she said to her partner, without bothering to lower her voice. They entered the opulent lobby. "There's more gold leaf and stained glass in this place than in an Italian church. All they need is a nun with a collection plate." She held her hat upside down with both hands, doing what she thought was a pretty fair impression of a nun trying to look pathetic and beatific.

Santos laughed, then took the hat out of her hands and put it on her head sideways and tilted at a rakish angle, homeboy style.

Thomas showed the concierge her badge. An array of television screens, built into his pulpit-like desk, covered all six elevators, the front door, and the three service or emergency exits. "Anything unusual this morning?" she asked.

"You're here about Mrs. Stein?" He had an Irish accent. "Wonderful woman."

"Oh, let me guess," she said. "Everyone loved her."

"She always had a smile and a friendly word." His voice had a hostile edge.

What does he have to be irritated about? she wondered. Not with his cushy job and fancy uniform, like something out of Gilbert and Sullivan. Christmas at a building like this must have been a bonanza. A cop never saw anything like that, unless she was in vice or something.

"Sincere," he continued. "You know, real. Not like some of them."

"Tipped well, too, I bet," Thomas added.

"Not as much as some."

That attitude again; what was with this creep? Maybe he needed a trip downtown to learn proper respect for authority. "See Mr. Stein this morning?"

"Not yet."

"Everyone love him, too?" Thomas yawned again.

"The wife is, uh, was the outgoing one. He never gives me no trouble, though."

"What apartment?"

"Ten B." He pointed to the elevator bank for the B line.

"Did the door open on the tenth floor this morning without anybody getting in?" Santos asked.

"Not so I noticed, but you're welcome to the security tapes."

"You okay?" Santos asked his partner as they waited for the elevator. "You look tired."

"I was up most of the night." She sighed. "My dad."

He returned her sigh. "Yeah, it's rough. Is he—"

"I'm losing him piece by piece, and there's not a damn thing I can do about it." She bit her lip. She didn't want to be thinking about her father now.

"You're doing great by him, keeping him in familiar surroundings and spending all that time with him and all. You should feel good about that."

"I guess."

"It's hard," he said.

"Isn't everything?"

* * *

Saul answered the house phone. "Yes?" He yawned as if just awakened.

"Mr. Stein, there are two police detectives here to see you."

"For me? You sure?"

"*They* seem to be."

"Okay, send them up." He smiled to impart a cheery tone. "Thanks." He paused. "Walter, are you okay? You sound, uh, troubled."

"Yeah, I'm fine, thanks."

Saul was tying the sash of his paisley silk bathrobe as he answered the door. "Hi, I'm Saul Stein. You sure it's me you want to talk to?"

The detectives flashed their shields one after the other, terrible choreography. "May we please come in?" Santos asked, polite as the choirboy he undoubtedly once was.

"Sorry about my…" Saul pointed to his robe and ran his hand along his unshaven face. "I was up late last night. Please come in." He extended his arm toward the living room.

"I'm Detective Thomas. This is Detective Santos."

He shook their hands. Thomas squeezed so hard it hurt. "What can I do for you?" He smiled like Josh.

"Wild night?" Thomas asked.

"Hardly. I was working." He wondered if he should be more annoyed that they woke him, or perhaps more insistent that they get to the business they came for. On the theory that cops, like everyone else, adjusted their behavior to conform to movies and TV, he'd been watching *Law & Order* to prepare for this encounter. However, he'd seen an entire panoply of emotional reactions. Usually the police were tenser than these clowns about having to deliver the bad news. "Can I get you coffee or something?" He walked down the long foyer and sat on the couch, intending to communicate that the coffee offer was just rhetorical. "I'm going to need to get cracking here."

"Your wife was murdered this morning," Santos said, looking him in the eyes, his voice just above a whisper.

Saul smiled crookedly. "No, she's at work." He stood, hit a speed-dial number, waited. "Hi, Karen, it's Saul. Is my wife available?" He ran a trembling hand through his hair. "Oh." He hung up. "She didn't come in," he said to the cops. He looked dazed—one of his better false expressions. "The love of my life is dead," he said silently to himself to create the proper mood. "What happened?" He shook his head. "No, there must be some mistake. Someone who looked like her?"

"Have you been reading about this invisible killer?" Santos's tone was soft and sympathetic.

"Oh, my God." Fighting back tears, he inhaled deeply. "What can I do to help?" he asked, thrusting his chin forward like F.D.R. used to. Saul regretted that he didn't have a cigarette holder between his teeth.

It appeared from Santos's glazed eyes that he hadn't the slightest idea.

"Did you and she talk this morning?" Thomas asked.

"We..." Saul buried his head in his hands, tried again. "We made love." He knew that the coroner would find evidence of that and it would enforce his image as the loving husband. Maybe they wouldn't even run genetic tests on the fetus. "Then I went back to sleep. We...she was..." His throat constricted. "Pregnant." The thought of the unborn baby brought on the tears.

"Can you think of anyone who'd want to hurt her?" Santos asked, then rubbed his bloodshot eyes.

Thomas put her feet on the Diego Giacometti coffee table. The little Degas dancer shuddered, and Thomas pulled her feet back.

"No. I'm sure not." Saul made his upper lip quiver, something he'd been practicing for weeks. "Did she suffer?"

"We think death was instantaneous," Santos said.

Thomas showed him a Polaroid. "Is this her?"

Saul believed he heard sympathy in her voice, but it might just have been fatigue. She stifled a yawn. Saul bit down hard on his lip, squinted and nodded. "How the hell can this maniac be invisible?"

"Unfortunately, there's some evidence we're not at liberty to divulge," Thomas said. She strode to the window, and Saul was struck by the realization that she was disarmingly pretty. Catching her face in profile, he noticed an endearing vulnerability that was so different from how she usually appeared to him. "You can see the scene of the crime from here," she said, breaking the spell.

Saul braced himself on the sill. The area was still cordoned off with yellow tape. He assumed the stain on the street was blood.

"If you think of anything." Santos took out his card. Thomas did the same, jockeying for position. Saul took both. "Is that a real Manet?" Santos pointed to the long painting over the oversized fieldstone fireplace.

"Monet," Saul corrected. "One of his *Water Lilly* series. It was Anne's, her favorite." He assumed they would discover that her death was a financial windfall for him. He thought it unwise to appear to be hiding it. He caught Santos's bloodshot eyes and decided to test Thomas's theory with a well-known quotation. "Human speech is so inadequate to…"

"Human speech is like a cracked kettle on which we tap crude rhythms for bears to dance to, while we long to make music that will melt the stars," Santos said; then embarrassment spread across his face.

Thomas's head jerked back as if she'd been slapped. She stabbed Santos hard with her elbow.

Saul considered eliciting other Flaubert quotations from Santos, but amusing though it might turn out to be, it probably wasn't a good idea. He stood with difficulty, the tears still coming. With Santos lending a stabilizing hand, Saul walked them to the door.

"We'll be in touch," Thomas said, more threatening than reassuring.

Listening after closing the door behind them, Saul heard Santos say, "Doesn't seem to be much there."

"I wouldn't be surprised if he did her," Thomas replied.

"Based on what?"

"I just know, okay?"

"It wouldn't be that he reminds you of the mope who killed your brother?" Santos paused. "I'm sorry. I don't know where that came from. I'm really sorry."

"You might be on to something." She sounded sad. "Doesn't mean I'm wrong, though. All I'm saying is we need to look at him closer. It's not like we've got a lot of suspects here." She sighed, then her voice turned tender. "Juan, you've got to stop coming to work high. Please. Try harder."

"I'm—"

"He knew."

"Oh, come on."

"He also knew you make literary references when you're stoned." It sounded as if she were speaking to herself more than to her partner. "How would he know that unless he'd seen you before?" She paused. "Watching you when you couldn't see him, perhaps."

Panic grasped Saul's gut.

"You saw that in his eyes, I suppose," Santos said.

"He saw it in *your* eyes; looks like you're auditioning for the 'before' in a Visine ad."

After hearing the elevator doors close behind the detectives, Saul cried. It felt good. He continued to do it until his voice acquired just the right rasping undertone. Then he telephoned Luriel.

"Hi, Saul. Thank you for a lovely time Saturday. Allen really liked meeting you. We both loved Anne."

"She's dead." His voice quivered. "I'm not coming in."

"What?"

"The Invisible…Anne was murd…I've got to get off the phone."

He hung up, and she called back. He didn't pick up. She left a message: "God, Saul. I hope I misunderstood what you were saying, but if there's anything Allen or I can do?"

Saul shut off his phone, put on Mozart's *Symphonie Concertante K* played by Jean-Pierre Rampal with the Franz List Chamber Orchestra and began reading *The Decline and Fall of the Roman Empire*, which to his embarrassment, he'd never read. With the help of a couple glasses of fine port, it turned out to be a pleasant enough way to spend a day when he was pretending to be home devastated, and actually was more upset than he cared to admit. He read a passage out loud that appealed to him: "The various modes of worship, which prevailed in the Roman world, were all considered by the people, as equally true; by the philosopher, as equally false; and by the magistrate, as equally useful."

* * *

Saul was flabbergasted that the two-hundred-and-fifty-seat chapel at Frank E. Campbell, New York's premier funeral home, was standing room only and, indeed, overflowing. He'd expected at most a hundred people and had rented it as an extravagant gesture to show how distorted his perception of Anne was.

He noted the presence of Santos and Thomas. From the way they spoke to Anne's relatives, it was clear that this wasn't the first time they'd talked to them. By then they must've already known that a three-million-dollar apartment, eight mil in art and north of forty mil in stocks and bonds were about to pass from Anne's control to Saul's. They might even have learned that he wouldn't have received a nickel in the event of divorce. Hell, if doing away with her was easy, he wouldn't have needed the invisible suit or had to kill two other women. It would be three others by the time he was done. He didn't want to kill again, but it would be suspicious if the Invisible Maniac's spree ended with Anne. Yet, here he was dawdling on the final killing, and he had yet to do anything to pin the killings on Josh. He told himself that he was waiting for inspiration, but it felt more like lethargy, and he knew he couldn't afford lethargy. That he didn't want to kill again was quite beside the point.

"Anne was the best thing that ever happened to me," Saul said to begin his eulogy, but he couldn't continue and had to be helped to his seat. He considered that he might be overdoing it, but if he gauged the reaction of the audience correctly, he was right on the mark.

He then had to sit through the speeches of Anne's sister, her brother and two of her three-dozen best friends. None of them understood that brevity was the soul of wit. It occurred to him that they might not have been striving for cleverness, but he rejected that hypothesis. Any normal person—himself, for example—would jump at any opportunity to impress an audience with his intellect, and humor was the way to do that without risking coming off as pretentious. He was pleased that, at least, all the speakers made favorable references to him and his excitement over the coming baby.

* * *

The day after Anne's funeral, Saul telephoned Josh while staring at a photograph of him and Anne at their wedding. "I need to cancel my appointment for tomorrow." His speech was slow and halting. "And all others as well."

"Don't you think that it would be helpful, maybe not now, but in a week or two, if we talked?"

"Thank you for coming to the funeral." Saul hung up.

He then called Luriel. "Just calling to tell you how much I enjoyed working for you." Painful pause. "And how much I enjoyed working with you."

"You sound…Saul. Saul, are you still there?"

He left the phone off the hook.

* * *

Saul woke but remained still. His memory returned in parts.

He heard muffled footsteps and whispered conversation. His head hurt. His stomach was gassy. He waited until he felt confident enough for his next big scene. He might have missed his calling by not going on the stage.

When he opened his eyes, Josh was at his side.

"Where am I?" Saul's voice was slurred, a nice touch, he thought.

"Mt. Sinai Hospital," Josh said. "You took a lot of booze and secobarbital. I gather you were trying to kill yourself."

He would have had to have taken three times what he had before there would have been any risk. "You heard about Anne?"

"I was at the funeral. We spoke yesterday."

"Did we?" Saul managed a vacant look. "She was my whole life. She and our child to be."

"We tend to be much more resilient than we think."

"Maybe."

"What you did was stupid and sinful."

"I…it wasn't exactly intentional. Just wanted the pain to stop. I thought…I haven't been thinking for…since Anne died. Was murdered, I mean. Have they caught the guy? Found out anything?" Saul's head felt foggy, but he thought he was putting on an Oscar-worthy performance.

"Not according to the press."

Saul called up the image of him and Anne in the early years of their marriage. They loved each other then. He began crying.

Josh sat on the bed and put his arm around him. Saul was startled by how good it felt. Just short of erotic.

"This would be a good time to call on your faith."

Saul lay back and closed his eyes. "I'm so tired," he whispered.

Luriel walked in. "Saul, what the hell did you do to yourself?"

"I'm sorry." He opened his eyes. "It was only half intentional."

"You will get through this, you know."

He bit his lip, shook his head.

"I had worse—well, as bad," she said. "Lost a child."

"You over it?" Bitter tone.

"I'm going forward." It was her turn to bite her lip. "You are coming back to work, aren't you? I really need you."

"Sure." He sighed. "I think so. I just…I need to feel stronger."

"Of course."

"How are you?" Josh asked her, sounding like a jilted lover.

Although still under the sedating influence of the barbiturates, Saul felt a surge of anger. How dare Josh come on to her?

"Good," she replied.

"Allen?" Josh asked.

"We may have some good news to report soon." She flashed her supernova smile.

That jolted Saul. He had to act quickly, dramatically and definitively.

XIII

Saul, invisible, stood behind the security desk at 441 Madison Avenue learning the patterns of visitors to the fourteenth floor offices of Banner Hastings, particularly the office of Allen Rosenthal, Esq., recently installed head of its corporate department. Some would find it tedious, but he always enjoyed detail work. The cavernous lobby—floor, walls and ceiling faintly veined white marble, sharp corners, no molding, hanging brass light fixtures—called to mind an Egyptian mausoleum complete with incense burners.

After a while, he followed a bike messenger, in Lance Armstrong U.S. Post Office Team regalia complete with hyper-aerodynamic helmet and carrying his wheel, seat and package. The elevator opened onto a reception area—dark wood paneling, oriental rugs, potted plants, couch and chairs covered in tartan plaid, prints of sailing yachts and racehorses on the walls. Apparently, they were striving for the Edwardian-sitting-room look. *Egypt, Britain, why is it that Americans have so little confidence in their own imperial destiny?* he wondered.

The messenger left the package with the receptionist, a squeaky clean Midwesterner. "Angel, honey bear," she said into the phone, "package for Allen."

Oversized walnut doors sprang open and somebody, Angel apparently, bounded out, took the package, and blew an air kiss to the receptionist. Saul followed him down the wide law-book-lined hallway. As computerized research had taken over, the books were retro décor.

Allen, feet on his desk, spoke on the phone while he responded to e-mails, keyboard on his lap. He put one Equal and one sugar into a mug of steaming tea. Saul intended to spend substantial time there; how could he get Allen to do the place up some? The sort-of-beige-not-quite-white walls were adorned only with diplomas in pretentiously thick gilded wooden frames—Duke undergraduate, Columbia Law School—and a large photograph of him and Luriel on top of a ski mountain. She looked great, errant strands of hair wisping across her face and her signature smile. As always, Allen looked as if he didn't belong; as if he'd stuck his head into a hole in a meticulously painted stage set. Allen was tall, broad-shouldered and slim-hipped with a full head of dark curly hair, but he had a thin vulpine face with uneven teeth, a long narrow nose, and close-set eyes that tended to look scared, insecure or both. He didn't deserve her. In a way Saul was about to right a wrong. The two of them together were an offense against nature.

The almost-square office had a large teak desk, a deep-maroon, leather, high-backed desk chair and two rickety-looking teak and maroon leather client chairs. File folders, lined neatly along the floor, ran the length of an entire wall. Saul sat across from them, between a file cabinet and a slender bookcase stacked with multiple copies of books that Allen had authored, published by obscure university presses—*Corporate Governance for the Nineties, Sticky Issues of Corporate Governance, Corporate Governance for the Twenty-First Century.* It was hard for Saul to imagine someone dedicating a third of his life to writing such twaddle, particularly as there were so many more interesting things to do, such as collecting tolls on the New Jersey Turnpike.

As soon as his cup was empty, Allen got up to get more tea from a watercooler with a hot water tap down the hall from his office. Saul noted the time it took for him to return. By the end of the day, a pattern had emerged. Allen left his desk for tea, to stretch his legs or to go to the bathroom—the constant consumption of tea—every forty-nine to fifty-four minutes.

During one of Allen's bathroom excursions, Saul checked the calendar on Allen's computer. During another he found, taped to the bottom of Allen's desk, the code for access to his computer and various passwords—"Luriel" for his ATM, "Benjamin" for Amazon and "A+L+B" for NexisLexis research.

At 7:15, Allen called Luriel. "I'm leaving in five minutes. Be home at the usual time." In fact, he left in fifteen minutes.

Saul had to visit several more times, but he'd made great progress. Already his life was so much more gratifying than it had been in the dreary Anne-and-practice-law era.

* * *

Saul spent tedious hours in a 42nd Street Internet cafe, under an assumed name, but he finally found just what he needed.

The New York City Department of Health and Mental Hygiene offered free confidential screening for sexually transmitted diseases, completely confidential. However, if you happened to be invisible, it wasn't much of a trick to walk in, look at the records, and sit in on telephone conversations and in-person interviews. The difficulty came in finding someone who wasn't HIV positive but who was suffering from that new strain of STD that Allen was considerate enough to reference over dinner. But that wasn't all, the person he was looking for also needed to have decided to leave her disease untreated (not having AIDS, she'd direct her attention from her health to more pressing problem such as scoring cocaine). But even that wasn't enough. That special someone he was searching for had to have supplied accurate enough information for an enterprising person—that excluded anyone who worked for the city—to locate her. Saul wasn't interested in someone who would divulge her real name or address. Such a person would be as unpredictably dangerous as someone who'd admit to an airline employee that she hadn't packed her own bags. Eventually his perseverance was rewarded. He found a promising candidate who had disguised her address by transposing digits, and her name by using a pseudonym based on her own initials, so Saul was able to identify her with reasonable diligence. He soon located her—well, he wasn't sure if "her" was the correct pronoun—and learned her habits.

* * *

On a enchanted late summer evening, Saul, invisible, stood on 52d Street between Tenth and Eleventh Avenues outside of Bethany's. He didn't go in because he had to avoid crowded places where people might bump up against him. But he didn't mind. The breeze from the river smelled of the sea. It changed direction, engulfed him in a sickly sweet odor so foreign to the city that it shocked his senses into sharp focus. What could it be? Then he recognized it: flowers—the little park at the end of the street.

An errant sheet of newspaper wrapped around his thigh. Saul yanked it away but not before drawing a curious look from a preposterously overdressed patron on his or her way into the bar. He had to be always vigilant. One wasn't invisible if coated with windblown newsprint.

The city had become dirtier since Mayor Bloomberg's austerity program; not that he had much choice in the matter given his predecessor's profligacy. It occurred to Saul that being mayor of New York could be a fabulous stepping stone. With his money and Luriel's political connections, the idea had definite possibilities. He loved the city and owed it a kind of debt, as it was, or rather would be, here that he'd found success. And, truth be told, he was no crazier than others who'd held that office. The Honorable Saul Stein.

A stick-thin black transvestite sashayed across the street. Two straight hookers materialized. "Hey, get outta here. Three holes are better than two."

"Not if you know how to use 'em, honey."

The front of Bethany's resembled that of a ramshackle clapboard house. Peeling gray paint revealed a coat of green on the splintered siding. The picture window had a diorama of a down-and-out extended family of urban poor enjoying the pleasures of bourbon and drugs; the expectation of violence and incest hung in the air. Six months before, the place was an auto repair establishment/chop shop. A couple million bucks later, it was a decrepit dive that appeared to date from the days of Mayor Jimmy Walker. New York moved so quickly that it couldn't wait for things to turn to shit by normal means.

Meri né Mark Daniels, a tall, slim blonde, emerged from Bethany's. Her black cocktail dress displayed ample cleavage and muscular legs. A gold-mesh choker covered her Adam's apple. A short, stocky, middle-aged man, wearing a designer black leather silver-studded outfit, had his arm around Meri's waist. She laughed so hard her augmented breasts shook. Saul recognized her from the Department of Health, where she had been so naïve or stoned that she had mentioned the bar as the place where she made most of her assignations. She'd told the bureaucrat that the bar was in the East Village, several blocks from the address she gave for her apartment, which—like many of the addresses used on *Law & Order*—worked out to be in the middle of the East River. He wasn't much of a TV watcher, but even before he had decided to kill, he'd rarely missed an episode—the original only, not the adulterated *Law & Order SVU* or any other of its too-abundant progeny. As a lawyer he understood that the TV show was hardly lapidary in its portrayal of the justice system; but as an observer of humankind, he knew that life adjusts to art.

Saul followed them. From the man's silence, in the face of Meri's chatter, the quickening of his step, and the brushing away of her clinging arm, Saul concluded that after three blocks, the guy had become as impatient as Saul. They stopped in the high vaulted doorway of a church. He handed her something. She spread out a cloth, daintily got down on her knees and opened his zipper and the top button of his pants with her teeth, a trick that impressed Saul as much as it evidentially had her companion. After some flicks with her surprisingly large tongue, she started in on spirited oral sex.

A well-dressed suburban couple, likely on their way from the theater to a low-priced parking lot, stopped to watch from a respectful distance. The stocky man waved, and they stormed off, offended.

When the act was completed, Meri and the man shook hands. He hailed a cab. She popped a breath mint and headed back toward Bethany's.

Shortly after she turned on to 52nd Street, Saul held a chloroform-soaked rag over her nose and mouth and dragged her into a doorway. He found a syringe in her purse, and after some difficulty, succeeded in finding a vein in her tracked arm.

* * *

Late the next afternoon, Allen got up from his desk for a bathroom run. Saul, invisible, emptied the contents of four Seconal capsules into his tea and stirred vigorously. While at it, he checked the closing stock prices displayed on Allen's computer screen. That both Hellenic Telecommunications and Apollo Group had hit new fifty-two week highs had to be a good omen. Then he went downstairs and, when the guard was distracted by the classified ads in the *Writer's Digest* he was studying, Saul did a decent job of forging Allen's signature on the sign-in/sign-out sheet. He pocketed the pen and left a pencil in its place.

When he returned, Allen had nodded off. Saul closed his door. After shaking Allen to see if he was fast asleep, Saul gently unzipped him and worked his penis out of his underwear. He lightly squeezed the head so the hole opened, then he sprinkled on and into it some grains of cocaine, the most readily available topical anesthetic, then inserted the tip of Meri's syringe, which he had previously coated with WD-40. Saul released some blood, waited until it flowed down, then squirted more. Allen squirmed, his mouth closed, his eyes opened. Saul stroked him, long and slow. His penis hardened somewhat, his eyes closed and his mouth formed a stupid smile. Saul gave another squirt. Allen hardened. Saul was getting a little excited himself, the result of the sight of blood. He injected the balance into the soft skin inside Allen's mouth. Allen woke, scanned the room with glazed eyes, then nodded off again.

At 7:30 that evening, Saul called Luriel from Allen's cell phone. When she answered, he hung up. A minute later, it rang. Saul hit start, rubbed the phone across his seven o'clock shadow to create static, then hit end. Allen's desk phone rang. Caller ID indicated that Luriel was calling from home. Presumably she was already suspicious, but not nearly as much as she would be when Allen came home the next morning with a lame story about falling asleep at his desk.

At the first hint of light in the eastern sky, Saul put some crystal meth on one of Allen's business cards—displayed in a black leather silver-trimmed card holder, part of a still-new-smelling desk set—and he held it under Allen's nose for him to inhale bit by bit as he snored. Saul wanted Allen to come home bright and perky rather than feeling as if he'd been drugged.

Allen signed out downstairs using the pencil Saul had left next to the sign-out pad. Saul erased Allen's signature, replacing it with something unrecognizable.

* * *

At Luriel's next appointment, Josh asked how she was doing with Allen. She paused before answering. Her face indicated that she was carefully framing her words. "Good, basically."

Josh bent his head forward while his eyes stayed focused on her.

"He came home at six the other morning, saying that he'd fallen asleep at his desk." Her smile was forced. "Actually, I'm quite proud of myself. A couple of months ago, I'd've been all over him, but I just accepted it. Relationships are, I've come to believe, a leap of faith."

Saul's smile was anything but forced.

"And your efforts to get pregnant?" Saul detected a hint of jealousy in Josh's voice.

"Still nothing." Now her smile was as genuine as a cat's stretch. "But we're having a hell of a lot of fun trying."

* * *

A month later, Luriel announced to Josh, "We're pregnant!" She raised her fist. Then she dropped her voice. "We're not telling anyone until after the first trimester."

"Congratulations!" Josh hugged her.

"Our fingers are crossed."

Saul's were, too.

* * *

Saul had wanted to accompany Luriel to the gynecologist, but feared being invisible in the close quarters of a strange doctor's office. He wouldn't even have known that she was going but for a cryptic note in her diary.

On her return, she yelled at her secretary for transposing numbers on a phone message. Saul hadn't ever before heard her even raise her voice to any of the staff.

A couple of days later, Saul, hearing a call from her doctor announced by the receptionist, rushed into her office ostensibly to discuss a case.

As she listened to what her doctor said, her face turned white. She picked up a pencil and broke it in half, then quarters. She stormed out without acknowledging Saul's presence or even taking her briefcase.

The next day, Saul called her at home. He got the machine and left a message: "You didn't come in, didn't call. I'm worried. Please let me know if anything is wrong. What can I do to help? You were so wonderful after Anne's, uh, murder. I'm sorry. I'm overreacting. I'm sure it's nothing, but please do call."

He then telephoned Allen at work. He wasn't in, either. "Yes!" He raised his fist.

Luriel didn't show up for her next appointment with Josh. Although it was her habit to check into the office whenever she was away from it for more than an hour or two during the work day, she hadn't once called in that entire period.

* * *

The following week, Luriel showed up for her appointment with Josh. She wore a loose black dress that reminded Saul of the garb of an elderly Greek peasant woman. Her eyes were red, her face careworn. Her hair looked like it hadn't seen a comb or brush in some time. She hadn't worn a coat despite a wintery early November wind off the river.

Josh hugged her. She rested her head on his shoulder and closed her eyes, apparently making an effort not to cry. "This is my first trip out since…" She paused as if speaking was a great effort. "A milestone."

Josh helped her to the couch. She moved like an old lady.

"Has Allen yet admitted to…?"

She shook her head. "I threw him out of the house," she said without affect.

"Don't you think that might be a little precipitous? After a pregnancy and an abortion, there are a lot of hormones—"

"Kicking his fat butt out of my life was the only thing I've done that's been the least bit satisfying."

"But you've shared—"

"What exactly have we shared?" she screamed. "What? Tell me? I want to know!" Before he had the chance to respond, she yelled, "A bunch of lies." She pounded her fist against her chest. "Josh, the man gave me VD and refuses to admit he was cheating on me." She spoke more quietly. "A normal strain of the disease wasn't enough for him. He had to find an extra-virulent variety that damaged our baby." Her tone became flat again. "He knew I wanted a child more than anything else." Her voice caught. "He couldn't even control himself while we were trying."

Josh's eyes turned a warm heather-gray. "Perhaps his disease dates back to after you lost Ben. I'm not saying that that would excuse anything, but if he flipped out a bit after that…I just think you need to have someone around, someone who can understand and share your grief." He grimaced. "My point is just that you shouldn't do anything precipitous."

"He'd had a blood test eight months ago, part of a general checkup. He's such an obsessive-compulsive little freak that he had them test for everything. Anyway, this strain just showed up recently." She was trembling. "And I haven't been one-tenth as precipitous as I'd've liked to be." She pointed at him. "But that's only because performing a penisectomy with a screwdriver would've been messy."

Josh frowned. "Possibly he contracted it in some non-sexual way. I only know him through what you've told me, but you always described him as being honest." He spoke barely louder than a whisper. "It's one of the things you admired about him."

"I suspected him of cheating. *You* persuaded me I was being paranoid."

Josh pointed to himself, a pantomime of incredulity.

"Remember me telling you that he'd stumbled in at six A.M. claiming he fell asleep at his desk?"

Josh nodded.

"I'm not proud of this, but I had someone check the office sign-in/sign-out sheets. He signed out at six in the evening. Didn't sign back in. Then I remembered he called me at seven thirty. He always calls from his office before he leaves, but that time he called from his cell phone. I called back on his cell. He didn't pick up. I called the office and got his voicemail. He never returned my call. He must have been quite occupied."

"But—"

"Don't you get it?" she screamed. "We had nothing. It was all lies."

"And when you confronted him with all this?"

"Deny, deny, deny. Like from that old movie, *A Guide for the Married Man*."

Josh's blank look indicated that he had never heard of it.

"One of Allen's favorites." Luriel began crying. Josh sat beside her on the couch and put an arm around her.

"I swear," Saul said to himself. "I'll do everything within my power to make sure that, in retrospect, her current setback will seem to her no more tragic than hitting a speed-bump at fifteen miles per hour. Hell, it's not like she's lost a child. It was an embryo, not yet eight weeks old; not even a fetus. It weighed less than a gram. I'll give her a kid soon enough, and a much smarter, better-looking one than would have been possible with Allen."

Finally, she stopped. "I'm sorry," she said.

"No reason to be sorry," Josh said, handing her a Kleenex. "Do you have anyone else you can talk to?"

She wiped her cheeks, then noisily blew her nose. "You've been great. All that time on the phone, stopping by." She sniffed. "I must owe you like a dozen more photos."

"We're not even close to even." Josh stood to indicate the end of the session, and she followed him to the door.

"Saul's been calling. I haven't been up to speaking with him, but it's been sort of comforting getting his messages," she said. "I think I'll take him up on his offers to console me. I'm not comfortable laying all my mishugaas on my old friends, but he's so recently been through a tragedy himself, he may understand. My friends pity me. I hate that. Also, I make them uncomfortable. If my life can so thoroughly turn to shit, theirs can, too. Saul isn't threatened. His life is already crap. Anyway, he's refreshing in an odd way; a breath of foul air." Her brow furrowed as if she'd had a disquieting thought. "Looking back on it, you seem to have been encouraging me to become friendly with him."

Josh responded with his usual inscrutable non-reaction.

* * *

After Luriel left, Saul stayed. He had over four hours of battery time remaining on his suit, and he still hadn't quite figured out how he'd close the trap on Josh. More information would be useful.

A few minutes later, Josh opened the door for a heavyset middle-aged man in a wheelchair.

"As I told you on the phone, Dr. Carpenter, three sets of doctors say that my nerves will never come back." The man, dressed in an expensive suit, conservative tie and a spiffy wide-brimmed fedora, had a pronounced German accent. "I brought my MRIs." He offered Josh a large flat envelope.

Josh didn't take it. "Everyone has disk abnormalities that show up on film, yet most of us can walk without difficulty."

"You really think you can cure me?"

"Yes," Josh said with granite-eyed confidence. He pointed.

In response, the man positioned his chair in the center of the room, coming within several centimeters of running over Saul. Although the man apparently had just met Josh, he looked up at him with reverence.

Saul realized that the reason Josh could be so compelling was that he truly believed in himself and his mission, whatever the hell it might be. Saul, in contrast, allowed himself to be swayed by doubts, and, in spite of repeated signs from the gods, didn't yet have sufficient faith to achieve greatness. It occurred to him that that was precisely what Josh had been trying to tell him at their first session.

"We never discussed fee, not that I'd begrudge you almost anything, if I could walk again."

"Give what seems to be appropriate to charity. I can't take a fee; I'm not licensed to practice medicine." Josh's now sea-gray eyes were even more enigmatic than usual. "Have you ever been hypnotized before?"

Brilliant, Saul thought, *what better way to get money out of suckers than to pretend you are uninterested in the stuff.* Saul believed in giving everyone the detriment of the doubt, that way you rarely went wrong.

"No."

Josh rested his large, scarred hands on the man's shoulders. "It will be quite pleasant." He massaged the man's neck and shoulders for several minutes, then rubbed his temples. He took from his desk the small, two-sided round mirror on a string, which Saul had noticed on his first visit to Josh's office, and swung it slowly in front of the man's face. "Relax. Look normally into the mirror."

Moments later, Josh said, "Yes, that's right." He sounded as if he himself were under a spell. His eyes, now the color of old asphalt, looked ancient.

"You are content. Soon you will be in a trance, and you will do what I say. Is that all right with you?"

"Yes," the man sounded as if he were far away.

Saul caught himself staring into the mirror. Careful, he told himself. Josh was uncommonly skilled at this. Saul examined each of Luriel's photographs in turn. She, too, was remarkably talented.

Josh chanted a quiet melodic incantation. Saul had a good ear for languages, but he couldn't place this one. Aramaic?

"You can walk," Josh said a few minutes later. "There's nothing wrong with your legs. Just a little muscle atrophy from not using them."

He spent a few minutes massaging the man's calves and thighs while he chanted, now *davening* like an Orthodox Jew in prayer.

"Get up, please," he commanded.

The man stood, bracing himself on the arms of his wheelchair.

"Go to the door and back."

The man moved like Frankenstein in the silent film, but he did it.

Josh, also sounding as if he were far away, said, "What are you doing now?"

"Walking."

"I'm going to snap my fingers. You will wake, fold up your wheelchair and carry it out of here."

He snapped his fingers, and both of them seemed to emerge from a deep sleep.

"I'm standing!" The man folded his chair and left.

Saul understood the power of suggestion, and Josh's charisma combined with hypnosis made his "miracle" cure understandable, but still it left Saul feeling unaccountably creepy.

The buzzer sounded.

Josh pushed the button to open the outside door, and the man returned. "I didn't thank you."

They hugged, both in tears.

An epiphany—Saul knew how to make Josh the dupe.

Josh busied himself on his computer and returning phone messages for over an hour. Saul, still feeling queasy and now desperate to go to the bathroom, yearned for an opportunity to get out of there.

At last Josh stood, about to leave, but then his phone rang and he sat and answered it.

"What's the subject matter?" he asked into the receiver. Saul had never heard him so formal or businesslike.

"Oh." He sounded unhappy but not surprised. "I have—" He looked at the clock on his desk. Saul realized that Josh didn't wear a watch. "About twenty minutes starting now. Are you in the area?" He blinked. "Okay, see you soon, then."

A few seconds later, he buzzed in Detectives Thomas and Santos.

"Detectives." Josh pointed in the direction of the couch.

From the rigidity of Josh's body language, Saul concluded that Josh was not comfortable in the presence of the police.

Santos stepped toward the couch, but when he saw his partner, arms akimbo, her eyes locked into Josh's, he stood at parade rest.

"You know, of course, there's nothing I can tell you about my sessions with Mr. Stein."

"We don't know anything of the kind," Thomas said. "You hold no licenses from the state. In fact, like your patient, there is very little record of your past."

"Oh, there you're quite wrong." Josh's eyes were a most mischievous shade of gray.

"Maybe so." Thomas's eyes also darkened, but they were malicious. No, sad and even sensitive. "In fact, you match the description of someone who escaped from a hospital for the criminally insane in Vancouver about two years ago."

If she or her partner turned up their stares one more notch, they'd be able to see his entire skeleton.

"The guy thought he was Jesus Christ," Santos added like a skinny kid talking tough because the biggest kid in the school was right beside him, although he outweighed Thomas by a good hundred pounds.

"Well, I can certainly see why they'd lock him up for that. Wouldn't want to repeat the nastiness he caused—all that preaching of love and peace."

"The Christ thing came while he was being held for trial for murdering a child abuser," Santos said. "He'd showed up in town shortly before the killing using the name Azrael."

"The Moslem name for the Angel of Death," Josh said, as if talking to himself.

"Curious, most people don't know who that is," Santos said.

Thomas handed Josh a cutout from a newspaper. "Oh, what do you know? Here's a picture of you from the *Vancouver Sun*."

Saul couldn't position himself to see it without risking discovery.

"Not much of a resemblance," Josh said, "but…" He waved his hand dismissively. "If you'd like, you can take my fingerprints and get a sample of my DNA."

"The part of the hospital where you were housed blew up." Thomas stepped toward him menacingly.

"Blew up?" Josh didn't sound surprised.

"Quite odd; all identifying evidence went with it," Santos said, staring again. "There doesn't seem to be anyone around who can—or, more accurately, wants to—ID the guy. There was a whole community of the pedophile's victims."

"Pity." Josh smiled. "So, what is it that brings you here?"

"We have our doubts about Stein's purported suicide attempt," Santos said.

"You think it was just a cry for help?" Josh mocked.

"More like a load of shit," Thomas answered. "He's already killed three times."

"I assume that if you had evidence of that, you'd arrest him," Josh said. "Or did that blow up, too?"

"You want the blood of his next victim on your hands?" Thomas asked, her face just inches from his.

"So, you have no evidence."

Right, Saul thought, his problem was Thomas's remarkably accurate gut. She suspected him because she was trained to suspect spouses, particularly those who came into money on their spouses' demise. Then there was his damn slip in his apartment where he'd gotten Santos to quote Flaubert, and Thomas realized Saul had observed Santos before and possibly while invisible. Well, none of that amounted to evidence and certainly wasn't probable cause to indict. She was sharp, though, he had to give her that.

She dropped her voice, "You can't really believe that he loved his wife. You think he's even capable of love?"

"He's far more capable than he realizes," he said. "So are you."

"He seems to have bounced back from her death quite quickly. I understand he's trying to get into Luriel Redding's pants."

Having spent considerable time observing him, Saul could tell, from the way Josh tilted his head back, that Thomas's missile hit its mark.

Thomas opened her mouth and eyes theatrically wide. "Oh, hey, she's another patient of yours, isn't she? Now there's one hell of a coincidence."

"Does it ever bother you that you have such an excessively romantic and spiritual view of life?"

"No, but it pisses me off mightily that I'll have to waste my time telling all your patients that you're a fraud. None of them will appreciate our hanging around as they go about their business."

Josh sat, caught them both in his stare and pointed to his couch.

Thomas stood firm, but then Santos complied, and she followed.

"The list of books he's bought, Internet sites visited, all under aliases, would make your hair curl," Thomas said.

"More than this?" Josh's hair was already pretty kinky.

Saul reviewed, in his head, his recent research. There was nothing that would tie him to the killings, and he didn't think that the cops could prove that the aliases were him, but they would have learned about his interest in the new strain of STD. Not that they'd be able to make the connection between him and Allen, but it still wasn't good news. How the hell had they gotten through his aliases? Hard work and good guesses and Thomas's damn gut, Saul figured, and, once again, guesses weren't evidence. It occurred to him that they were telling this to Josh because they wanted him to tell Saul how maniacal they were in their pursuit of him. They hoped the increased pressure would cause Saul to screw up. This undoubtedly was a technique they'd picked up from watching cop movies, so Saul needed to respond in kind, perhaps with extreme prejudice.

Santos was alternately squinting at the window photo and staring at it wide-eyed.

"The man pisses on everything Western culture holds dear," Thomas said.

"That's an amazing amount of wasted urine," Josh said. "It could be put to so much better use."

"In 1849," Santos said, "Flaubert spent a night at the Great Pyramid of Giza and was awakened by the sound of Jackals pissing on it."

Thomas pinched her partner's arm so hard that he winced. "Quiet," she hissed.

"Flaubert said, 'Hatred of the bourgeois is the beginning of wisdom.' You probably ought to find a more democratic role model." Apparently noticing Santos's bloodshot eyes and dilated pupils, Josh continued, "You do understand that your body is the temple of the holy spirit, and to pollute it is an offense to God?"

"His is a tent," Thomas said. "We're going to get Stein for serial murder. When he hits the wall, the shit will splatter on anyone close to him."

"I intend to love him and lead him on the right path, and, by the way, to do the same for you."

Thomas stood. “You’re not my type,” she said. She walked out with Santos following.

* * *

It was late morning, but Allen couldn’t get himself to go to work again. He continued sitting on the bed. For quite a while now, he’d been drinking tepid vodka straight from the bottle and looking out the open window of the Thorndale Hotel. He wasn’t normally a drinker, but lately he couldn’t sleep without it.

The place was a dump, the kind of room that, in an old movie, would have a neon sign blinking outside the window. When he rented it two weeks earlier, he thought it would be just for one night. He’d always been able to reason with Luriel before. Didn’t she know that he wanted a child as much as she? Didn’t she know how awful it was for him that they had to abort their child? Didn’t she know how much he wanted to be there for her? Hadn’t he proven his love for her over and over again?

His face itched. He considered shaving. Decided to scratch because it gave him something to do. After all, if he shaved, then what? He took a few more short gulps. It felt as if it were burning away his stomach lining.

A cold wind was blowing in. He considered closing the window. Instead, he had another drink.

How could he have caught an STD? Probably was a mistake to respond to Luriel’s accusation with one of his own. That was what had finally gotten him tossed out, but from whom but her could he have gotten it?

There were four empty bottles on the floor. He was on the fifth and last one. In a way he’d gone through them quickly, less than a week, but time crept by so slowly that in another way he’d been moderate in his consumption. As he learned, and later taught, in law school, there were two sides to every question; little that was black or white, few bright lines and many shades of gray. It seemed that Luriel had missed those classes.

He survived the Ben tragedy because he had Luriel. He wouldn’t survive this.

He held down number one on his cell phone, activating speed dial. He heard the satisfying ringing sound. “Hello, this is Luriel; please leave a message.” Her voice sounded so cheery, he took a celebratory gulp of vodka. “Listen to that voice,” he said out loud. “Quite obviously she hasn’t just had an abortion, hasn’t thrown her husband out.”

He called again just to be sure. "If she answers," he said to himself, "I'll beg her to let me come back. I swear I'll meet whatever condition she sets, do whatever she asks."

He repeated his vow.

His skin had a peculiar greenish yellow tinge, very subtle; the only subtle thing in his life. His life? He couldn't live without Luriel. He wasn't with Luriel. So he wasn't alive. That was a tautology. Hermetic. He was quite well educated, well read, thoughtful. Turned out none of that meant dick. None of it contributed a scintilla of significance.

He had the last sip. Just when he thought things couldn't get worse, he was out of vodka. Much to his surprise, he tossed the bottle out the window. Then, his body hanging out in the cold, he watched the bottle fall end-over-end toward Broadway. He envied its seeming purposefulness. No, like him, it was in free fall. Not free, of course; it was in the grip of gravity, but weren't we all? Most of all he envied that the bottle was rapidly reaching an end. No, a fresh new beginning, an existence as shattered glass.

From his eleventh-floor vantage point, it made just the slightest pop as it hit the sidewalk, barely perceptible over the din of traffic nose.

Pedestrians must have been cursing, wondering what kind of nut would do something like that. Allen smiled for the first time in weeks. He liked being thought of as a nut. All his life he'd been such a straight arrow. Look where it got him.

When he summoned up the energy, he'd toss out the other four.

He began crying. Luriel. He loved her. She had promised till death do us part. Ben. Their new baby. He could never recover from this. It would've been hard with her, but it was impossible without her.

He called her again.

She screamed, "Allen, go to hell!"

"Okay." He had made a solemn vow: whatever she asked.

He dove out the window.

XIV

Luriel hadn't slept all night. She'd drifted off in the early morning only to be roused by her asshole husband's incessant calls. Now, finally having gotten back to sleep, she heard a commotion in the hallway. As she sat up, she realized someone was banging on her door. Who the hell was making such a racket? Why had the doorman let them up? What were they shouting?

Emerging from her bedroom, she heard, "Mrs. Redding, it's the police," a woman's voice. "Please open the door. We need to talk to you."

Luriel yanked the house phone from its hook, but then replaced it. It probably wasn't the doorman's fault, she decided. That Thomas had been around a couple times before. She had enough testosterone flowing through her veins to fuel an entire football team.

She opened the door. "Go downstairs, have the doorman announce you, then I'll think about letting you up." She locked eyes with Thomas.

"We're so sorry to bother you," her partner, the sweet one whose name she never remembered, said.

"Fine, don't." She tried to close the door, but Thomas held it open.

"Please let us in," the male detective said. "We have some bad news." He bent his head.

She motioned for them to enter. When they did she closed the door behind them, but stood by it, hands on her hips to communicate that they weren't invited beyond the foyer. "What is it?"

Thomas met her gaze, but the other one continued to avert his eyes. "Your husband jumped out of a window a couple of hours ago," he said quietly.

"Oh, my God!" She covered her mouth. "Is he..."

"Yes."

She couldn't breathe, but somehow made it to the couch. A couple of hours? It must have been right after they'd spoken. Tears pressed painfully against her eyes.

Without being invited to sit, Thomas plopped into the chair across from her, not bothering to clear the old newspaper off it. It wasn't clear if Thomas was being insensitive or was just tired. Her face looked careworn, but when she noticed Luriel looking at her, she replaced her frown with a tight smile.

"We're terribly sorry for your loss," the other one said.

"Thank you." Luriel nodded. "Please." It was an effort to speak. "I'd prefer to be alone now." She tilted her head toward the door.

"Of course," Thomas said. "We'll just leave you with these." She handed her a sheaf of papers. "Internet sites visited by your friend Stein. Seems he was quite interested in this new industrial-strength STD." She shook her head, immediately realizing it seemed, that she'd been insensitive.

"Get the hell out of here." Luriel rushed to open the front door.

The detectives slowly followed.

"Look, I'm sorry," Thomas said. "I…I need to learn to be more tactful, but there's something you ought to know. Stein is due to inherit about fifty million bucks from his wife."

Luriel hesitated but then shoved her out the door, then slammed it so hard behind them that the plaster cracked.

She collapsed to the floor and cried.

* * *

Saul had resorted to watching the local news, although he had Schubert on in the background. He was vaguely disappointed that his invisible alter ego had faded from the public consciousness. He was restless, even depressed. He regretted killing. It wasn't that he was feeling guilty; what he had done was sanctioned—no, demanded—by the gods. He just wished he could become invisible from himself.

He always got downhearted when inactive, but, even taking that into consideration, Josh had been having a particularly pernicious effect on his psyche. The other day Josh, seemingly apropos of nothing, said, "For great wrongdoing there are great punishments from the gods." Was Josh screwing with him by quoting Herodotus, knowing Saul would recognize it? Repeating

Josh's words to himself they sounded innocuous, but his eyes were black when he spoke them, and they chilled him like an arctic blast.

Then, he'd said, again in his usual breezy style, "A few weeks ago I was watching these three young women running together in the park. They radiated such happiness, it seemed to affect everyone around them." It was almost as if Josh knew that Saul had killed one of them. It seemed that Josh was systematically manipulating him, but Saul had no idea of what he wanted from him. He asked several times, but each time Josh just responded with his damn Mona Lisa smile. "We are both better served if we let things take their natural course," he once said. Saul didn't ask what the hell that meant, because that was what he thought Josh had wanted him to do.

Saul couldn't even say why he continued to see Josh. None of his original reasons for going to him still applied. He felt as if they were bound together and could be separated only by death. It wasn't that he liked Josh, although he did. It was more that he was profoundly attracted to him, but not in a sexual way. Well, soon things would take their course, natural or not, Josh would take the fall for the murders and Saul, hand in hand with Luriel, would go on to his glorious destiny.

This inactivity was driving him crazy. Just that morning, waiting on the subway platform to go to work, he saw the usual homeless man singing for tips. The man sang the world's most annoying songs, "New York, New York," "Memories," "Somewhere Over the Rainbow," all accompanied by his snapping fingers and a saccharine smile. When anyone passed, he'd stop to turn up that damn smile and wish them "the most wonderful, stupendous day." Saul had found him irritating in the past but had always managed to tune him out. That morning, though, Saul put his face a few inches from the man's, gave him a fifty, and screamed, "Here, take this. Now, get the hell out of here and never come back! Plague some other station with your treacle."

The man's face fell. His already-yellow eyes reddened.

Saul felt awful. He'd always made it a point of honor that he never abused those who acknowledged their social inferiority to him. He'd never before raised his voice to any of them. What he did to the poor man was inexcusable and grossly out of character. It ate at him almost as much as killing did.

The one good result of his shortness of temper was that he finally took Anne's advice and threw his impossible client, Mrs. Feld, out of the office, but now he had almost nothing to do at work.

He needed to move forward with his new life with Luriel, but so far all he'd managed was a few inconsequential telephone conversations. It had been *weeks* since her abortion. In his plan she was now needy, vulnerable and psychologically open to his advances. But in the real world, she still hadn't even returned to work, so there was no point in him going there himself—hence, his inactivity. All Saul wanted was the opportunity to help her through it. He repeated to himself what he'd been telling himself daily: "I will do enough good to far outbalance all the pain I caused."

Watching the news was torture. Sensationalism upon tripe sensationalism—a story about some creep who jumped out of a window and landed on a two-year-old and her nanny, killing both.

Saul grabbed his coat and rushed out the door.

* * *

"Tell Luriel Redding that Saul Stein is here to see her," he said to the doorman, a stout man of about sixty with a friendly Slavic face and a nose like a failed creampuff.

"She left strict instructions. She'll see no one."

"I'm a friend."

"She particularly doesn't want to see friends." He paused. "Sorry."

"It's been rough for her?" Saul said.

The man grimaced but otherwise didn't respond.

Saul took out his wallet. "Benjamin Franklin thinks it would be good for her to be with a friend now." He handed the man a hundred dollar bill.

The man gave it back.

"I gather the police came by today?" Saul asked.

The doorman winced, which Saul took as an affirmative.

He shoved the hundred into the doorman's breast pocket. "Just tell her I'm downstairs and insisting that I see her, making a scene. Ask if she wants you to call the police to throw me out or if she'll see me."

After a minute's hesitation, the man pushed a button on the house phone. Getting no answer, he tried again. He turned his back to Saul and, in a soft apologetic tone, conveyed Saul's message. Then he turned back and said, "Apartment 12 C. She'll talk to you through the door." He paused. "Be gentle with her. She's good people."

"I know. Thank you."

* * *

"I saw it on the news," Saul said through the door. "Please, Luriel, let me in. You know you shouldn't be alone." His warm, concerned tone sounded as good as, or perhaps even better than, Josh's. "I refused visitors after Anne was killed. You saw where that got me—Mt. Sinai Hospital."

Saul heard her sigh, then the sound of a chain coming off the door and two locks being unlocked. She opened the door but stood blocking the doorway. She was wearing flannel pajamas and a bathrobe, her feet bare, her toes and fingernails barely hinted of vestigial polish. She had on no makeup and her eyes were red, her hair tangled. She stood before him like a heretic about to be tied to a stake set in a pile of dry wood.

Saul couldn't remember a more erotic vision. The specter of regret that haunted him in his apartment disappeared like a whiff of smoke in a gale.

"Please, let me come in." He rested his hand on her shoulder. She flinched but didn't remove it. "You know that you need a friend." He looked at his feet. "And I need to be a friend." He paused, wondering if he was capable of delivering his next line with Josh-like sincerity. "We've suffered similarly; we're kindred dispirits."

She shrugged his hand off and frowned, then shuffled down the hallway, which was festooned with photographs of her and Allen interspersed with sailing scenes and breathtaking photographic abstracts, some even better than those that adorned Josh's office. Saul followed her into a large living room with a view across 78th Street into another apartment.

Dust covered everything, and the place was past due for repainting. Much of the furniture was frayed, even torn along the seams. Saul concluded that, not only was she quite broken up over recent events, but also she was likely never much of a housekeeper. Also, with Allen out of a job and her starting up her not-for-profit firm, money had been tight for a while.

"I brought dinner." He removed from a Zabar's bag a roasted chicken, a quart of gazpacho, several portions of beef Wellington, a large asparagus and artichoke salad, and a spinach soufflé.

"That's nice of you, but I'm not hungry, and I'm sending you home in five minutes. You've been calling every day. That's nice, too, but I don't want nice. I don't want anything, just want to be left alone." She began to put the food back in the bag, but soon lost the energy or interest to complete the task.

"Come on, Luriel, don't be childish," he said more harshly than he'd intended. "Let me help you through this."

"I briefly considered doing just that, but then I realized I'd have to tell you what happened, and I couldn't bear doing that." She paused. "Fact is, I just don't feel like being with anyone, and, well, we're not even friends. You and I."

"I saw it on the news. You and Allen separated, and he killed himself. I don't have to hear any more than that. It's easier to talk to me than a friend." He shrugged. "I'm dispensable. Doesn't matter what I think."

"What about the subject of why he did it; why he was living in that dive?"

Saul decided it would be impolitic to comment on her inadvertent pun.

"Don't you think that might come up?" she continued, then shook her head violently as if trying to force away unwanted thoughts. "Saul, it's nothing personal, but I just don't want you here."

Her telephone rang, stopped for the answering machine to give multiple beeps indicating that it was full, then rang again.

"Have some dinner," he said. "Lot's of good stuff has been happening in the office. I'll bring you current."

"I don't care about the office."

Just as well, as Saul would've had to make something up, and that would have violated one of his most closely held precepts: never lie about something that is verifiable. He went into the kitchen, which was large but still contained the white enamel appliances, now badly chipped, that it had when the apartment had been a rental. Most occupants would have upgraded it when they bought the place, as part of its conversion from a rental to co-operative ownership. Copper pots hung from a trendy ceiling-mounted iron rack and dusty appliances—a juicer, a Cuisinart and several whose function Saul couldn't even guess at—crowded the expansive counter. There were two kitchen windows. Out of one he saw an air shaft; out of the other a regatta on the Hudson.

"Fine," he said. "Eat. Just start eating with enough flourish so I believe you'll have a decent meal, and I'll leave."

Luriel continued to sit on the couch, gathering the energy, he suspected, to throw him out.

He took dirty plates and silverware from the dishwasher, washed and dried them, then set the little butcher-block table in the kitchen—more intimate than the large dining room table. Was he pushing too hard? No. Great deeds are only wrought at great risks. He opened the bottle of 1994 St. Estephe that he'd brought with him, washed two dirt-encrusted crystal wine goblets and poured as much as they could hold.

When he had dinner set up, he returned to the living room, pulled her gently into a standing position and led her to the table.

"I'm sure your intentions are admirable," she said. "But I'm getting angry."

"Anger is good for you, better than lethargy. All I insist on is that you eat. We don't even have to talk. You visited me in the hospital, helped me through the darkest days of my life. I don't like owing people."

She sat, then covered her face with her hands.

He lifted his glass as if to make a toast. She didn't respond, so he had some wine and started on the soup.

She removed her hands from her face and scowled at him. She had a spoonful of soup like a petulant child condemned to eat her vegetables.

"Bon appétit," he said.

She gripped the edge of the table so hard her knuckles turned white. Saul went over to the extensive CD collection—rather, collections. Roughly half could be oxymoronically described as classic rock arranged alphabetically by artist and within that by date of issue. The other part was jazz of the type he approved of—no big bands or dance music—entropically arrayed so only about a third of the titles showed. He'd given himself a the-lady-or-the-tiger choice. If he picked Luriel's music it would help lubricate the evening, but Allen's would likely get him tossed out. He took a deep breath, then put on Miles Davis's *Kind of Blue.* He thought he noticed a fleeting appreciation in her eyes, but at least there was no increase in her displeasure.

"How are you doing dealing with Anne's death?" she asked. "It's been, what, four months?"

He drank some wine. Under the force of his stare, she followed. "Better than I ever thought I would be," he said. "When I'm busy, I'm fine. Not joyous but, you know, okay." It sounded to him as if he had captured the right tone, so he continued. "When I stop, images come flooding back: our honeymoon, of course, but also silly things like the memory of her mimicking me when I shave. She was an excellent mimic. I cry, sometimes even in public, but that passes."

Saul paused as if to get control of himself. He tried to look miserable, but he was so happy about how the evening was progressing, it was hard to be sad. He drank more wine.

She followed. "I'm sorry you felt compelled to waste such an excellent wine."

He shrugged. "I saw the news and rushed over. It was the first thing I grabbed. Anyway it's not wasted. I'm having some."

Her smile wilted before it had the chance to bloom.

“The worst time for me is at night,” he said. “I’ll wake up at like three or four in the morning feeling unbearably lonely.” This was the only topic he was sure she was interested in, so he leaned into it. He had an agenda he needed to cover, but that would have to come later.

“Yeah.” She winced. “You think it will ever be better than okay? Like it was before?”

“Josh says it’s appalling how quickly we recover from even the worst of tragedies. We’re genetically hardwired to grieve but then to forget.” Saul paused, wondering if he could seamlessly make the segue into a new subject. “He’s been very helpful, by the way.”

“It’s frightening to think how miserable I’d be without him,” she said.

Saul regretted that her tone was so peremptory. He’d hoped that she was as fascinated by Josh as he was, and that Josh would be a fertile subject for a mutually bonding conversation.

They finished their soup and sipped their wine in an increasingly awkward silence. Noticing that the sailboats he was watching out the window hadn’t moved, he realized it was a photograph.

Her brow furrowed in concentration as it did when she had a difficult strategic decision to make in a litigation. Her lips quivered. Her eyes moved back and forth. What was going on in that head of hers? Whatever it was, Saul had the feeling that it had nothing to do with Allen or her lost embryo, and that at least was progress.

He cleared away the soup and topped off their glasses.

“I love him, but I have the feeling there’s something not quite right about Josh,” she said. “Is it just my perception, or do you feel it, too?”

If Saul had used that just-a-little-too-casual tone, it would’ve meant that he was trying to suck someone in. But, he realized, Luriel wasn’t devious or manipulative, certainly not in her current condition. The important thing was that she’d taken his bait.

“I know this sounds bizarre,” Saul said, “but I’m pretty sure he had some ugly run-in with the law.”

“I know.” She sounded hoarse as if her throat constricted.

“And, I’m sure you noticed those scars on his hands, like bullet holes.”

She composed her face as if preparing to say something about which she had grave doubts. “I’ve seen them,” she said, and she pulled her chair closer to the table as if about to propose that they enter into a criminal conspiracy.

Saul, dizzy with delight, sat in calculated Josh-like silence. But the ridiculous sensation that she herself was calculating and plotting intruded on his peace. Josh was right; Saul needed to be more confident, particularly in times like these when, viewed objectively, he was succeeding. He said to himself, "Apollo, golden archer whose arrows never miss their targets, thank you for my success so far. Please give me the serenity to accept it and put my faith in you." Did he truly believe in the Greek gods? He wavered, but it comforted him to pray and the appearance of the suit on the day he learned of Anne's unfaithfulness did smack of divine intervention.

"Do you ever have the feeling that Josh thinks he's Jesus Christ returned?" Luriel asked after a considerable silence.

Saul had never expected that such a thought would have crossed her pragmatic mind, and it threw him to have misjudged her. Or was it something else that was quietly gnawing at him?

"Worse, I sometimes have the fleeting sense that that's exactly who he is." Saul glanced at his wine glass as if it had just thrown its voice. What possessed him to say that, or, even, to think it? he wondered.

She stroked her chin, an incongruously masculine gesture. "I know just what you mean."

She ate, then drank, while Saul considered her last statement. Perhaps they had more in common than even he had thought.

"You quote from the Bible a lot," she said. "I gather you grew up in a religious household?" She leaned forward.

Her interest in him made him giddy. "I'm an unusually spiritual person," he said.

"In what way?"

He so wanted her to understand him that he actually considered saying, "As the result of a painful adolescence, I started praying and sacrificing to the Greek gods. The gods responded with signs and epiphanies. I've recently given myself over to them and, with their blessing and encouragement, I kill people to fulfill my destiny." Instead he said, "I believe in God and that He has a plan for us all."

"If what I've been through is part of God's plan..." Her smile looked misplaced, like an elderly man who stumbled into a Farrelly Brothers movie having purchased tickets for the Merchant–Ivory film playing in the theater across the hall. "What would you do if you knew for a fact that Josh actually is Jesus Christ returned?" she asked, her voice trembling.

"You mean the son of God?" He could barely believe how spectacularly he was doing. They were actually conversing, and it had nothing to do with Allen's demise. "I guess I'd follow him." But Josh was going to die and take the rap for four murders long before he had the opportunity to ride into town on a donkey and declare himself to be King of the Jews. "And you?"

A cloud of indifference passed across her face, leaving only sadness and anger in its place. His time was running out.

He gave her his most endearing smile. "Are you going to give Allen a funeral?" he asked. "Sit shiva?"

Her eyes opened wide, displaying anger, which Saul chose to read as passionate fury. "Saul, I'm *really* not up for this. This ersatz romantic dinner is, frankly, it's insulting and infuriating. In about a minute, I'll have the energy to throw you out of here. If you really want to be nice, you'd leave now."

"You don't have to talk to me about it, but you do need to have answers," Saul said as he imagined a real friend might. "Your phone hasn't stopped ringing. People have expectations."

"I truly don't give a flying shit about their fucking expectations."

He'd only once heard her curse before, when she'd said "fuck" in Josh's office and then was embarrassed by it. "And a month from now, will you still not care? Life goes on, you know."

"Why are you here, bringing me dinner, forcing yourself on me?" Veins bulged in her neck and her face reddened.

He sipped his wine while he contemplated her question. Aware that in a matter of seconds she'd demand that he leave, unless he came up with something enticing, he adopted a desperate and radical strategy—the truth. Not the whole truth, of course, but a version of it. "I want, solely for my own selfish reasons, to be there for you because it will make me feel good. There's this huge hole in my life that I'm desperately trying to fill. You're brilliant, funny, sensitive, kind, and, most importantly, we truly communicate on many levels. You even seem to understand me. You're the only one I could imagine replacing Anne, so I'm trying to seduce you."

Her mouth dropped open. She sounded as if she were choking.

"The beef Wellington is superb, by the way, have some," he said. "Also the spinach soufflé. You'll find the wine goes quite well with both."

She swallowed, which solved the choking problem, but she was now hyperventilating. Not being used to that particular tack, he might have gone overboard with the honesty thing.

"That was the single most outrageous statement I've heard in my entire life," she said, but, to Saul's relief, she laughed. She looked at him through slitted eyes. "Do you have *any* idea how strange you are?"

“Far weirder than you even suspect.” No, he was still on board, and it was clear sailing ahead.

Her laughter grew louder until it almost bordered on madness. “So,” she said, recovering control, but her eyes flitted rapidly, “how do you rate your chances?”

“When I say seducing, I’m not talking just about sex. For me, sex and love are intertwined.”

“Oh, of course, like all men.” She drained her glass.

Saul refilled it. “I figure my odds at about seventy-one to twenty-nine.”

“You know how the distribution of molecules in the air is the random result of Brownian motion?” Her tone turned serious.

He nodded, pleased. He didn’t know where she was going with this, but not many women he knew understood physics, so he considered her reference a good omen.

“The chances of all the oxygen molecules in this room accumulating in that corner,” she pointed, “and us suffocating while being hit by meteors, one for each of us, are far better than you reaching first base.”

“Then you can relax and let me help you through this tragedy.”

She shook her head in disbelief.

“You really do need to focus on what you want to do about a funeral,” he reiterated. “You don’t *have to* do anything, but that should be the result of a conscious decision.”

“And this is your business because?”

“It’s what’s expected of me as your future lover.”

After several minutes of eating in silence, she said, “You are leaving after dinner, even if I have to get the police to escort you out.”

“Fine. It’s crucial that our relationship be based on trust.”

She frowned with her entire face; eyes, mouth, even the sides of her nose became arrows pointing down.

There were no recently used dishes in the dishwasher, the garbage hadn’t been taken out in days, there were no order-in cartons, and her refrigerator was empty except for items so moldy they might have dated back to Alexander Fleming’s discovery of penicillin. So it seemed that she was drinking on an empty stomach. It must’ve been getting to her big time.

He sat in Josh-like silence.

“Right before Allen jumped,” she said, pausing between each word, “I told him to go to hell.” She sat back, then pushed away from the table. “I told you that only so you’d get a hint of…” She shook her head. “Please, don’t even try to understand. I certainly don't want to talk about it with you." She scowled. "Or anyone else."

"That was pretty nasty of him. Why did you throw him out in the first place?"

"Maybe he left me."

"Inconceivable."

"You know, Saul, I sometimes find you entertaining, but I don't think I like you." She sounded as if she were making this judgment as she articulated it. "There's something terribly odd, even repellent, about you, and, my laughter jag before notwithstanding, I'm not currently in the mood to be entertained."

"You really don't need to feel constrained to be quite so honest with me."

"I mean, look at this ridiculously excessive spread." She extended her arms. "I'm surprised you don't have a single rose in a crystal bud vase."

He hit his forehead with his palm. "I'll be right back."

He returned from the kitchen, and set the vase and black rose on the table. "It's Waterford, by the way," he said.

She forced her mouth closed, then, seemingly against her will, laughed heartily.

"An hour ago, did you think you'd be laughing any time in the coming week?" he asked.

She shook her head. Tears were streaming down her cheeks.

"I read a story once about a very expensive cathouse where girls are hired by the month," he said. "Their job is to break the johns' hearts. Men need that every now and then."

"What *are* you talking about?"

"Just something I found interesting." He twirled his fork "Eat, eat."

She sipped some wine, then crossed her arms over her chest.

"Anyway, we were talking about the funeral," he said.

"No." Both her hands came forward perpendicular to the table. "*We* weren't." She then made a gesture like an umpire ruling a player safe. Then she sat up straight, pushed her plate back, crossed her utensils and held up a single finger.

Her gestures reminded Saul of a theory that early humans spoke with their hands for hundreds of thousands of years before they invented language. She had articulately communicated that she was gathering her energy to throw him out. He leaned forward, turned up the corners of his mouth and widened his eyes, mimicking Josh when he looked preternaturally concerned and compassionate. Too bad Saul didn't know how to make his eyes go lighter.

She leaned forward. "He gave me an STD." She looked as if she were about to spit. "I was pregnant, and had to abort the baby, who'd been damaged by the disease and wasn't going to develop. I've told you about losing Ben last year? How losing him broke my heart; how desperately I want a child?"

Saul nodded.

"He refused to admit he cheated on me. I threw him out, told him never to speak to me again." She sighed, then drew her hand across her face as if erasing a chalkboard.

"Thank you for telling me that."

"My point is that I hardly feel like giving him a eulogy. And shiva? You mean like a Jewish wake, but with prayers for the dead and all?" She wiped her mouth with her napkin. "I'm not Jewish. He was."

"We could modify it so there are no prayers. Reform Judaism is like Unitarianism; it means never having to do anything that makes you or anyone around you uncomfortable."

"I know you're trying to help me, and I appreciate it, but..." Without warning she was crying again.

Saul put his arm around her and whispered, "I'll do anything I can for you. You don't have to like me or even trust me. Use me. You need help to get through this tragedy."

She shook her head.

When she stopped crying, he returned to his seat. He fought back a smile but felt as if he were glowing. "Funerals and shiva are for the living," he said. "For closure and to occupy them. All religions and cultures have comparable rituals. I'll do the heavy lifting; you get involved as much as you can bear. It will make you feel better and be healthier for future relationships with your friends and family. Believe me, I just went through this."

"Saul, I may be weak and depressed, but I'm not going to let you work yourself into my life like some sort of parasitic worm."

"Parasites rarely kill their hosts. They'd then have to find somewhere else to live."

"Does this aggressiveness tempered by studied vulnerability ever work for you?"

"Never did it before." He shrugged.

"If I were single and emotionally available and you were, too," she said, "I wouldn't even consider giving you my phone number."

"In that case, I'm glad then that you're not emotionally available and that I already have your number."

It looked as if she might laugh again, but then her face became a steel mask.

"I'm abnormally intelligent, deficient in my ability to empathize, and don't feel constrained by social norms," Saul continued. "Otherwise, I'm pretty much a regular guy."

He got up to clear the table.

She also stood.

He motioned for her to sit. "Finish your wine. We're having Chateau d'Yquem with dessert."

"Oh, of course, I wouldn't expect anything less than one of the world's greatest wines when dining with a self-described sociopath."

He returned with the dessert wine, a plate of exotic cheeses and an assortment of small pastries.

"Saul, do you even have any idea how inappropriate—"

"As I said, I'm not good with social norms." He poured her some of the famously golden wine. "So, about the funeral?"

"Saul, stop!"

"I'm diverting you from your grief."

"In a peculiarly irritating sort of way."

"Would it've been better if I'd brought McDonald's and Snapple?"

"Don't you get it? Nothing would've been better." For the first time that evening she raised her voice. "I don't need anything from you."

"Of course you do."

She glared at him and bared her teeth. Her face became flushed. Then tears collected in her eyes, and she adjusted her silverware.

He pointed to her glass.

She hesitated, then took a sip.

"The funeral and shiva?" She grimaced. "How exactly do you envision me responding when people ask what happened? Or even what he was doing in that vile fleabag in the first place?"

"Probably would shut them up if you said something like, 'He gave me syphilis, and lied about how he got it. I had to abort our baby, so I threw him the fuck out.'"

She laughed. "You seem to have made me feel better in spite of myself."

He smiled with a spontaneity unmatched since his first kill. Next chance he got, he intended to sacrifice a pure-white unblemished ram to Apollo and distribute the roasted meat to the homeless. "You do know that Allen wouldn't have done it unless he was about to anyway and that you had a good reason to kick him out?" He rested his hand on hers.

She slid her hand out from under his, but he took comfort in the fact that she had hesitated for several beats before doing so.

He continued, "Of course you're a bit freaked out by it all, but—"

She stared at him as if he were a Kafkaesque cockroach. "I'm a hell of a lot more than *a bit freaked out.* I'm so fucking out of my gourd that I'm putting up with your insulting, ridiculous seduction ploy just because it's a distraction." She picked up a piece of a mini-napoleon with her fork. "How the hell do you think you'd feel if our positions were reversed?"

"If I'd decided I didn't want him to be in my life, I'd be relieved."

She dropped her fork. It hit the plate and spun toward the floor. Saul caught it in midair. He held it up, like a center fielder showing off a diving catch.

Her eyes opened wide. "That stuff before about you being deficient in empathy wasn't just chatter."

"I'm not a chatterer."

She took a big gulp of wine, then said, "By the way, two detectives were here this afternoon."

"They don't suspect that you—"

"They asked about *you.*"

On second thought, with those two detectives sniffing around, he had better postpone the ram sacrifice. They might consider it suspicious. He studied her, trying to determine if they'd planted any ugly thoughts in her mind.

She had some pastry, cheese and wine, all the while staring at him. "My first reaction was to think they were misguided, but now I see where they were coming from."

"I'm about to inherit a good bit of money from Anne, and there seems to be something not quite right about me." He popped a mini-cannoli into his mouth then licked his fingers. "But as you can plainly see, I'm not invisible."

"But you'd be able to figure out how to shoot an axe head of frozen oxygen at someone from a respectable distance."

"I love that you listen to what I say and remember it. I said that like months ago."

"You say plenty that's memorable." She shook her head. "Just to be clear, I don't mean that as a compliment." She had a reluctant bite of pastry. "They told me that you did Internet searches on new strains of STD under another name."

His gut clenched. "You're talking about that mad dog Thomas and her drug-addled companion?"

Her face showed that she didn't like them any more than he did.

"As best as I can figure, their strategy is to put pressure on all possible suspects and see what shakes out." He thought that he'd hit just the right combination of sadness and outrage. "Sort of the way the British in India used to rub salt in the eyes of possible suspects to force a confession rather than go out into the blazing sun and actually investigate. Josh showed me what they gave him, stuff from some God-awful Internet café on 42nd Street. I mean can you imagine me in one of those places? And, of course, none of it was under my name or linked to me in any way." He raised his voice. "Ask them if they have any real evidence." He paused. "I'm sorry to rant like this, but they piss me off so. It's not their slanders, but they just don't seem to be doing enough to find Anne's real killer." He made his upper lip quiver.

His pulse was racing, his heart pounding. She seemed to buy it, but he wished she'd say something.

After a long silence, she sighed. "You. This." She pointed to the table. "Allen. All of it."

He got up to clear the table.

"I'll do that. Just get out of here." She stood. "Please."

Something about her eyes or the set of her mouth reminded him of Med. Saul suppressed the memory. He stepped toward Luriel. In bare feet, she was just a couple of inches taller than him. The attraction he felt for her was so strong that she had to feel the same way.

He tilted his head slightly, parted his lips, and partially closed his eyes. Although he saw her only through slits, she appeared to be doing the same. He stood on his toes and leaned forward to kiss her good night.

She slapped him hard across the face. The sound of flesh hitting flesh echoed off the walls like a gunshot.

He stumbled, caught himself and prepared to accept her apology.

"Get out!" She pointed, her finger trembling. "Don't you *ever* try that again."

"I'll e-mail you about the funeral arrangements."

He was out the door before she had the chance to respond other than to slam it so fiercely that the hallway walls shook. His face burned. She'd chipped one of his teeth. He couldn't remember ever being hit that hard. His dick was rock-hard and aching. He pulled it out and gave it a few strokes.

He was in an apartment building hallway. There were a half dozen doors, any of which might open at any time. Didn't matter. He was so turned on he couldn't restrain himself. It just took a few more strokes. He barely got a Kleenex out of his pocket. It was an amazing feat of self-control that he didn't scream out with pleasure. Smiling, he drifted back against the wall, then, in slow motion, slumped down into a sitting position, knees up. His breath was coming in gulps. The walls were moving in and out. God, gods, that was incredible.

He wanted to go back in there. He needed to be next to her. If he kept ringing the doorbell she might call the police, but she might just be angry enough to open it and beat the crap out of him.

Amazingly his dick stirred again. He'd just come, but he was still turned on like crazy—exactly like crazy. He had to do something to dissipate his libido. He couldn't allow his cock to lead him around by the nose. His cock leading him around by the nose? Words used to be his friend.

He had to get going. He had a funeral and a shiva to plan.

XV

Red-eyed but perfectly put together and ravishing in her conservative black suit, Luriel greeted everyone who worked their way through the overcrowded reception room to the bench on which she was perched. All expressed sympathy. *Tragedy,* Saul observed, seemed to be the operative word of the day. Sometimes it was coupled with *incomprehensible*, *senseless* or *terrible*.

"Thank you," she said to Saul. "You did a fabulous job. You were right. It was the appropriate thing to do, and I couldn't have done it myself."

"Of course you could've. Just know I'm here for you."

Others came over to her to express their sympathy, and Saul, delighted by her words of appreciation, drifted back into the crowd.

Detective Thomas stuck her nose into his face. "Oh, how interesting seeing you here."

Santos sardined between them, as if breaking up a fight.

"Terrible, senseless, incomprehensible tragedy," Saul said. He opened his mouth and widened his eyes as if he'd just had an unsettling thought. "You think Allen's demise resulted from foul play?"

"Yeah," Thomas said. "Thought occurred to me when I learned you were paying for the funeral." Her face lit up in a grotesque parody of a smile. "We had a fascinating conversation with Luriel the other day, didn't we?"

"That's an understatement," Santos said.

"We gave her a listing of Internet sites you visited—you know, the ones on that industrial-strength clap, and, well, it was the strangest thing; she told me that Allen Rosenthal had caught it, probably like just a couple of weeks after your search. Now, you paying for the funeral and all. Well, the pieces are all falling into place. She's this far from rolling over on you." She held her thumb a hair from her forefinger.

"Any progress finding my wife's murderer?" Saul asked.

Santos slipped on a rubber glove then picked a hair from Saul's jacket. "As a matter of fact, we just got some of his DNA."

Saul yawned.

"Oh, look who else is here," Santos said, pointing toward Josh.

"Please excuse us," Thomas said to Saul. "Don't worry, we'll have plenty of time to chat once you're under arrest." She patted his cheek.

"Now you'll have to wash your hands," Santos admonished her.

Saul noticed Thomas's shoulders slump when she walked away. Was she putting on the macho toughness to keep her own fear and sadness at bay? He needed to find out more about her so he could use it to destroy her.

The funeral director herded the lingering multitude into the already-full chapel, the décor of which appeared to have been inspired by Chartres—same deep-blue starry ceiling.

A rabbi supplied by the funeral home—Allen wasn't religious—gave the kind of eulogy one would expect from someone who didn't know the deceased. Saul noted with pleasure the fidgeting in the audience.

Then Luriel, dignified and self-possessed, strode to the podium. One of Saul's subsidiary goals for this event was to alienate her from Allen's friends and family. The more alone she was, the more welcome his attention would be. During the pre-funeral gathering, he'd overheard whispers implying that she had contributed to or even caused Allen's suicide. There were hints that she had been cheating on Allen. She wasn't in any shape to speak, and at least some would find her mawkish presentation to be inappropriate.

"Thank you, all of you, for coming," she began. "I'd say 'Allen would be pleased,' but the truth is I'm not sure I know how he would have felt." Her voice was strong, not even a hint of the quiver that was *de rigueur* in this situation. That was fine with Saul, she would antagonize some by not being sufficiently devastated. He made a mental note to patch up her relationships with Allen's friends and family once he and Luriel became a couple.

She spoke of their pain at losing Ben, then, almost clinically, told of learning of Allen's infidelity and having to abort. People shifted uncomfortably, looked at each other and whispered. Saul controlled the urge to smile. Both Thomas and Santos were staring at him. Curiously, so was Josh.

"So, maybe you should blame me for pushing him to his death," she continued. “I truly don’t know. It turns out that there’s quite a lot I don’t know.”

Saul gauged the audience’s reaction as ranging from confused to downright hostile. Things could hardly have been going any better.

“On our fifth date, his birthday, I got him tickets to the final game of the Stanley Cup. His beloved Bruins were playing. An impossible ticket. As we were walking to the Boston Garden, we noticed a young man scaling the outside of a brownstone/walk-up. We later learned that he’d lived there but lost his keys. He fell. Five flights to the concrete sidewalk. He broke his neck and his back and was bleeding from his mouth, nose and ears.

“Allen ran to him. I called for an ambulance. Allen lay next to him holding his hand, whispering into his ear. By the time the paramedics showed up, an eternity later, Allen was covered with blood. The young man asked Allen to stay with him. I reminded him about the game and that the guy was now in the hands of professionals, but Allen insisted on staying. We were still at the hospital the next day, dealing with the boy’s immigrant parents, insurance issues, etc. One of the doctors said it was a miracle the man had lived, and he ascribed it to Allen’s warmth, caring and support.

“I went out with Allen because of his brilliance and wit, but fell in love with him for his kindness and decency.

“Allen’s father left when he was fourteen. My mother died a few weeks after my thirteenth birthday. We both grew up feeling not quite whole. As a result, I guess, we desperately desired kids of our own. Maybe we wanted them too badly. Life poses a lot of questions and offers few real answers. That’s just the way it is.”

She paused, seemingly not knowing how she wanted to continue.

“He was a wonderful, kind and generous man, a brilliant scholar, an inspired teacher. He enriched the lives of everyone who knew him. He would have been a superb father, but at the age of forty-eight, he jumped out of a window.”

On the way out, Saul hooked up with Josh and said, “I think Luriel’s doing as well as can be expected.”

“A pair of detectives were questioning me about why you paid for the funeral.”

“A friend in need.” Saul shrugged.

“One of them told me that you’re trying to worm your way into her pants,” Josh said accusingly.

“How did that make you feel?” Saul thought he did a pretty fair imitation of a TV shrink. "Personally, I don't like the word 'worm.' I'd've preferred it if they'd compared me to a long, really thick snake."

Josh didn't smile. He was getting almost as tiresome as the two detectives.

"They see a murder and think the spouse did it. Then their *modus operandi* is to get his friends to turn on him, all part of a concerted effort to harass him into confessing." Saul sounded so angry and resentful that he almost scared himself. "Meanwhile, the real killer goes free."

Realizing the edge in his voice had been inappropriate, he smiled. "I thought they'd get off my case before they got around to pestering you. I'd very much like to talk about all that at our next session."

Yes, Saul had big plans for that session. They were in the endgame. But right now he needed to devote his full attention to his seduction and winning of Luriel.

* * *

Thomas, after suggesting that Santos do some work back in the station house, caught up to Josh just after Saul departed.

"Oh, hi." She punctuated her greeting with a friendly smile. "May I walk you back to your office? You never know in this town when you might need police protection."

"Or protection from them."

She shrugged. "If you don't want to talk, then I'll be off." She turned away.

"You love your partner; that's nice to see."

"Not like you think," she said as she turned back.

"Oh, exactly like I think," he said. "But you might need to do more to help him than just worrying and chiding him when you see him high."

"I've been doing a lot of research," she said. "Twenty-eight years ago, a five-year-old Jewish boy in Montreal was orphaned when his parents wrapped their car around a tree racing friends to their lake house. The boy was taken to the hospital with minor wounds but was totally amnesic."

"So, because I don't remember that, I'm that boy?" Josh stopped at a don't walk signal even though there were no cars coming.

Caught off-sides, she stepped back onto the curb. "He was adopted by these backwoods fundamentalists. No TV or radio; only thing to read was the Bible. He was one of a dozen kids, some by blood, some not. To distinguish himself, apparently, he got into self-mutilation. Went so far as to drive wooden stakes through his hands."

"And I bet he doesn't remember that, either?"

Thomas was struck by the intelligence in his ash-gray eyes. "It's a sin to believe oneself to be God, or even God's son," she said.

"Jesus spent his entire life discovering aspects of his identity, and he never quite came to terms with that one." Josh had such a warm and compelling smile that Thomas could easily imagine how someone might be taken in by him. "I get the feeling that you're leading up to something."

She shook her head. "Just chatting; thought it would be nice to get to know you."

"It's quite agreeable to me. Is it to you?"

"Very." She tried to match his smile but failed.

"You're so much more likable and real when not playing the tough cop."

Most people didn't realize that she was playing. More and more, she didn't even know which role was the real Susan Thomas, or even if there was a real Susan Thomas. "Hey, enough about me. What are we going to do about your problem? When Stein kills again, and our investigation proceeds, all of this will come out. Maybe with embarrassing results."

"Thanks for your concern," he said. "But I don't get embarrassed much. Perhaps it's that maple leaf backwoods vigor." His face turned serious. "I bet this stirring things up often works for you. You're good at it."

She found herself liking him even if he was somewhere between deluded and stark-raving mad.

He stopped short at the window of an antiques shop, causing her to again come to a clumsy halt. "Look at that amazing icon," he said. "Russian, looks like it might be from the time of Catherine the Great."

Could he possibly have known that she collected them? And, yes, damn it, it did look as if it was from Catherine's reign, although only a handful of people in New York would have known that. "Come on, Josh, we both understand that Stein is a psychopath who never loved his wife," she said, trying not to sound thrown by him.

"We're all so complex. Context is so important that that type of characterization simply isn't useful."

"So the whole *DSM-IV*, the official psychiatrists' diagnostic manual," she explained just in case he hadn't heard of it, "is a crock?"

"Pretty much." He shrugged. "My guiding principle is that we're all capable of being transformed by love. I find it works much better than trying to fit a person into a diagnostic box."

That shit about love transforming people was true enough, but Thomas didn't see that as a positive. When her brother was shot, her love for him changed her from a peace-and-love flower child into a hard cop. Her love for her slowly dying father was turning her into an angry depressive. Her love for her partner was worrying her to death. Her love for her ex-girlfriend had made her incapable of loving anyone in the present. They walked in silence.

When they were a block from his office, she said, "You do know that this is going to end badly for you?" She'd intended to sound threatening, but it came out sounding concerned.

"Yes." He smiled. "Like last time."

* * *

There were almost fifty people in Luriel's apartment already. It was only six fifteen, and the shiva—or the pallid form of a Jewish wake that Saul had organized—had been called for six. Saul, sensing that she was becoming annoyed with his overdoing it, had acceded to her request that he go easy on the food and drink. The two bottles of wine he'd brought were already empty. Many of the guests contributed food, especially dessert, but none supplied any booze.

Josh was moving through the crowd like a minor celebrity. He ended up in front of the street-facing windows of the living room. A respectful arc formed around him. Saul and Luriel followed. Josh, *sotto voce*, asked Luriel, "Is Peter Simonson coming? I'd very much like to meet him."

Why is that? Saul wondered.

"Maybe later. His son has taken a turn for the worse." Then she whispered something Saul couldn't make out because an overweight lawyer type stepped between him and them.

Josh nodded in response to whatever she'd said but for the first time since Saul had been observing him, looked uncomfortable.

After accepting multiple condolences with grace, Luriel said, "Please help yourselves." She held her hands out palms up toward the tables on which the food and drink were set.

The rotund lawyer asked, "Is there any more wine?"

Luriel looked toward Saul, apparently forgetting that she'd specifically told him to go light on the stuff.

"I'll run out and get some," Saul said.

"Don't bother. I can do without," the lawyer said, his tone signifying the opposite.

"Please bring over a large pitcher of water and some glasses." Josh spoke in a quiet but commanding tone.

What right did he have to take over? How did he suddenly become the center of attention? Josh's and the lawyer's eyes met. Luriel smiled gratefully, then turned to comply. Saul and the attorney went along to help.

She presented the pitcher to Josh as if she were holding out a baby to receive a priest's blessing. Saul and the attorney stood by, like busboys, with the stems of wine glasses between their fingers. He had a disquieting premonition about what was coming.

The lawyer coughed and lost his grip on the glasses but recovered it before any fell.

Josh slowly drew a hand over the water, and it turned deep red.

Saul gasped.

"Anyone care to join me in some wine?" Josh asked.

The servile three filled and distributed glasses. When the pitcher was empty, Luriel, now beaming at Josh, refilled it, and gave it to him to repeat the process.

The lawyer took a sip. "A little young, but it has a long, fruity finish," he said.

"Perhaps it needs to breathe a bit," a fellow denizen of the bar said. He swirled it around in his glass then sniffed it. "Nice nose, an aroma of blackberries and minerals." He took a sip. "Good clean fruit character, well-integrated tannins, long, caressing finish. It has possibilities."

One by one the participants chimed in with their opinions. This was New York, Saul realized, no one was going to be impressed by a parlor trick, eerily reminiscent though it might have been. This was particularly true of lawyers who were too impressed with themselves to notice much else. Then he was caught in Josh's ice-gray stare and felt the temperature drop by ten degrees. Saul gulped his wine. It felt like vodka as it rushed down his esophagus, but drinking it made him lightheaded, even happy.

"Josh believes we are due for a new religious awakening," someone announced as if there were some importance to what Josh believed.

"Sure," an entirely bald man with a single large ruby earring and the build of a weight lifter said. "We're all about to join the Christian Right: gun control, abortions by coat hanger, wars of aggression in violation of international law. Do any of these clowns ever consider what Jesus would have said about all that?"

A shimmering golden light seemed to surround Josh's head.

"There's a study by this historian at Princeton or somewhere that ranks religion on a par with bubonic plague, and well above megalomaniac tyrants, in terms of numbers killed," Saul said. "Look at bin Laden and his crew.

They're cut from the same cloth as the Christian Right. The last damn thing we need is more religion."

"Because some pervert God's word, it is not a failure of God," Josh said in his usual benign tone.

"Perhaps not." Saul wasn't sure why he was competing with Josh, but now that he was, he was committed to winning. "But organized religion needs a hierarchy, and who is going to rise to the top of an organization but the most ambitious and ruthless?" He held out his arms like an eagle about to take flight.

Nods of the multitude, Luriel's in particular, encouraged him.

Josh was unabashedly staring. An enigmatic smile clung to his face like a mask.

"The problem with the religious is that they aren't content with living in accordance with their faith; they insist on regulating what others do." In contrast to his often awkward conversational style, Saul was a commanding speaker when he addressed a group. He could hold this crowd's rapt attention reading the phone book, or even one of George W's speeches.

Mr. Well-Integrated-Tannins jumped in. "The Reform Jews, Unitarians, Episcopalians, Quakers—none of them try to change others." He paused to accept the praise of his fellows.

No one acknowledged his contribution.

Luriel smiled at Saul, then refilled his glass as if presenting him with kudos—the awards given the winners of the ancient Greek Olympics.

"This wine is really improving, by the way," the previous speaker said before slinking back into himself like a snail seeking the safety of its shell.

Josh seemed to glow and shimmer. Saul realized that his unusual feelings were *just* the aura that preceded a migraine. He took a gulp of wine even while realizing that that was the worst thing he could do in his condition. He needed to go home and lie in his darkened bedroom. No, he had a few minutes.

"Yes," Saul said, "and that's why all those nice, gentle religions are endangered species." The aura receded. "Christianity is all but dead in Europe, and in this country all sects that mind their own business are losing members in droves. Want to be alone sometime, walk into a Reform synagogue on a Friday night or an Episcopalian church on Sunday. You can't have a successful religion without a message of hate." The assembled gazed with rapt attention. "Well, that may have been a bit strong, but people want to think of themselves as the in-group, the chosen ones, and the rest can all go to hell. We'd all be far better off if religion went the way of smallpox and polio."

Luriel was now staring unabashedly. This, Saul realized, was a battle between him and Josh for the attention of a woman. It was immaterial whether it was Josh's parlor trick against Saul's rhetorical skills or butting heads; it was a primal Darwinian conflict. Saul had no more interest in modern organized religion than he had in the yurt building techniques of Mongolian nomads, but he was an autodidact who prided himself on being able to discuss any subject intelligently.

"Are you content?" Josh asked the multitude. He extended his arms like Pat Robertson. His large, scarred hands were steady as steel. "Is anyone you know content? Is there one of you who doesn't ache with emptiness? Does the pursuit of material goods and sexual conquest fulfill you?"

Saul raised his glass, and having done so, felt compelled to take yet another drink. "Let's solve our woes with a crusade or pogrom." Saul pointed east. "Death to the infidel. On to Mecca."

"Your solution?" Mr. Well-Integrated-Tannins asked Josh.

Luriel refilled Saul's glass and those of the others. She looked at Saul provocatively, then at Josh.

"Love your neighbor as you would yourself," Josh responded.

Amazingly, no one laughed. While Josh got no points for originality, Saul was impressed with the sincerity of his delivery.

"We are on the verge of a great religious awakening. It will start here." Josh's outstretched arms encompassed all attending, but his pale eyes locked onto Saul's and darkened until they were black holes pulling all light into them. "The Messianic Age will start slowly and quietly in New York. From *you,* and it will spread throughout the world, because it is right, and because it is the will of God."

"I agree with Saul," one of the lawyers said, his hands in front of his mouth. "I distrust anyone who claims to know the will of God."

"Love thy neighbor like thyself too much of a stretch for you?" Josh fixed him with a stare.

"No," he whispered. It looked as if he were about to fall on his knees and kiss Josh's feet.

"Nice sentiment," Saul said, "but that message always gets perverted. Jesus, a monotheistic Jew, would be appalled if he heard that people were claiming that he was the second person in the Trinity. And the history of spectacularly unloving behavior among the various sects claiming to follow him would be beyond his ability to comprehend." Saul's head, back and shoulders ached but not from a coming migraine or even the wine. He was concentrating with all his might. He drank more, knowing he shouldn't.

"Boys are dying in Iraq because a group of the followers of the Prince of Peace decided it was His will to fabricate claims of weapons of mass destruction and use it as a pretext to go to war."

"Well, Saul," Josh commanded, "your job is to see that this time the message doesn't get perverted."

Saul laughed, but no one joined him. In the ensuing all-pervasive silence, everybody seemed to be expecting him to do something.

"I'm going to go help myself to…" Saul pointed toward the food, then backed away in that direction. He caught his leg on the bridge table on which the picked-over remnants of the lox and bagels were arrayed, and it crashed to the floor. Josh rushed over, and Luriel followed, as did the portly lawyer.

"Don't test," Josh whispered to Saul.

"Only losers are afraid of tests," Saul whispered back.

"But are you testing me or yourself?"

Luriel righted the table, and, with the clumsy assistance of the lawyer, began to clean up. Only five quarter bagels and two slivers of nova survived.

Saul turned his attention from Luriel and the lawyer to Josh, who slowly spread his arms over the table. He then took a stack of paper plates from an adjourning table and distributed lox, cream cheese and bagels. Somehow it turned out that, from that meager amount, there was enough to feed the multitude.

No one but Saul appeared to think it strange that the food was renewing itself. They thanked Josh for their ample portions with casual arrogance as if they were addressing a waiter. Luriel, though, beamed at Josh, occasionally making eye contact with Saul as if egging him on to create a miracle greater than Josh's. Saul considered that he might be imagining all or part of this. His stomach was churning; his hands and feet were cold, yet he was sweating.

"We should talk," he said to Josh, then headed down the long hallway.

Josh followed him into the bedroom.

"Do you trust me?" Saul asked.

"Far more than you do yourself." Saul took from his pocket a round mirror attached to a thin silk cord. "Enough to let me hypnotize you?"

"If that's what you want to do." Josh sat on the plush down comforter that covered Luriel's king-sized bed. "And if you're prepared to live with the consequences, I'll make myself as receptive as I can"

Saul plopped down next to him. *Luriel must be overwhelmed with loneliness every time she crawls into this huge bed,* Saul thought. Usually he was blind to other people's feelings, but now, Saul felt lonely in sympathy with her. With two night tables, two reading lamps, two dressers side-by-side, and a stunning photograph of a pair of twelve-meter racing yachts so close that their sails almost touched, it was difficult not to think of the couple that had, until recently, shared this room.

"You are susceptible to hypnosis?" Saul swung the mirror in front of Josh's eyes. This was to be a dry run, the penultimate step on Josh's road to dupedom.

"Like you, I imagine."

Their eyes met. A shiver ran through Saul. The wine thing was a parlor trick, nothing more, but the loaves and fishes thing was inexplicable. He was deeply bothered that everyone else took it in stride. He couldn't shake the feeling that it was meant only for him. At least the pre-migraine symptoms had disappeared.

Josh continued staring at him—lovingly.

Saul continued to let the mirror swing. As he stared into it, he saw his own image swinging back and forth. His mind drifted to Allen, drunk, desperate and so in despair that he jumped from a window. Saul regretted having driven him to do it.

The curtains were open and the extra-bright crime-fighting street lamps bathed the otherwise unlit room in a ghostly glow. He heard the grinding of the gears of a Number 5 bus working its ponderous way up Riverside Drive, then a foghorn off in the distance. With each oscillation, the mirror threw a rapidly moving reflection across the wall. The now total silence was palpable.

Josh's eyes were a slate-gray blank. His lids fluttering, he was about to go under.

Saul himself felt drowsy. He stared at the swinging reflection.

He forced himself to look away. Josh's hands were on his lap, palms up. Both had similar jagged scars, fronts and backs.

When Saul was sure that Josh was under his power, he said, "You are very attracted to Luriel."

Josh responded with a child-like nod.

"When I snap my fingers, you will sprint out of here, grab Luriel's breasts, kiss her open-mouthed on her lips, and then rush from the apartment." He paused. "Repeat what you are going to do."

Josh complied.

"Then you will get a cab and tell the driver to take you to Bethany's, a bar at 52nd Street between Tenth and Eleventh Avenues. Mid-block, south side of the street. You will go inside and ask for Meri. She is a tall, thin, blonde transvestite with hair very much like Luriel's. When you find her, you will buy her a double Grey Goose cosmopolitan and get one for yourself. Talk to her about whatever comes to your mind, but be sure to make an impression on the other patrons."

After Saul snapped his fingers, Josh staggered out of the room, then followed Saul's instructions. Luriel was so shocked that she didn't raise her arms to push him away until he'd disengaged and darted out her door.

Saul needed to use the bathroom, but the guest bathroom off the entrance hallway was occupied, so he went back toward the bedroom. The hallway was peculiarly long for a one-bedroom apartment. There were several doors. Believing that all knowledge was useful, he opened the first—a linen closet with neatly stacked sheets, towels and blankets. The next one was locked. His interest was piqued. He leaned against the wall, so anyone coming from the living room would see his back and be unable to determine what he was doing, and, using a credit card, Saul fiddled with the lock. When it sprang open, he looked over his shoulder and, seeing no one, jumped inside, shut the door behind him and turned on the light.

He feared he might weep. He'd been in rooms that took on the personality of their occupants, but this one had the essence of someone who'd never lived there. It was pale blue and adorned with colorful decals of dancing cartoon characters, others hung from the ceiling as components of mobiles and still others pranced along a frieze. A wicker crib, with a tiny blue quilt and a dark-blue crocheted blanket, was against one wall. Over it was a large framed needlepoint with the letters BEN made by bats, hockey sticks and balls of all description—the product of many hours of painstaking labor. Along another wall was a white dresser with a built-in flat countertop covered with a fresh towel. Infant-sized pampers, wipes and a tube of Desitin, coated with dust, were neatly set up in one corner, and a Diaper Genie, still in its box, waited by the dresser. A comfortable-looking white wicker rocking chair was parallel to the crib. In one corner was an edifice of neatly stacked, boxed gifts with faded wrapping paper and bows hanging loose. On top of them were forlorn teddy bears and elephants.

The single-gram embryo that Luriel had to abort seemed to Saul as heavy as a collapsed star.

He tiptoed out of the room as if afraid of waking a sleeping infant, turned out the light and shut and locked the door.

Shortly afterwards, a tall, handsome man, pushing a twisted five-year-old in a wheelchair, entered the living room. The crowd parted. Luriel introduced

Peter Simonson to those whom she apparently perceived to be worthy of his company.

Not making the cut, Saul emptied his wineglass to drown his disgust at the sycophantic behavior of the chosen ones. He willed himself not to think about Josh. What was done was done; back to Simonson. Having recently formed a charitable foundation that managed a multi-billion dollar fund whose twelve-member board was a who's who of American money and influence, he wielded more power than all but a handful of world figures. Saul tried to derive pleasure from the realization that he'd thwarted Josh's fervid desire to meet the man.

Simonson began talking to someone Saul really wanted to meet, Raymond W. Kelly, the police commissioner, who must have come in while Saul was off with Josh. Luriel, with her not-for-profit law firm, seemed to have made some pretty impressive—and useful—connections.

As he strolled over to them, Saul heard Simonson say, "I just read an authoritative study that credits most of the decline in crime to *Roe v. Wade*. With abortions legal, there were less unwanted children who would've otherwise turned to crime."

The commissioner grimaced.

Saul stared at Luriel until she, reluctantly it seemed, introduced him to both men.

"Why does your name sound familiar?" Kelly asked.

Saul looked at his shoes. "My wife was murdered by the Invisible Maniac," he mumbled, using the name the tabloids had given him.

"My God, that's awful. Don't worry, we'll find the guy. Our best people are on the case."

"Of the two detectives I've met, one, Juan Santos, has been stoned out of his gourd whenever I've seen him, about four times now. He's always spouting off about Baudelaire, Proust, Flaubert, while his partner yells at him to shut up or IA will get him."

"Those are quite serious charges, Mr. Stein."

"Yes, I know. Proust is incredibly boring." Saul shook his head; the wine was having an inordinate effect on him. "My wife was murdered; that's pretty serious, too. Have him tested. If it turns out I'm wrong, I'll publicly apologize and contribute a million bucks to the Patrolman's Benevolent Association." Saul handed him his card.

"The contribution *quid pro quo* is unnecessary," Simonson said, looking at Kelly.

"I'll check into it. Someone will report back to you." The cop *capo di tutti capi* glanced at an efficient-looking young woman by his side, who took a pad from her shoulder bag and made a note.

Satisfied with what he'd accomplished, Saul took his leave. "I'll be by tomorrow night," he said to Luriel. Shiva was scheduled to run for another four nights.

She hesitated but then said, "Thank you for everything."

He raised his hand to stroke her cheek, but when she flinched, he settled for shaking her hand. "I live to serve."

* * *

Saul couldn't get to sleep. Although he knew he should stay home, he felt a compulsion to go to Bethany's.

He sat naked on his bed, smoking. He'd given up the habit back when he had begun his quest for Anne. However, he started again shortly after killing her. Usually it helped him to relax, but it wasn't doing anything for him tonight.

His effort not to think about what was happening downtown caused images of the women he killed to march through his head. For about the twentieth time in as many minutes, he turned the television on, then off.

Cigarette still dangling from his lips, he rolled a joint and put on a vinyl—he loved his old record collection and was vaguely suspicious of CDs—of Helen Huang playing Mendelssohn's *Piano Concerto No. 1* with the New York Philharmonic. He repeated to himself Euripides's advice not to waste fresh tears over old griefs.

Saul had been overwrought since he'd first killed. Nothing wrong with that; indeed it would have been terrible if killing hadn't affected him. The solution was to bring this phase of his life to a favorable conclusion. Then his anxieties would recede. After tonight he would have no trouble pinning the murders on Josh. As for his immediate problem, he'd let the gods decide what he should do. He took a couple more hits on the joint and smoked yet another cigarette, then said, "Apollo, I serve you as I pursue the destiny you've chosen for me." Pacing in the dark room, he continued, "Why do I feel so troubled, even guilty?" He stopped at the window and looked down at the site of Anne's murder. "Tell me if anything I've done is not pleasing to the gods."

He took a major toke, held his breath and heard nothing. The gods weren't displeased.

"I feel the need to go downtown," he continued. "Yet I fear that would be a mistake. Please give me a sign." His prayer, the nicotine and the THC were calming him.

A pigeon flew by his window on its way south, and, just before it left his field of vision, it joined up with a second bird. Could there be a clearer sign that he should go downtown to check if Josh had done his bidding?

* * *

A cold, foggy drizzle kept the street deserted, an undeserved good break. It wouldn't do for a witness to later come forward and tell the police that he'd seen Saul and Meri together. Having enough sense not to go inside, Saul waited in a doorway across the street until he saw Meri emerge from the bar. "May I talk to you?" he said as he strolled up to her.

"Depends." Showing no concern at the appearance of a figure from the fog, she stuck out her silicone-enhanced chest and wiggled her skinny hips. "You a cop?"

He unzipped his pants.

"I guess not," she said.

"I'm curious about someone who might have been down here tonight." He handed her a twenty.

Her upper lip twitched. She squinted like someone who was having trouble with her contact lenses. In his previous observations of her, she'd never appeared to be nervous.

"A little shorter than me," Saul continued, "mid-thirties, strange gray eyes."

She handed him back the money.

He held out a hundred.

She didn't take it, turned away.

Hand on her shoulder, he spun her back toward him. "I gather you met him?"

She nodded.

"I'm a P.I. hired by his family. There's a lot I can't tell you, but take it on faith, he's a *very* troubled and dangerous man." He gave her two hundred. "We want to help him. Just tell me what happened tonight. It could be very important."

She took the money but said nothing.

"He came to the bar about nine thirty," Saul said, his voice soft and tender.

"He appeared to be looking for someone, saw you, called you by name, then ordered a couple of Grey Goose cosmopolitans, one a double, which he gave to you. Am I right so far?"

She nodded again, but showed no surprise. Apparently, what she'd been through earlier had been so astonishing that Saul's clairvoyance seemed commonplace by comparison. She wiped her hand across her face, thrust out a skinny hip and rested a hand on it. "You're really looking to help him?" she asked.

Saul responded with a warm smile.

"Can we get a drink?" she asked.

"Sure."

Saul hesitated but then stepped toward Bethany's.

"Someplace else," she said.

They hailed a cab. "Twenty-fifth and Broadway," he said to the driver.

They walked south from where the cab dropped them off. At 23rd Street, they descended to the subway. The acrid odor of urine beckoned them forward. Neither asking where they were going nor questioning the reason for the hike after they got out of the taxi, it was almost as if Meri was in a hypnotic trance. Just before the turnstile, they stopped at a closed door covered over with sloppily painted black boards and a window that looked like a closed storefront covered with old issues of *Pravda*. There was a rough-hewn wooden sign over the door that looked as if it had been painted by a seven-year-old: *Gulag*.

Saul hesitated then stepped into a room about the size of a New York City studio apartment. She followed. A black unfinished plank, casually laid over some wooden sawhorses, served as a bar. The only light came from dozens of votive candles. An anorexic blonde dressed in black stood behind the bar all attitude, but not the New York kind. Behind her, resting precariously on slanted black wooden shelves, was one of the most extensive selections of vodka in New York.

"A lot of design effort went into making the place look decrepit," Saul explained to Meri, who stared ahead like a zombie manqué. "What are you drinking? They have anything you might want as long as it's straight vodka, Russian or Eastern European."

When she failed to answer, he said to the waitress, "A bottle of Moskovskaya Pepper in shaved ice and two glasses."

Saul filled each of their glasses and chugged about half of his.

She downed hers with a sudden robotic motion.

He poured a refill, and she chugged it as well.

"I gather Josh made quite an impression," Saul said.

Saul's intention was that Josh be seen in public with her, so, after she is murdered, there would be witnesses to assist the police in making the connection between the two of them. Also, Saul wanted to test Josh's susceptibility to hypnosis. Having learned that Josh had followed his instructions, there was no longer any reason for Saul to spend more time with Meri. In fact to do so was worse than unnecessary; it was dangerous.

A bottle slipped from a shelf and crashed to the floor—an unmistakably bad omen. Yet he had an inexplicable compulsion to talk to her. At least they were here and not at Bethany's, but, he reminded himself, that was just because Meri suggested that they go elsewhere.

She took a deep breath. "A pile driver makes an impression." Her gravely voice sounded neither like a woman's nor a man's. "He did more than that." She again emptied her glass.

He refilled it. "Tell me. It will help to get it off your chest."

"We talked and drank."

"Talked? About what?" Saul kept his tone low-key and unthreatening. He had some vodka.

She followed. "He goes something like, 'This is an evil generation: they seek a sign.' I agreed; I mean that's a no-brainer, right?"

Ignoring the unreasoning panic that exploded in his gut, Saul shrugged. "Sounds pretty quotidian."

"Quotidian?" She paused. "Not coming from him, it didn't." She slid her empty glass away from her. "Then I…"

"Yes?" Saul pushed it back and refilled it.

She pushed it away again.

He rested his other hand on hers, and their eyes met.

"You seem like a nice man," she said. "Nice, but troubled."

"Troubled? Yeah, aren't we all?"

"He said he loved me," she whispered.

"Lots of people say a lot of things."

"Not like he said it, they don't."

"What did you do?"

"I'm going to have to tell you, aren't I?"

She was squeezing his hands so tightly he lost feeling in his fingertips. Even in the darkness, he could see the white of her knuckles.

"You do for your own well-being," he said.

"I got up to use the facilities, but realized I didn't need to." She took a deep breath. "Then, out of the blue, I started like going all weepy. Gobs of tears, like when my mother died. I knelt in front of him. He was stroking my head, telling me he loved me, and that his father loved me." She licked an errant tear, and with it a hunk of make-up, off her cheek. Her Adam's apple protruded from her faux gold choker. "My tears were falling onto his feet. I took off his shoes, but couldn't stop crying."

"This is all in the bar?"

"I…I guess I made a scene, but it was like, uh, no one else was there but us."

Not wanting to hear any more, he pushed away from the bar. He gave her another fifty. "Thanks." He had to get home. His face was slick with sweat.

"Please stay," she said. "I know you're not a private dick; don't know who you are, or why you're asking, but you're right. I need to tell you."

Who gives a crap about her/his fucking needs? Saul asked himself, but—and this was the strangest thing to happen in the entire damn bizarre evening—it seemed that he did. He sat.

"Thank you," she said.

He smiled weakly, but her thanks was as exciting as an appreciative gesture from Luriel would have been.

She smiled back. "So, I kept crying; tears were like pouring out. His feet were like soaked."

"Oh, my God, no," Saul said to himself. "I know what happened next."

"Yes, it was like déjà vu," she said.

Saul hadn't any idea what she meant, but apparently he wasn't just talking to himself. He'd unwittingly said it out loud. He saw spots before his eyes.

"You're so empathetic," she said. "You feel my pain."

"Yeah, empathy is my middle name."

"I don't want to know your name," she said. "I want to know you."

"Right." He wanted to know her, too, but he intended to kill her, he reminded himself. His plan was unfolding perfectly. She and Josh had made a public spectacle of themselves. There would be many witnesses.

He had to steel himself. She'd die. So would Josh. Then he'd never kill again. From there on in, it would be just good works. He was sickened by the thought of killing her or Josh, but he would push through it. The gods and he desired that he achieve his destiny, but the argument that resonated most with him was that to maintain his sanity, he needed to put this hellish phase of his life behind him, and he'd never be able to do that until the murders were cleared. Until then, Thomas would be on his ass. She would continue to try to turn Luriel against him, and might succeed if only because Luriel would come to hate her obnoxious presence. The public pressure for a conviction would grow, and he suspected that Thomas was fully capable of planting evidence on him, if she were unable to find any by doing it straight. Beneath her cynical veneer was the soul of a zealot. She'd already decided that he was guilty, and that was sufficient moral justification for her to do anything, no matter how immoral.

"What are you thinking about?" she asked.

"Uh, nothing. Just you, Josh—what we were talking about."

She put a hand on his thigh. He reached down to remove it, but ended up resting his hand on hers. Their eyes met. She smiled. "Please tell me," she pleaded.

"Why do you care?" he asked.

"I really don't know."

They both reached for their glasses, lifted them and put them down without drinking. Their eyes met yet again. They laughed.

"I'm…well, you know what I am," she said. "It's not useful in what I do to make emotional connections. My friends growing up, the few of them, aren't friends anymore. Many of my comrades from the bar and the street are dead. One even got married, and to her, now I'm dead."

"I'm pretty much on my own, too," he said.

"I think I knew that." She stroked between his legs.

He moved her hand away, but continued holding it. He liked the way her hand felt in his, strong but soft.

She said, "If you'd like to spend the night…"

"No. No, thank you." He realized he hadn't had sex since Anne died. "Not my thing."

"If we use a condom and don't kiss, it's perfectly safe," she practically pleaded.

"I'm in love with someone else."

"Does she love you? Is the sex good?" she asked. "I don't mean to pry; it's just that I don't meet guys in good relationships."

"Sorry to disappoint. We haven't had sex, and she tells me she doesn't like me much."

"I knew that, too."

"What else do you know?"

She turned his palm up and traced the lines with her fingernail. They both giggled. It had been quite a while since he'd last giggled—longer than since he'd last had sex, and, he realized, he'd missed it far more painfully.

"I don't think most people try very hard to be good," she said.

Saul shrugged.

"Hardly any try as hard as you do," she said.

"I'm smart, ambitious, not very good, though." He paused. "I plan to change that." He realized he was squeezing her hand. "Am I hurting you?"

"It's okay. I'm going numb."

They laughed again.

"This is quite lovely," he said.

"Amazing. Awesome. One of those magic moments," she replied. "They feel too real to be really real. But for me, anyway, they're all that makes life worthwhile."

"That and laughing with someone, really laughing," Saul said.

Her eyes became dreamy. "I was in a fraternity in college. Deke, this like major league animal house. You think I'm playing a role now—imagine what that was like for me."

Saul, always the outsider, found it unsettlingly easy to imagine.

"Anyway, sophomore year, before I dropped out, me and my fraters would get all shitfaced. At like two, three in the morning, only a couple of us were still conscious, and time would get all soft, round and fuzzy, and sometimes there'd be this magic connection, like." She held her hands out, palms up, her fingers pointing toward him. "But now when it happens, once a year if I'm lucky, it's so much more, I don't know, profound or something. Am I even making sense?"

"I've been drinking all night, smoked some dope too," he said.

Her eyes narrowed.

"Yes, perfect sense," he admitted.

"So that explains our connection?" she asked, looking as if she fervently cared what he'd say, like he sometimes looked at Luriel.

He might kill her, but he sure as hell didn't want to hurt her. "No. It's laughing together and knowing why. And, yes, it's special."

She beamed. "You do feel like totally close to me?"

"Absolutely."

"I'm sick. I look pretty good, but I'm rotting inside. I'm going to die soon. Will you remember me after tonight?"

"For the rest of my life."

"You swear?"

"I do." If only he could connect like this with Luriel. If only he'd had this feeling with Anne, maybe she wouldn't have cheated.

"Two lost souls meet in a bar, connect and go their separate ways." She paused. "Why is that such a poignant and compelling story?"

"Because the whole thing can be shot on a very low budget." And there was also the fact that he was going to kill her.

She grinned and shook her head as if she admired him. "You're much nicer than you think, and you really want to be better."

"You were telling me about what happened between you and Josh."

"Oh, right."

He filled her glass.

She took the daintiest of sips.

"Please hug me."

He did. She hugged him back. On disengaging, she said, "I feel like the world has changed, just a little bit." She held her thumb and forefinger close together.

Saul responded with the identical gesture.

"So, I was telling you about me and your friend," she said. "Where was I? Oh, right. So then I started drying his feet with my hair."

"Your hair?"

"I felt like compelled to do it. Strange, huh?"

Saul nodded.

"I think there's a story somewhere," she continued. "Something my mommy read to me when I was young about someone doing that."

"There is," Saul said. "You didn't by any chance then massage his feet with ointment?"

She took a tube of K-Y jelly from her purse and raised it.

Saul laughed. "History repeats itself, first as tragedy, then as farce," he said. He was certain that everything Josh did since the start of the evening was solely for his benefit or, more accurately, detriment. He concentrated on that idea until anger surged through him. He needed that anger to complete his task.

"How did he react when you anointed him?"

She stared straight ahead, seemingly gathering the strength to tell him. "He goes, 'Your sins are forgiven for you loved much.' I looked up at him, about to make a joke back. You know, something about love not being the most precise word or something. But he seemed to be like glowing, you know, like in a medieval painting. It was totally weird."

"Then he said something to you along the lines of, 'Your faith has served you, go in peace'?" Saul asked.

Her eyes opened wide. "How did you know?"

"A lucky guess."

"It made me feel like warm and, well, peaceful." She paused. "Who is he?"

"Did you ask him?"

"He said that I already knew who he was. I just had to open my heart to him."

"And did you?"

"I think so." She bit her lip and shook her head, looking almost like a little girl. "I'm scared." She intensified her stare. "My life's about to change."

Saul put a fifty on the bar and handed her a hundred, which she refused to take. He kissed her forehead and, without another word or a look back, left the bar.

XVI

Meri, her long blonde hair shimmering under the unnaturally white glare of the high-pressure sodium streetlights, knew that she looked almost beautiful, and certainly more classy than usual. Being an artifice herself, the artificial light was flattering. It spotlighted the cleavage between her too-perfect breasts, glinted off her Adam's-apple-hiding gold mesh choker and made her heavy makeup glow. It was a freakishly warm late fall night. She had just seen a newfound friend to a taxi and, after brushing off her knees and straightening her black cocktail dress, was on her way back to Bethany's. She felt sultry and feminine, but she wished she wouldn't sweat so much during sex. It was weird to be sweating outside in November, or was it December? The two hits of ecstasy in her purse seductively called to her.

She had the lovely feeling that the odd man she had met the other night was thinking about her, even watching her. She hoped he'd find peace of mind. He deserved to be happy.

A homeless man was crumpled in a sitting fetal position on the sidewalk; a beaten-up wooden picture frame rested on his shoulders. The sign in front of him read, "I've been framed." Feeling a joyous burst of energy, she broke into a run and vaulted him, clearing him by a good eight inches. She then stuck her landing and returned to her smooth, excessively feminine wiggle on the next step.

A trio of college boys hooted and applauded.

A Latino woman in her early fifties scolded, "That wasn't nice."

Meri smiled sweetly. "Suck my clit."

"Yeah, mine too," one of the young men, who was wearing an *I Survived the TriDelt Pledge-Fry Weekend* T-shirt, chimed in.

Warming to her audience, Meri put her face close to his, purred and flicked her tongue at the tip of his nose. She threw one leg over his and mimed intercourse.

The woman stared like a superhero employing deadly laser vision.

"She's a guy," a muscular boy in a too-tight *Kiss My Ass I'm on Vacation* T-shirt stage-whispered.

"I know." TriDelt stepped, back blushing. "I was just, uh. Hey, it was just a goof."

"Part of you doesn't seem to care." Meri pointed to the bulge in his crotch. "I can do stuff that would dislocate a TriDelt's jaw."

The boy's companions laughed. He joined in, but it looked as if his facial muscles had been paralyzed by a sudden stroke.

"You guys want to buy me a drink or four?" She pointed in the direction of Bethany's.

"When in New York, do as the New Yorkers do," the previously silent boy said. His T-shirt—*Beer, It's Not Just for Breakfast Anymore*—clashed with his corn-fed, pink-cheeked baby-face.

"I feel so sexy this time of year." Meri performed a clumsy pirouette, but managed to stay on her toes most of the way around. "Maybe it has something to do with being a Libra. I bet at least one of you is an air sign."

Beer Breakfast raised his hand as if shamed into volunteering for a dangerous mission.

The four of them turned on to 52nd Street. Beer Breakfast's arm was draped across Meri's shoulders and On Vacation's clung to her waist the way a five-year-old holds on to his mommy on his first day of school.

TriDelt-boy was looking behind him as if afraid that his mother was about to be transported from her Peoria kitchen to the street corner.

He froze, terrified.

* * *

Saul's blow was perfect. Meri fell in a clump. Her fingers and toes twitched for a few seconds, then quieted.

The silence was profound and terrifying.

The three boys were statues. A crowd rushed out of Bethany's. Working girls materialized from several doorways, but they maintained the silence.

"She was sick. She herself said that she'd die soon, and she seemed to be ready for it," Saul told himself. Then he flat-out admitted that he'd committed an appalling crime.

The EMS people appeared along with a gaggle of uniformed police and a swarm of CSU geeks in NYPD jackets. The uniforms set up yellow-crime-scene-tape boundaries. The flashing lights from the police cars reminded Saul of a discotheque, and he re-experienced the alienation that he used to feel at them; he was an outsider, unable to talk over the noise and dismayed that everyone else seemed to know each other and be having a good time. He decided to go home and get insensibly stoned and drunk, but he couldn't seem to move.

He strained to find a consoling thought. He'd read somewhere that people can't accurately be characterized by personality traits because their actions are merely reflections of the context in which they find themselves. There was a study made of seminary students who had been divided into two groups. Group One were those who had chosen their career because they wanted to help others; Group Two had been primarily motivated by the desire for personal salvation. Those in Group One were asked to prepare a speech to younger students on the parable of the Good Samaritan and later notified that they were expected immediately at the lecture hall. Those in Group Two were asked to speak on the relationship between the lay clergy and the professional clergy and, when they were each about to leave to give their presentation, were informed that they had several minutes to spare. As each subject separately made his way to the hall, he was confronted by an actor, dripping movie-blood, who passed out at his feet. Sixty-seven percent of Group Two stopped to help, while ninety percent of Group One stepped over the poor soul even though they had wanted to help people and the example of the Good Samaritan was fresh in their minds.

Following the logic of that experiment, Saul told himself that he wasn't inherently evil. He was merely reacting to the unfair and humiliating situation in which he'd found himself. With money and love, he would be transformed. He wondered if many other serial killers derived comfort from that article.

By the time Thomas and Santos arrived, the vortex of realization and self-loathing had taken him to a glum and dangerous place. In spite of his suit, he felt a cold wind and shivered.

"Could it possibly be that Josh really was the Second Coming?" he asked himself, desperate for diversion. No. First, Saul didn't even believe in the first coming. If Jesus had been the messiah—*christos* is messiah in Greek—he would have brought on an age of peace, and quite obviously that hadn't happened. Jesus was a good man, a religious Jew, who, for the most sterling motives, was involved in a deception. Entering Jerusalem on the back of a donkey in order to shoehorn himself into the ancient prophecy was but one of many examples of his outright manipulation. And what about the fiction that he was born in Bethlehem, Mary and Joseph having gone there for a census? There was no record of such a census nor of the Romans ever requiring their subjects to return to supposed ancestral homes to be counted. So then, if Jesus were *merely* a remarkable man of God, then, Saul wondered, why couldn't Josh be the same?

He directed his attention at the detectives. "Completely different kind of victim," Santos said to Thomas. "The others were conspicuously classy."

"Conspicuously, Juan?" Thomas's eyes were as red as those of her partner. "You high again?"

He looked down.

"I'll set up the command post," she said, pacing off a rectangle like an alpha-dog marking barriers with pee. "Go back and take another shot at the witnesses." Then her tone changed from commanding to entreating. "And please, don't use any word of more than two syllables."

He departed.

"She was a he," Santos told her on his return.

She shoved a bystander back. "Hey, give us a break here. We need space." The civilian, after barely recovering his balance, blinked repeatedly. "Get these jerks outta here," she yelled to one of the uniforms. "I'm in a baaad mood," she gratuitously explained to the guy she shoved and to everyone else on the block who didn't have a hearing deficiency.

Santos shielded his eyes from the flashing lights. "You almost had me buying that Stein did the first two as a cover for doing his wife."

"He did this one so jerk-offs like you would think it wasn't him." She looked disheartened. Then she rubbed a hand across her face and her usual tough expression returned.

"Sure, only wimps let the facts get in the way of a good theory. If you had balls, they'd be the size of grapefruits." He covered his mouth as if the last part had escaped by accident. "Seems a helluvalot more like a psychopath branching out than a guy killing his wife."

"That's what he wants us to think." She squinted. "When we figure out why he chose this particular person, we'll have him."

"Could be a copycat."

"Yeah." She nodded. "One invisible guy copying the other. Pretty soon we'll have a regular plague of invisible murderers." She sighed like one who'd recently had a death in her family. "If you're going to show up stoned, keep your mouth shut and nod whenever anyone says something that sounds halfway intelligent."

"The invisible thing *is* a problem."

"Yeah. I think you've gotten right down to the nub of it. Only trouble is we've been at that particular nub since the beginning."

"Is there anything you can take for this PMS attitude affliction of yours?"

"If you must know, I was breaking up with my girlfriend when I got the call," her voice cracked.

"Another one," Santos said, resting a hand on her shoulder. "Christ, talk about revolving doors; yours should come equipped with a tachometer." He smiled. Apparently he was trying to cheer her up. "As Flaubert observed, life is a pile of shit in which a few gold coins are buried. To get at them, we have to bend down and pick them out with our teeth."

She shook him by his shoulders. "Juan, listen to me. Listen, very, very carefully, please. You've got to stop this. You can't come to work high." Her hands slid around to his back, a modified hug. "Understand?"

"How did you know?"

She rolled her eyes. "Any of the witnesses have anything interesting to say?"

He shrugged. "Three college kids, each of whom has already tossed his cookies. There's one I want to have another go at."

"Good idea. Maybe he'd like to discuss with you the theme of illusion versus reality in *Madame Bovary*."

His face lit up with pleasure. "Ah, you do know Flaubert."

"Please, go talk to the kid," she said, sounding drained.

When her partner left, Thomas pushed a speed dial number on her cell phone. "Look, I'm sorry. I screwed up. I do that sometimes. But, and this is the important thing, I really care for you, and I want us, our relationship, to work."

To Saul's astonishment, her voice cracked. He'd never heard her sound so soft, contrite or human. Then she listened for a long time, also uncharacteristic. Finally a tear rolled down her cheek, which she blotted with a handkerchief as one would swat a mosquito. "Okay, I understand," she whispered, although it was apparent that she didn't.

Unaccountably, Saul felt the urge to hug her, stroke the back of her head, and tell her it would all be all right and any other fib that would make her feel better.

She placed another call. "Hi, everything okay?" She made a lazy circle on the sidewalk with her left foot as she listened. "May I speak to him, please? Hold the phone at his ear." She frowned. "Hi, Daddy, just saying goodnight," she said, forcing a smile. "I'll be home soon." She pushed the end button and again looked like she was about to cry.

"Susan, you gotta hear this," Santos said on his return with TriDelt-boy in tow.

The witness looked at his Nike-clad feet.

"Come on, tell her." Santos sounded as if he were talking to a young child. "You're the hero here."

"Yeah, hero," Thomas snorted, fully back in character.

"You ever watch *NYPD Blue*?" Santos asked the kid.

He tilted his head but didn't speak.

"Well, she's our Sipowitz: tough on the outside, inside as warm as the great outdoors."

"Spit it out, cornpone," Thomas said. "We got lives to get back to."

"I saw him," TriDelt-boy said. "The Invisible Maniac, I saw him."

"Can you be a bit more oxymoronic?" Santos said.

"When you go polysyllabic, it's like a fuckin' billboard that says, *I'm stoned, suspend me*," Thomas whispered to Santos. "Let me handle everything tonight. Stand there thinking deep thoughts." She pointed to the police cars. "Groove on the pretty colors."

"I was hanging with my kid, you know, reaching out," Santos explained. "I didn't expect—"

"Ah. There's an excuse Internal Affairs will just eat right up," she whispered. She turned to TriDelt-boy. "Tell us what you mean, son." She put her arm around the boy's waist and directed him toward the other side of the street. "Come into my office." When they reached a parked car, she hopped onto the hood and patted the space beside her. "Not many tourists get to break the biggest case of the year. Tonight you're talking to a real live homicide detective. Tomorrow, maybe Geraldo."

"I am not a hick. I'm a senior at IU, mechanical engineering."

She wiped a piece of vomit from his cheek with her handkerchief. "So, I guess hanging out with a she-male whore was research for your senior thesis."

He looked frightened. "You won't tell anyone, will you?"

"Of course not."

"He stepped from the penumbra into the halogen light." TriDelt-boy paused. "You know what penumbra means?"

"Yeah. Like with eclipses."

"I saw him lift his axe." His voice shook. "He stepped back into the penumbra and brought it down on her, uh his, head."

"You saw this?" Thomas motioned for Santos to come over.

"Please tell us both exactly what you saw."

He scrunched up his face, apparently organizing his thoughts. "It was just a wispy sort of image, sorta like a ghost in an old movie or something, a hooded figure like, you know, a monk or something. I think he was wearing some sort of suit that, I don't know, like reflects what's behind him or something. When he moved through different lighting conditions, it didn't quite adjust right away. I saw him for maybe a second in each different kind of light."

Saul's knees buckled.

"You're sure?" the two detectives said in unison. Then they looked at each other and the briefest of smiles passed between them.

"Positive." He gained confidence in direct proportion to the interest level of the detectives.

"Would you mind coming to the station and giving us a statement?" Santos asked.

"I'd be glad to." His BMOC voice. "The guy was about," he held up his hand, "five eight, definitely a couple of inches shorter than me."

Saul stood on his tiptoes.

Santos said, "Designing such a suit would take a lot of smarts and a lot of cash. Stein has both. Shit, *I'd* kill for the kind of money that fell into his lap on his wife's death."

"Let's get a warrant."

A man in an ill-fitting dark suit, dark tie and starched white shirt appeared from the night. "Detective Juan Santos." He showed Santos his badge. "I need you to come with me downtown."

"What the hell is this about?" Thomas looked as if she were about to punch the guy.

"IA. Stay out of this, Thomas. You're on our list."

"I'd be embarrassed not to be on your cheese-munching, ass-licking, chickenshit list."

"From what I understand, you know quite a bit about licking."

"What the fuck's that supposed to mean?"

"It means butt the fuck out of my business, stop harassing victims and find the goddamn killer or there's going to be a ton of shit flowing on you from downtown."

"Flaubert wrote quite eloquently about the tide of shit beating against civilization's walls," Santos said, making a poor attempt to strike a defiant pose.

"Come on." The man grabbed his shoulder and yanked him along.

Saul smiled, but even that pleasure was fleeting.

"Say nothing until your representative arrives," Thomas called out.

The man pointed at her. "Obstruction."

"Juan," she yelled to his receding back.

He turned his head, causing the IA creep to yank his arm.

"Great work tonight." She tilted her head toward the witness, who appeared to be having a hard time understanding what was happening.

Most of the police personnel had left. Thomas and the college boy went over to talk to his pals. Saul, too dejected to care what they said, didn't follow them. But after a while, the other two kids sauntered off, and Thomas led TriDelt boy to her car and opened the door for him. Then she said, "Please excuse me for a minute. I forgot something."

She went back to a now-deserted part of the block and looked around to see if anyone was watching her. Then she drove her fist through a car window.

XVII

Detective Susan Thomas wasn't comfortable in her Bergdorf tweed suit, a present from a former girlfriend. It didn't suit her self-image, but the shit was rolling down on her from downtown and desperate measures were called for. The key to getting results was knowing one's talents, playing to one's strengths, and hiding one's weaknesses. Thomas's strengths were doggedness, toughness and intuition. She was about to display one of her special skills. She called it *stirring the pot*, not that she'd done so well with it in her previous attempts on this case. Having weaseled past the doorman, she was pounding on an apartment door at 7:30 A.M.

"It's Detective Thomas. Sorry to burst in on you so early, but we really need to talk."

Luriel Redding opened the door. Thomas wondered how Luriel managed to look so sexy in a suit. Shouldn't she still have been crushed by her tragedies?

"I'm on my way out." Luriel's tone made it clear that no time would be a good time for her to speak with Thomas.

"You have a few minutes before your appointment with Dr. Carpenter." Thomas congratulated herself on not putting ironic stress on the man's phony title.

Luriel shrugged.

"Look," Thomas said. "I was impolite—well, downright rude—the last time we talked."

"Oh, really? You think maybe breezily telling me about my husband's suicide, then immediately hectoring me with your unbaked theories about Mr. Stein may have been a bit insensitive?"

"I'm sorry." Thomas bent her head. "I have a job to do, trying to catch your husband's killer. I don't do it in the most sensitive way." She made eye contact. Even Thomas's use of the word *killer* seemed to have had no effect on her. "May I come in, please?" she asked gently.

"This is as good a place as any to talk. I assume you won't be long."

"Are you alone?" Thomas asked.

"Isn't everyone?"

"I just thought that with you and Mr. Stein spending more and more time together. Well, you know, I'd hate to intrude on anything."

"The more time I spend with him, the more kindness, gentleness and decency I see in him." Luriel glared.

Her tone was so pointed that Thomas felt it stick into her gut. "But you *have* been thinking about what I told you?"

"Unsupported suspicions don't move me to flights of fancy." Luriel looked at her watch. "Speaking of moving, I've got to go. Too bad I don't have time to chat." She placed her hand on the door. "Anyway, you have killers to detect, sleuth, frame or whatever you do with them."

After a long, hard look, Thomas concluded that Luriel operated on a deeper and more subtle level than most of the mopes Thomas spoke to in the course of her day, and was likely a step ahead of her. The question was, in what direction had that step taken her?

"No problem. I'll walk out with you."

Luriel shoved her arms into her coat and yanked on her hat and gloves, all of exquisite fur-lined black suede which, in contrast to her disaster area of an apartment, had not a stain, crease or mark. Her husband had been unemployed for a year, Thomas reminded herself, during which time Luriel was putting together a non-profit law firm from which she'd only just started to draw a salary—seventy-five grand, which was less than Thomas made if overtime was included. Thomas had read that the average price for a New York co-op apartment exceeded one million bucks. Luriel's place was spacious, well above average, yet maintained as if it were a thousand-dollar-a-month rental. Juan—it had been just a day since his detention, and she already missed him like crazy—used to say that if the math didn't work, something was wrong, and here nothing added up.

"Your law firm keeps turning up in my life," Thomas said. All people like to hear about themselves, and lawyers like to hear and talk about their work, but Luriel's face betrayed not the slightest interest. "You got my brother's murderer out on parole—Malcolm Jones."

"He'd already done nineteen years, found God and completely reformed," Luriel said.

Thomas realized this wasn't the time for that argument. "And you got my dad back on Medicaid."

"Oh, he was part of that class? That was a good case."

"Must be satisfying doing so much good work." Thomas paused for the answer that didn't come. "I may not be as educated or sophisticated as you, but it seems to me that you, Carpenter and Stein make an odd little triangle."

Luriel strode toward the elevator. "You're about the only one I've ever met who'd profit from etiquette lessons given by Saul Stein."

Thomas followed, having to take almost two steps for every one of hers. "I have some facts for you to cogitate on." She paused, but Luriel didn't even look at her. "A she-male prostitute, a Meri Daniels, was murdered with an axe by an invisible killer a couple of days ago."

Luriel glared at her watch.

"She had the same exotic strain of VD that your husband had."

The elevator doors opened, but Luriel didn't step in.

"I assume you already know how blessedly rare it is, at least so far," Thomas continued.

They each pointed to the elevator cab—you first. They both hopped in just as the door was about to close. Their eyes met, and they exchanged brief smiles. Thomas certainly understood what Stein saw in her. Worth killing for? Perhaps.

"Where does that particular factoid take you?" Luriel's eyes were boring into Thomas.

At the next floor, they were joined by a mother with twins about five years old. Thomas made faces at the children, who reacted with delight. Luriel looked straight ahead, then, almost as an afterthought, one-upped Thomas by gaining the kids' attention with a comic expression of exaggerated surprise.

On the street, they were caught by a gust of wind. "It's got to be ten degrees colder on these blocks between Riverside and West End than anywhere else in the city," Thomas said.

"I take that to mean you haven't connected Saul to that coincidental factoid, and you just dropped it on me for its shock value?"

"You're partially right. We've been unable to link Stein with the vic." Thomas cleared her throat. "But she and *Dr.* Carpenter had an odd sort of thing going."

Luriel stopped walking. "Josh?" She raised her perfectly trimmed eyebrows. "You've *got* to be kidding."

"He was with her a week ago at Bethany's, a Hell's Kitchen hangout for she-males and their johns. Something Carpenter said or did made her cry. Several witnesses tell us that she went completely to pieces. People in her profession tend to get hardened pretty quickly, but she was bawling so hard she wet his feet. She dried them off with her hair."

"Her hair?" Luriel was staring at her, seemingly trying to read every nuance. "I assume you've asked Josh about it."

"He has no recollection. Claims he was at your place earlier that evening, then went home to bed."

Luriel turned and began walking again. "So all you have is a couple of disparate dots with no lines between them."

"He's killed once before." Thomas, having to jog to keep up with her, handed Luriel the article from the *Vancouver Sun*, which she read without breaking stride. She wondered how Luriel managed to move so fast yet gracefully in those skinny high heels? "Hard to tell from the picture one way or another, isn't it?" Thomas said.

"What have you done to be sure?"

"Dead end." Thomas frowned. "But it is food for thought, isn't it?"

Luriel returned Thomas's frown and doubled it. If this had been strip poker, Thomas would have been standing there in her Hanes cotton boy shorts.

"A transvestite in Hell's Kitchen is…" Luriel indicated with a rolling hand motion that she was searching for the right word.

"Quite different from the other three. Yet she was killed by an axe blow from someone wearing a suit that made him invisible. Someone around the height of Stein and Carpenter."

Luriel's face became a question mark, head tilted, eyes narrowed, mouth pursed.

"A witness made him out during a change of light conditions." Thomas spun on her heels. "Well, I've taken enough of your time." She said over her shoulder, "My advice is, when talking to either of them, remember the other may be there invisibly listening."

"Susan?"

Thomas turned back to see Luriel smiling at her, and what a smile it was. The wind stopped blowing and the temperature spiked.

"I apologize," Luriel said. "I underestimated you."

"Most people do," Thomas replied.

That could hardly have gone better.

* * *

It was Thomas's day off. For the past three hours, she'd been parked on Central Park West, staring into her side-view mirror, which was focused on the entrance to Saul Stein's building. How long was she prepared to continue?

As long as it took.

Sure, Juan had been coming to work stoned, and that had to stop, but he was one of the world's last great innocents. Certainly the last innocent with a gold shield. And she'd been placed on earth to protect and care for him. Stein was her enemy, and he had to be beaten, and for that to happen, he had to be broken. But what about justice? Well, that would be the judge's job. Anyway, the Saul Steins of the world were represented by high-priced lawyers. A little cutting of corners barely evened the score. And if he was innocent? Well, she had to go with her gut. True certainty, like true justice, existed only in heaven. A place she was certain didn't exist.

And Luriel? She was also the enemy. Apparently, she'd made some calls downtown, bullshit harassment charges. But why? Their meeting the other day had ended so well; Luriel had even apologized for underestimating her. Thomas hit her head for being so stupid in not realizing it right away. That was why. Luriel didn't want the cases solved. But why would that be?

Oh, shit! Luriel planned to marry Stein for his money. Somehow the two of them were in this together. The key then was to make them turn on each other. But she seemed too classy for Saul. Perhaps, but she wasn't too classy for fifty mil. She'd been a successful corporate lawyer and then brilliantly built this non-profit bleeding heart thing from nothing. One didn't do that without ambition. And would someone with such ambition be content to live in a run-down dump, with so little savings that Stein had to pay for the funeral? And Josh? Well, under that theory he was the fall guy, the one to take the rap.

Not on Thomas's watch he wouldn't.

* * *

Saul got a call from a Ms. Healey, who introduced herself as an assistant to Commissioner Kelly. "Detective Santos has been suspended, and Detective Thomas removed from the case," she said. "The commissioner asks that you please accept his assurances that it is not departmental policy to blame the victim. We'll find your wife's killer."

"I have complete confidence in how it will turn out," Saul replied. He felt no pleasure. Santos was an amusing fellow. But wasn't it good to get rid of that pit bull Thomas? He supposed so.

He lit a cigarette from the one he'd smoked down to the filter. He'd been through most of a pack, and it wasn't even lunch time. He'd put on a CD of Gregorian chants by the Benedictine Monks of Santo Domingo de Silos that he usually found soothing, but that morning they only added to his disquiet. He decided he'd rather listen to a vinyl—Pachelbel's *Canon in D-minor* but couldn't pull together the energy to make the switch.

The only thing standing between him and a full-fledged depression was the pleasure he derived from hanging out with Luriel. He'd abandoned hope of seducing her in the near term, but her grudgingly growing affection for him gave him unimaginable pleasure. Just the previous night, she'd told him he was, "A good and true friend; better than I probably deserve."

Feeling trapped inside the confines of his commodious apartment, he went for a walk in Central Park. He needed to think things out. Did he really have to close the trap on Josh?

He stopped at a playground to watch a group of children chasing each other over climbing apparatus. He lit yet another cigarette. The clouds darkened; the wind picked up. The kids didn't have raincoats. Did he care? He seemed to.

He continued on. A pure white egret flew overhead toward the reservoir, a good omen. He followed. As he crossed the Park Drive, a blonde runner reminded him of Chris, the woman he'd killed in the park. If he'd had it all to do over, he wouldn't have killed anyone except Anne. And, it now occurred to him, probably not her, either. He sighed. Maybe he just wasn't cut out for greatness. There was a sudden scurrying through the dead leaves. He jumped. A rat. Another omen. He had to end it here. There was an undeniable elegance to his plan to frame Josh, but was it really necessary, particularly now with Thomas having been brought to heel?

With one exception, he hadn't slept through the night since he'd killed Meri. Even sleeping pills didn't help anymore. He tripled the dosage his doctor prescribed and had to supplement the legally available pills with those purchased from the receptionist at his office for ungodly sums, but still they'd knock him out for two or three hours at the most. The one glorious night he'd slept was the one he spent on Luriel's couch, so close to her that he could hear her breathe through her bedroom door. But even that night, as he reviewed it now, had a disturbing undertone:

They'd been at her place drinking port. At around eleven, he, following a now established protocol, got up to leave. "Please don't go yet," she said. "I..." She wrapped some strands of hair around her fingers, then looked down. "Could you just stay a bit longer?"

He stroked her cheek, a natural reaction to her obvious discomfort, but she didn't flinch. She put her hand around his wrist and held it.

They stood there looking at each other. It crossed his mind that she wanted him to kiss her, but he didn't want to make the same mistake he'd made the day Allen died.

The moment passed. She turned away and poured them each more port, although their glasses were only half empty, or rather half full. She was shaking so badly she needed to use two hands and still spilled some. Unlike herself, she didn't jump to clean it up.

Saul got a paper towel. "Is something wrong?" he asked.

She shook her head and sat at one end of the couch. Saul sat in the middle. She moved over next to him, yet another thing she'd never done before. He put his arm around her shoulders. She smiled a tight and twisted smile, but it was a smile just the same. Saul's heart was pounding. He put his hand under her chin and turned her face toward his.

"Please don't," she whispered.

"You're shaking," he said.

"It's a little cool in here, don't you think?"

"Not really." He was sweating but couldn't tell if it was from Luriel or the temperature. "Please tell me what's bothering you."

She took a deep breath. She played with her hair.

"You do know how much I care for you and want to be your friend?" he asked.

"Yes." She examined the ends of her hair.

"Then?"

"I can't."

"Of course you can."

She shook her head. "I don't know that I want to talk about it. But the fact is that I can't. I can't express it."

"Just try. Please."

"Detective Thomas came by last week."

"Something's seriously wrong with that woman," Saul said. "I'm really sorry. She's been pestering everyone I know."

"That, uh, transvestite prostitute who was murdered by the invisible killer?"

"Terrible thing." Now, Saul had another reason to be sweating.

She had some port, took yet another deep breath, exhaled. Saul didn't know how to move the conversation forward. His arm slipped off her shoulders, and amazingly she moved it back.

"According to Thomas, she had the same strain of VD Allen had," she said.

Saul willed himself not to react, but his stomach did an ungainly somersault.

"She and Josh had some sort of weird interaction a few nights before that left her crying very publicly," she continued.

Saul leaned forward. "Surely she doesn't believe that Josh killed that, uh, person?"

"I don't know what goes through that head of hers."

"Come on, really, Luriel. You can't think that Josh would kill anyone."

"She showed me a newspaper article."

"I saw it. Did you think it was his picture?"

"Close, maybe. I don't know." She emptied her glass.

Saul did the same.

Both of them reached for the bottle at the same time. Their eyes met. They smiled. Saul had thought that after killing Meri, he'd never smile again, but he could hardly contain his delight. Luriel snuggled up to him, actually needing his comfort—what could be better?

He said, "I can understand how seeing that picture and the article on the Vancouver killing might have been upsetting, but—"

"That's not it."

"What then?"

"In one of our conversations, you'd told me that you believe in the Greek gods."

"Not, uh, not the way you probably think of them. I'd had some, uh, trauma in my early adolescence." This was neither the time nor the place for that story, he'd realized, if only because he didn't want to upstage Luriel's upset. "And you? We've never spoken about your beliefs."

"I'm a deeply committed agnostic. Or at least I used to be."

Saul turned to face her. "Used to be?"

"Thomas's visit got me thinking of that night. The first, uh, shiva."

"I don't know what got into him." Saul paused. "That wine *was* pretty strong."

She opened her eyes wide. "Did you see what he did?" She gesticulated wildly. "Water into wine? And then, I mean three little strips of nova served like fifty people. It was almost as if…"

"I thought I was the only one thrown by that."

She shook her head again. "I thought it was just me." She took a deep breath. "The victim…"

Saul nodded.

"She dried her tears off his feet—with her hair," Luriel said.

"You mean like—"

"Exactly." Her eyes were pleading to him. Had he known what they wanted, he'd have given it to them. "That night he called for a great religious awakening."

"Are you saying that you actually think he might be…" Saul was unable to complete the sentence.

"I'm saying that it all leaves me profoundly unsettled, and I don't know why. But there *is* something incredibly compelling about him."

"Yes," he agreed, "there is."

"And his eyes. You notice how they change color and show emotions in a way that normal people's don't?" She swirled the port in her glass. "You look tired."

"I haven't been sleeping well."

"Me neither." She bit her lip. "I mean just, assuming *arguendo*, as us lawyers say. If he is Jesus?"

"Yes?" Saul wanted to tell her about the miracle he saw Josh perform. The one with the man in the wheelchair, but he couldn't come up with a way to explain how he'd come to see it.

She shook her head. "Nothing."

"What?"

"Well, apparently the police are after him."

Saul drank so it wouldn't be obvious that he was at a loss for words.

"I mean, just following the line of thought," she said. "If he were soon to die?"

"I don't know."

"He exerts this, like, pull on me," she said. "He's like no one else I ever met."

"Me, too."

"I'm scared."

"I am, too." He took her hand.

"Would you mind sleeping here tonight?" She pointed to the couch, clearing up any ambiguity in her question.

"Not at all."

Now, as he walked through the park, he reviewed his conversation with Luriel for maybe the fifteenth time. That they shared the same fears and thoughts made him hopeful that she might turn out to be the love of his life. He'd come to believe that his marriage with Anne had failed because he wanted her for what she represented, not who she was. That he now understood that was yet another thing for which he had to thank, or curse, Josh.

He admired Luriel's razor-sharp mind. If she too saw the divinity in Josh, could it be that he actually was the Second Coming? It was one thing to want to kill your wife. Quite another to kill Jesus. Indeed, if Josh really was Jesus, shouldn't he follow him?

He took another cigarette out of the pack, but, no longer feeling like smoking it, slid it back. Maybe he was just overtired. Once he killed Josh, he could put it all behind him with finality. Needing to be alone, he headed for a small wooded area.

No, he wasn't going to kill Josh. It must end here. He'd never kill again. He'd make an effort to befriend Josh. He wanted very much to get to know him, even if he did blame him—and Luriel—for planting and nurturing the seed of guilt inside his soul.

* * *

Thomas followed Stein into the park.

He stopped in front of a playground. Adults unaccompanied by children weren't permitted. One step inside, and she'd nab him for child molesting.

But he walked on. He was watching the runners. Perhaps he was planning another murder. *Someone should stake out this area,* she thought. Unbelievable that she had been kicked off the case. Fucking brass knuckling under to pressure from a killer. Outrageous. Or was it push from that stuck-up bitch Redding? Well, either way, she would set it right. When she got pushed, it was her nature to push back harder.

With Stein, Carpenter and Redding on her radar screen, this was getting to be a full-time job in addition to her real job. She was exhausted. Getting up three times a night to feed her father through a tube was wearing her down, particularly as she couldn't even pretend any longer that he recognized her. At least she'd soon be getting some healthful relaxing exercise.

Stein was on the move again. He was the killer; she knew it. If only she could prove it. Her new steel-toed combat boots made a crunching noise on the old leaves and twigs. She surveyed the area. There was no one around but joggers and an occasional rider on the bridal path. Off to the right was a brick bathroom and equipment shed. She closed her eyes, willing him to go behind there. If he did, he'd be invisible from the Park Drive and the paths. *Invisible*. She smiled. She might not have been the smartest cop on the force, but when she latched onto a case, she didn't give up. Not when the victims reminded her of her murdered brother—a more and more frequent occurrence. Indeed none of these victims were the least bit like him, but just the same, the connection was there, innocents killed for no reason.

Yes! He stopped behind the shed. He seemed to be lost in thought. She approached quietly as she used to when hunting deer with a bow. She grabbed Stein's shoulder and spun him around.

"Thom—"

She drove her knee into his groin. As he bent forward, she rammed her knuckles into his eyes, and he fell to his knees.

She kicked him in the face, and blood spurted from his nose and lips. She liked her new boots.

Grabbing his ears, she yanked him to his knees. "I guess you heard, I'm officially off the case, but, as you can see, unofficially I'm still all over it."

He sat up slowly, wiped blood from his face and blinked his bloodshot eyes.

"I'm curious if you're planning to file a complaint against me?" she asked pleasantly. "If so, it would make sense for me to kill you here and now."

"And if not?"

"Well, then, we've had this pleasant little talk and bygones will be bygones. That is until I put together a case against you, and you get the needle with me sitting in the front row of the audience eating popcorn and clapping."

Stein grimaced. "This is all about what I did to Santos?"

"That and general principles."

"But you do agree that he deserved it? Detectives shouldn't come to work high."

"I just noticed that my last kick landed a little to the right, rather than square on the chin." She pointed to the spreading black and blue mark on his cheek and chin. "For the sake of symmetry alone, I owe you another one."

"Please tell me."

"Why you askin'?"

"Lately I've been trying to get a handle on what makes people tick. You, in particular, interest me."

It unnerved her that Saul didn't even sound angry. Why was he focusing on that of all things? She must have scrambled his brain. "He didn't deserve to take shit from you and Luriel Redding's highly placed friends."

"Granted, but why do you care enough to put your career on the line?"

"Because I don't like you." She raised her left foot.

He didn't even shrink from her. "But…I still don't understand. Why do you care so much?"

"Same reason you do."

"Hmm."

"I've had some fascinating chats with *Dr*. Carpenter and that Luriel. She's quite a little hottie in her way."

Stein didn't respond. Maybe he was trying to appear uninterested. Maybe she'd just beaten him into semi-consciousness.

"Maybe you didn't do it," she continued. "I'm open minded."

He still didn't respond.

"Strange that the grieving widow jumped into her so-called doctor's bed before the dirt even settled on hubby's grave."

His eyes momentarily widened, he opened his mouth, then he grimaced. Apparently he'd tried to fake a yawn but his jaw hurt too much to do it. "How long does it take for dirt to settle?" he asked. "I guess it must depend on the amount of rain."

Stein almost pulled off sounding like a wiseass, but one's throat doesn't constrict when mouthing off; neither does an already red face become yet more flushed.

"Well, just thinking out loud," she said, "if he were slipping the kielbasa to her all along, it could be that the two of them decided that it was time for Allen Rosenthal to take his place in the past tense."

Stein rubbed his swelling face. "You're smart, you work hard and you have a finely developed sense of irony. I respect that, but you're only a mediocre liar, so you should do it less."

"Perhaps you could even help us and yourself at the same time." She paused for three beats. "Seems this recently deceased she-male and Allen both had the same exotic form of clap." She paused again. "A few days before she was murdered, Carpenter did something that set her off on a world-class crying jag. If you could provide some explanation…"

It was hard to tell if he smiled or grimaced, but she wasn't going to get anything useful from him. Maybe she'd succeeded in planting a seed of distrust, maybe not.

"So, you underestimated me?" she asked. They all did.

"No, overestimated. I thought I hated you."

"We're done for now." She threw him a card. "Call me when you're ready to confess."

She stood over him, waiting for a smart-ass response.

His irregular breathing caused blood to bubble from his nostrils.

* * *

Saul took an inventory. He had several loose teeth. His ears were ringing. His nose probably wasn't broken. His vision was blurred, but it was recovering.

Thomas wasn't about to go away until the murderer was killed or convicted. He didn't want to frame Josh, but it was a choice between Josh and himself. Even factoring in the remote possibility that Josh was the son of God, Saul knew where he came out on that one.

Just the thought of Josh and Luriel sleeping together, preposterous though it was, made him furious.

He found it quite curious that Thomas was willing to jeopardize her career just to avenge her drug-addicted partner. Exponentially stranger, however, was the affection he felt for her even after she'd so brutally beaten him. He was changing rapidly. Was this what it was like to approach a great and glorious destiny? Somehow he doubted it. He was certain, though, that his rate of change would continue to escalate; but not, of course, nearly as quickly as Josh's.

XVIII

Saul, invisible, followed Luriel into Josh's office.

While enduring one of Josh's trademarked silences, she smiled that brilliant smile, which had been all too rare since Allen had died.

"What is it?" Josh asked.

That was the first time Saul had seen anyone break through Josh's silent treatment.

"I'm having dinner with Saul tonight. We're getting together with some of my oldest and closest friends. I just realized how much I'm looking forward to it."

Josh looked as if he'd just swallowed a live fish. Saul had warned Luriel that he might have to cancel because he thought he'd felt the initial signs of a migraine coming on, but now he felt terrific. Anyway, headache or not, he'd be there. And Josh wouldn't. He'd be nowhere.

"That's, uh, wonderful." It didn't sound as if Josh considered it the least bit wonderful. His silver-gray eyes narrowed, displaying uncharacteristic confusion.

"I can't quite believe it, but we're becoming close. I can really talk to him. That's very important to me. He makes me laugh, and that's what I need more than anything these days. And, well, I think he truly loves me."

Bewilderment spread across Josh's face.

She laughed.

"You're not considering…" Josh rolled over his hand.

"Maybe." Her tongue darted across her lips. "I consider quite a few things, as you know." Her feral stretch was followed by an erotic moan so faint that Saul wasn't quite sure if he'd heard or imagined it.

Josh swallowed hard.

"I told him that I was planning something wonderful for tonight. I could just feel his desire for me. It's *very* sexy to be desired."

Saul's heart was pounding so loudly that he feared they would hear it. He tried to control his breathing. He offered a silent prayer of thanks to Apollo. With Luriel by his side, he could learn to deal with his guilt. He might have a conscience now, but from his experience observing others, he knew that consciences were surprisingly accommodating.

"I need a man in my life," Luriel continued. "He's not someone I'd choose for the long term." She paused. "But I'm hardly capable of a serious relationship at the moment."

A guttural sound, part sigh, part protest, emanated from Josh's throat.

Saul comforted himself with the thought that short term had a way of drifting into long term without anyone quite noticing.

"Hey, haven't you always told me that I have to go where my heart takes me?"

Josh fingered a shirt button. "I didn't mean…"

Saul reminded himself of all the times he'd misread her, but his entire body was certain that this time he had her right. When he'd finally given up all hope of consummating their relationship, she started to come around. Wasn't that just the way it always happened? He would respond totally and completely, holding nothing back. He noted that the gods were coming through on their end of the deal. He had to come through on his.

After the session, Josh left, as usual, failing to turn off his computer. Saul backdated it then made an entry on Josh's alphabetical client list for Christine Hall, the runner Saul had murdered in Central Park. After typing her contact information, he put in, "I can't treat her; I'm terrified that if I'm alone with her I'll kill her." He set it to another date and made an entry for Meri/Mark Daniels, where he wrote "I'm so drawn to him/her. I hate/love him/her." He then revised the entry for former patient, Lorraine Reno, who, his research had revealed, was tall, blonde, slim and pretty: "I'm having trouble controlling my lust and hostility. I need to get help." Finally, to the entry for the diseased David Jaskiel, he added, "David told me about an incredible suit that makes the wearer invisible. He won it in a high-stakes poker game in Macao and swears it is untraceable. He promised to give it to me. I told him I don't know if I want it. I fear what I'd do if I had it."

He reset the computer's internal calendar and checked Josh's schedule. He had appointments until three and nothing for the rest of the day. None of these patients fell alphabetically close to the notations Saul had just typed, so there was little danger of Josh seeing them. He left the computer precisely as it was when Josh left. On his way out the door, he pushed the button in the lock so he'd be able to re-enter without buzzing.

* * *

Josh saw his final patient out and went to the bathroom. When he returned to his office, Saul, visible now, threw a net over his head, and pulled the drawstring so tight that Josh had trouble breathing.

Offering no resistance, but rasping like a marijuana smoker holding his breath, Josh said, "You know not what you do."

Saul swallowed hard, but he was beyond being thrown by Josh's biblical references. "Believe what you want." Saul led him to his chair, sat him down and tied him to it. "You've been fucking with my head."

"How's that?" Josh asked.

Saul loosened the drawstrings. His hands were sweating in his latex gloves.

Josh took a series of deep breaths.

"The wine, loaves and fishes—"

"Bagels and lox," Josh corrected.

"Meri, the tears and ointment."

"Detective Thomas seems to think you killed her," Josh said.

The thought that a few hours hence he and Luriel would be making love calmed him and steeled Saul to his task. "I want to hypnotize you to get to the bottom of this once and for all."

"I've been preying on your mind?" Josh asked.

"You have," Saul admitted.

"Have you been thinking about what you said at the shiva?"

Saul nodded, unsure of what part of their conversation Josh was referring to or, more important, why Josh had asked.

"I was quite impressed not just with what you said but how you said it," Josh continued.

Saul, unaffected by the irrelevance of Josh's statement, stared into Josh's eyes. They were pale gray and not the least bit intimidating. Saul had read that animals, once they realize that death is inevitable, cease to struggle.

"You can untie me, you know," Josh said. "I'm not going to resist. If this is where our destinies finally cross, so be it."

Confident that, if it came down to it, he could overpower him, Saul did so. Also, he thought that Josh, with his martyr complex, would welcome the opportunity to put himself in harm's way. He took Josh's mirrored pendant from his desk and began to swing it in front of Josh's face. He looked at Josh's willing gray eyes, confirming that they were following the mirror.

As Saul slowly swung the pendant, it took all his energy to concentrate. The objects on Josh's desk rearranged themselves. The helmet floated off its pedestal.

"You're relaxed," Saul said, forcing himself to ignore the signs of an oncoming migraine. "As you know, this is going to be quite pleasant." He found himself reciting the chant Josh had used when hypnotizing the wheelchair-bound man.

Josh continued to stare at the mirror as if willing himself to go into a trance.

Glancing occasionally at Josh, then turning away, Saul saw Josh's eyes darken.

When sure that Josh had gone under, Saul said, "At exactly seven thirty this evening, you will put on this suit." He showed him the invisible suit. "Go to Broadway and stroll up the middle of the roadway from 80th Street to 125th. Don't worry about traffic; the suit will protect you. When you walk into busses or trucks, you'll go right through them. This is a test of your faith."

You can't get someone to do under hypnosis what he wouldn't do normally, but Saul was sure Josh would do most anything to test or demonstrate his faith. Also, given what Saul had had him do on the night of the shiva, he knew Josh would do what he directed him to do. Strolling through traffic in the belief that he was immortal was more in character for Josh than forcing himself on Luriel.

Saul stowed the axe under Josh's couch—for the police to find later—then brought Josh out of his trance.

The prickly sensation, which he'd felt earlier in the day, reemerged. He took a Naratriptan, a cerebral vasoconstrictor that, if taken at this phase, generally stopped the headaches from developing or at least limited their severity. He went home to shower and nap, which, in concert with the drug and his optimism over the evening's promise, would make him fine by dinnertime.

* * *

At seven, Saul rang Luriel's doorbell. He was troubled by what he had done to Josh, even though he had repeatedly reminded himself that it was the only way with Thomas on his ass and that it was the price he had to pay to the gods for Luriel.

She looked terrific in her simple black cocktail dress, although it occurred to him that it was merely a more expensive, better-fitting version of the one Meri used to wear. He leaned forward to kiss her cheek. Instead, she gave him parted lips and darting tongue.

Moments later he was leaning against the doorframe for support, breathing hard.

"Oh, God, I'm *really* looking forward to later tonight," she said, holding his face in her hands. "To showing you just how much I appreciate what a good friend you've been to me."

He felt her breath on his face. She was almost as turned on as he was. "That kiss was, uh, really something." It took all his concentration to put together a coherent sentence.

"Wasn't it?" Her smile lit up the room. She ran her tongue over her lips.

He stared, trying to permanently implant the vision of her in his head.

"I'd have you in for a drink," she said, "but we have a seven thirty reservation, and I'd like us to be the first to arrive, since I'm the only one who knows everybody."

"Fine." Anything and everything was fine with him.

"Anyway, the way I'm feeling now, if you come in, I might never let you leave."

Saul, thinking he must look stupid, tried to stop grinning. "Where are we going, by the way?" he managed to say.

"Damascus."

"Damascus?"

"Not an easy reservation to get," she said. "*Time Out* just wrote it up, calling it one of the most beautiful in the city and the first truly gourmet Middle Eastern restaurant on the continent. Anyway, I thought it would be fun to go downtown. You said you wanted to get out of the neighborhood."

"Great," Saul said. "Is Peter coming?"

"Of course not. Some new problem with his son. Making plans with him is truly the toughest reservation in town."

* * *

In the cab to the restaurant, the symptoms, which had tentatively begun that morning, had then receded and then modestly reappeared in Josh's office, now returned in full force. Oncoming headlights blinked. He was bathed in sweat.

"Saul, are you okay?" Luriel put her hand on his thigh.

He couldn't see her: he'd lost his peripheral vision.

"No. I'm getting a migraine."

"Should I take you home?" She stroked his cheek.

"We're closer to the restaurant than to my apartment, but I might need to sit in a dark closet or something. Maybe it will just pass. Sometimes it does." He reminded himself that he wanted to be around other people and to be far from the scene when a speeding truck crushed the life from an invisible Josh.

The taxi stopped in front of a Doric-columned building with First Union Bank engraved in the portico. A bright red awning said "Damascus" in squiggly Arabic-like gold lettering.

Inside, the bar area was an Arabian Nights setting of floor-to-ceiling Oriental rugs and swinging brass lamps. In his pre-migraine state, it made Saul feel as if he'd taken several doses of bad LSD. Then his vision cut out entirely. The pain hit the right side of his head like one of Thomas's steel-toed boots. Then it landed on his left and the two forces made a pincer movement. His brain was being compressed, and his eyeballs felt as if they were about to be expelled from their sockets. He screamed.

"What should I do?" Luriel's arm was around his waist. "My companion needs to get to a dark room, even a closet will do," she said to someone, presumably the maître d'.

The pain was now going in and out like a European two-tone siren, but awful as it was, Saul felt his panic more acutely. "What time is it?"

"Seven twenty. Why?"

Being struck blind on the road to Damascus was the last straw. He took a deep breath, which momentarily cleared his head. He considered that maybe Josh had hypnotized him. Maybe his symptoms were a guilt-based psychotic reaction. But, no, there had been far too many coincidences.

After a moment of silence, he heard a click, then the words he feared he'd hear. A disembodied voice seemingly coming from all around him. "Saul, Saul, why are you persecuting me?"

He had to get uptown and had to do it right now; he had to save Josh. Sure, Josh might not be the Second Coming, but Saul was now convinced that he might be, and he was not prepared to kill Jesus, even for Luriel.

"Please, Luriel, help me into a cab."

"I'll come with you," she said. She screamed, "Taxi!"

"No. There's something I have to do alone."

"You're in no condition to—"

"I have to."

"Eightieth and Broadway," he told the driver when the cab arrived. "Please, go up the West Side Highway, get off at 72nd Street, then head up Broadway. I'll tell you where to stop. As fast as possible, please."

As the taxi raced, he regained his vision, but the pain was even worse. He tipped his head back and looked up through the cab's window. The dark clouds were the color of a giant swirling pus-filled bruise. Josh's voice kept repeating, "Saul, Saul, why are you persecuting me?" Each time he heard it, he pulled tighter into himself until he was compressed into the smallest possible space that his bones would permit.

The taxi stopped at 79th Street. Rotating flashing lights shot out from a pride of police cars and burned their way through his eyelids.

Squinting, he threw the driver a twenty, or maybe a fifty. "Keep the change. I'll walk from here."

He forced his way through the growing crowd, pushing people aside. "What happened?" he asked a uniformed cop. His head still ached, but he cared only about Josh and undoing the horrible thing he had done to him.

"Truck hit something, swerved into the divider."

A spasm shook his entire body. "What kind of something?"

"Hard to say. It was beaten up pretty bad."

"A person?"

"Get back." A policeman shoved Saul as a couple of men in ill-fitting suits walked by, detectives presumably.

"Keep the whole area clear," one of them commanded. "Street's closed until I say otherwise."

Lightning flashed repeatedly. Saul didn't know if it was real or in his head. He smelled ozone. Peels of thunder so loud that they landed with convulsive force were followed by a deluge. Josh's voice had stopped; he wasn't quite sure when. Saul slogged home through the downpour.

He was soaked through and cold. His eyes burned, and his head was being painfully compressed. Yet he could see himself more clearly than he had at any time since he was given the invisible suit. He now knew that he had in fact been chosen by God—God, not *the gods*—for a special destiny. But until now he'd tragically misunderstood the nature of his mission. His adolescent vision of the Greek gods—and most particularly Apollo, the dispenser of severe unwavering justice without forgiveness—was immature to the point of wrongheadedness. Fate wasn't immutable as the Greeks believed, but the result of one's own actions and, even after a lifetime of sin, was within one's capacity to change.

He called Luriel on her cell.

"Saul, I was worried. How are you?"

"Great," he said, meaning it. "I need to ask you a question." As soon as the words were out of his mouth, he realized he didn't need to ask her anything. He had to tell her. He was more sure of this than he had ever been about anything. "Josh really was—no, is—Jesus returned."

"Yes, I know."

He looked at the phone. She knew? Last time they'd spoken about it, she was full of doubts.

"I need to ask you a huge favor," he said. "Would you call me when you're at a phone you can comfortably talk from?"

"That's not such a huge favor."

He could hear her spectacular smile but no longer felt the erotic longing that it generally engendered. "No, but what I plan to ask of you is."

He fought his way out of his soaked clothes and, before hanging them up, dialed Thomas's number.

She answered on the fifth ring, "This better be pretty fucking important."

"Meet me for breakfast tomorrow, eight A.M., the Hotel Grande. Come alone. Bring no recording equipment."

"Who the fuck is this?"

"The man of your dreams. I'll be wearing a gray-and-black camel's hair and cashmere jacket, a custom-made blue-on-blue checked shirt and a red geometrically patterned Hermès tie. Make an effort to look presentable for a change."

He sat naked on his couch. He better be totally sure of this. Tomorrow morning, the die would be cast.

He was grinning. He was sure. And Luriel and the role he had chosen for her? He was sure of that as well. She fit in so perfectly that his meeting her had to be part of God's plan.

She called him a couple of hours later, and, after initially expressing understandable reluctance and begging him not to do anything precipitous, she agreed to his proposal.

He was awakened by the morning sun streaming into his living room. Apparently, he'd fallen asleep on the couch as soon as he got off the phone with Luriel and slept peacefully until it was time to shower and dress for his breakfast date.

XIX

Saul was sitting alone. Woody Allen was dining with Mayor Bloomberg at a table to his right, and Sandy Weill, the chairman of Citibank, was on his left regaling a nobody whose jacket sleeve buttons were undone to show off that his suit had been custom made. The others in the room were so rich and powerful that Saul couldn't afford to recognize them. The floor was robin's-egg-blue marble. The walls were hung with monumental paintings, each of which had originally hung in the palace of a king or grand duke. The coffee, kopi-luwak, was the most expensive in the world, every bean having traveled through the digestive system of a certain species of Indonesian monkey. The juice, all freshly squeezed, came from fruit specially cultivated at a secret location. Special baffles on the walls and ceiling and a high-tech hiss from the HVAC system made it impossible to overhear the conversations at the next table unless they were using bullhorns. The deals made in this room had changed the face of the financial world.

Saul had never been here before and wanted to try it before going away. Anyway, he thought his guest would get a kick out of it. A waitress wearing Chanel poured him juice and coffee, while a waiter in Prada brought over a steaming basket of fresh-baked croissants and brioches and an array of specially made marmalades, preserves and jams. Saul, staring toward the entrance, pointed to what he wanted. But for his headache, which had receded to the point of being background noise, he felt terrific.

The waitress returned Saul's smile with one of startling sincerity. Then Thomas stomped in. Saul was surprised how attractive she was in her simple black skirt and white shirt.

Saul waved, and she flipped him the bird.

A waiter held her chair, while others rushed over. "Coffee black, ham, hash browns, two eggs sunny side up," she said. "The *gentleman* is paying."

"Virginia country cured, or would you prefer our own prosciutto?"

"Virginia is fine." She turned to Saul. "So, okay, what do you have to say?"

"You haven't read me my rights. You agree you can't make use of anything I say unless we reach a deal. We've both agree not to record." He raised his glass. "The coffee is quite good." He decided she wouldn't be favorably impressed with the monkey-shit story.

"Once something is in my head, I can't get it out."

"Understood."

She had some juice. "You look like you've recovered from our last interaction."

"Interaction? Another four syllable word, and I report you to IA."

She laughed grudgingly. "Santos is in rehab. Best thing that could've happened to him." She looked around the place. "Trying to impress me?"

"Is it working?"

"I'm impressed all right, but not favorably."

"I'm prepared to plead to four murders."

Her face betrayed no emotion. "In exchange for?"

"No death penalty and a right to parole in, say fifteen years." He tore off a piece of croissant and spread marmalade on it.

"Why you coming to me?"

"Thought you'd like to be a hero. The one who cracked the case. Get you out from under your problems with the brass."

"So this is to reward me for being so good to you? Turns out that deep down, you're just nice?"

"Yeah, like you."

Saul felt gratified by her full-bodied laugh.

She squinted. "You do seem different. Relaxed, confident, almost human." She had some more juice. "Why should you avoid the needle?"

"'Cause you can't prove dick and never will."

"You'll slip up."

"No. I'm done."

"Why the plea?"

"Guilt."

She started to laugh but cut it off, presumably realizing he was serious.

"Anyone hurt in the accident on Broadway last night?" he asked.

"We got your suit and forensics is going over it."

"If you find anything on me, you can take the deal off the table."

Saul had always worn latex gloves when handling the axe or suit and full-body cotton underwear under the suit, Hanes's most common style which he'd effectively disposed of. Just the same, before giving the suit and axe to Josh, he'd washed them in almost every solvent known to man. While by now they were undoubtedly crawling with Josh's DNA and fibers, there was no way they could be tied to him.

"The oldest trick in the book is to talk plea with a detective, then bring in a high-priced mouthpiece to renegotiate."

"The oldest trick in The Book," he gently corrected, "is when Jacob put the sheepskin on his arm to mislead Isaac into choosing him over his other son, Esau."

She held up her hand. "My psychopath-led Bible classes are on Tuesday morning. This is Wednesday."

He smiled. Why did he find himself liking her? "We have a deal?"

"I'll take it to the D.A."

The waiter brought her breakfast, and she dug into it as soon as the plate made contact with the table.

"If he starts to give me a hard time, I'll get a lawyer."

Hungry, and realizing he hadn't eaten the preceding night, Saul gobbled down most of the croissant. A waiter brought over another.

"Including my art and everything, I've got just north of fifty mil," Saul said. "I'll give three each to the beneficiaries of the women I killed, other than Anne. I'm her sole heir, so it would just come back to me. Her will, as you know, had no alternative provisions so there's no one to challenge it, except possibly the state, and it will sign off on the plea. As part of my plea, my victims' beneficiaries will also agree to accept the payment in full settlement of all claims, known and unknown."

"Why would they do that?"

"Because without my plea, they'd be unable to prove a case, even considering the lower standard of proof in a civil matter than in a criminal one, and I won't plea unless they agree."

"So you get to keep all the rest of the money even though you got it by murdering your wife?" She pursed her lips, leaned her head back. "No way." She shook her head. "Try again. I'll never be able so sell that."

"A good negotiator wouldn't have bothered with that pursed-lips thing." He broke off a piece of croissant and spread a generous amount of marmalade on it. "Take it or leave it. But, if it makes you feel any better, all the money will go into an irrevocable charitable foundation, which I'm in the process of forming." He put the morsel into his mouth.

"With you as sole trustee, no doubt."

"Actually, I persuaded Luriel Redding to take the job. She and Josh Carpenter will have complete authority as to how to distribute the money. I won't control a cent—that'll also be part of the plea deal."

She swallowed a huge forkful, then said, "I assume that, being dead, Mr. Carpenter's role will be primarily passive."

Dead? "Have they found his body?"

"Not yet. Maybe you'll tell us where to look now that you've become such a nice guy and all."

They ate in silence.

"Why do I have the feeling that you have a plan and that turning yourself in isn't quite what it might appear to be?" she asked.

"Probably because I have a plan, and turning myself in isn't quite what it appears to be."

The waitress looked over. Saul pointed to Thomas's juice glass, then to his own.

"What was your impression of Josh?" he asked.

"Phony as a six dollar bill."

"I thought so."

"Yours?"

"Jesus Christ returned."

She laughed, but a cloud passed across her face. "You setting me up for an insanity defense?"

"My plan is less subtle than that." He had some croissant. "You know, Susan, I like you."

"Sure, I can see why. Given the nature of our past interactions and all." She had some coffee. "Hey, this stuff isn't bad; almost as good as Starbucks."

XX

At Attica prison near Buffalo, a guard with two black tears tattooed on his left cheek and wearing a black baseball cap with the legend "Jesus saves" led a handcuffed Saul down a long row of cells. Apparently that was what passed for entertainment up there, as most of the inmates were pressed against the bars.

"Hey, psychobitch," someone yelled. "You ain't going to like it in here."

Several blew obscene kisses; others spat. One of the prisoners tossed a steaming turd, missing the guard by no more than a couple of inches.

"We've got a special cell for you befitting your exalted station," the guard said to Saul. "Oh, small world. Turns out we have a friend in common. I was in the police academy with Juan Santos. Told him I'll look out for you."

The guard stopped, unlocked a cell, then the handcuffs. "Hey, Jacques," he said to the man inside. "Got some tight, fresh white meat for you. Don't say I never gave you nothing."

A huge black man sat up on his cot and licked his lips. His sleeves were rolled up to reveal Schwarzenegger arms covered with ribbed tattoos, symbols the meaning of which Saul decided he was best advised not even to guess at.

"Turn around, boy." The guard grabbed Saul's shoulders and twisted. "I want Jacques to see what he's going to be getting into." He pushed Saul down, which resulted in his behind jutting toward the man's face. It saddened Saul to realize that there was yet one more bad act that he'd have to do.

"Looks might tasty," Jacques said. "I owe ya."

"Ole Jacques here is a very powerful man, ain't you? All the jigaboos look up to him."

"If you say so." He smiled threateningly at Saul. "New guy don't seem to talk much."

"Maybe he's just nervous. You'll loosen him up."

Jacques laughed. "He don't smile, either. Can't tell if he got teeth."

"Probably won't for long. You'll share him with your friends, I hope." The guard shoved Saul. "In you go." He slammed the door, then grinned at Jacques through the bars. "Free time at three today. We're taking a little cigarette break when you fellas get settled."

"Heard you pled, though they couldn't prove shit?" Jacques asked Saul after the guard had departed.

Saul shrugged.

"Biggest mistake of your life. Never seen a rich white dude like you last six weeks in here."

"I killed four people." Saul saw from Jacques' facial expression that his answer didn't explain anything. "I thought I'd enjoy the comradeship and relaxed pace of prison life."

"You coulda gotten some fancy Jew-shyster to tell them you crazy, don't know right from wrong."

"But I'm too crazy to do that."

Jacques didn't smile.

"You get high in here?" Saul asked. "Drugs are called *tits*, right?"

"For the right price, I'll get you whatever you want."

"I got something for you, if you treat me right, roomie." Saul sat on the lower bunk, bouncing to test its non-existent resiliency. "I'll take this one. You take the top."

Jacques punched Saul in the face. Saul's head hit the wall four feet from where he'd been sitting. Over the ringing in his ears, he thought he heard, "You got a lot to learn, bitch."

Saul saw stars. "You've just lost out on the best high of your life, boy," he said.

"What you talking 'bout?"

"I know hypnosis. I can put you in a trance and activate the pleasure center of your brain to release dopamine, like cocaine does. But I can give you ten times as much. It would make a gram of Florida snow seem like a thimble of beer."

Jacques swung again, but Saul managed to slide out of the way so he was just caught with a glancing blow—sufficient to send him crashing to the floor.

"Bad idea to lie to me, bitch." Jacques recocked his massive fist.

"Sure, that's it. I want to share a fifteen-by-fifteen cell with a peculiarly smelly three-hundred-fifty-pound black dude who's mad at me." Saul waved his hand in front of his nose. "But it don't matter. It won't work if you're scared." He shook his head. "As my mother always told me, bullies are big scaredy-cats."

Jacques rocked back to put all of his weight into his next punch.

"If I do hypnotize you, and it's the best you ever had, then you'll protect me?"

Jacques looked at him as if he realized that Saul was truly insane. "Sure."

Saul held out his hand. The man's paw wrapped all the way around it with plenty of room to spare.

"You have something shiny?" Saul rubbed his throbbing jaw.

Jacques worked out from the mattress stuffing a razor blade stuck into a toothbrush handle. He passed the blade to Saul. "Don't get no ideas."

Saul cut a piece off the sleeve of his prison jumpsuit and made a string, which he tied through a hole in the blade. "Sit comfortably and relax." He swung it in front of the man's eyes. "Look at the blade."

"Relax," Saul repeated. Then he chanted Josh's incantation.

When Saul brought him out of his trance, he asked, "How do you feel?"

"Relaxed."

"So, you'll be my protector in here."

"It's more like you'll be my bitch. This hypnosis shit will be just a tiny little part of your job description." He hit Saul in the stomach and laughed as Saul writhed on the floor struggling to breathe. Then he kicked Saul out of the way and used the toilet in the corner of the cell. When he was done, he commanded, "Wipe me, bitch."

Saul complied, then climbed into the upper bunk. His new life was starting pretty much as he had thought it would.

The cell doors opened. "Come on," Jacques said. "Time to meet your new friends."

The prisoners were lined up along a wall and marched down to a large open room with tables and chairs bolted to the pitted linoleum floor.

"What's over there?" Saul pointed to doors at the far end.

"Showers," Jacques said. "You could probably use one."

"Good idea." Saul smiled. "Thanks."

The guards left the room.

Jacques and a half-dozen large black men trailed behind Saul. The rest of the prisoners, nearly a hundred men, followed with their eyes. As soon as they got through the doors, inmates grabbed each of Saul's limbs. Jacques tore Saul's jumpsuit. They bent him, exposing his buttocks to Jacques, who was stroking his huge uncircumcised penis.

XXI

Wind and salt spray rushing through her hair, it occurred to Luriel that she liked being rich just as much as she thought she would when she was growing up poor and resentful in blue-blooded Greenwich, Connecticut.

She executed a series of perfect turns as her shoulder glanced across the azure water. She'd begun planning to acquire Saul's money from the day Allen jumped out of that window and Detective Thomas had planted the thought in her mind that Saul had some hand in the matter. That night, when he'd shown up at her apartment laden with gourmet food and wine and revealing himself to be insane, she was open to believe the worst. He'd told her that Josh saw himself as Jesus returned and apparently found that to be quite unsettling. She thought she could use his superstitious nature to her advantage, and her probing that evening confirmed it.

Her adolescent dream had been to sail a twelve-meter yacht in the America's Cup and do a photographic book on it. However, when she was finally in a position to carry through on it, she'd instead bought a big chunk of a tropical island off the coast of Brazil, one of the best places in the world for her newly chosen sport. She'd wanted a total break with her old life.

In the past seven months, she'd missed only eighteen days of windsurfing, and she was in the best shape she'd been in in a decade. Quite an accomplishment as, nine weeks before, she'd given birth to a gorgeous, healthy boy.

Another surprise was that she needed other people much less than she used to think she did. She had plenty of friends whom she'd flown out—and flown back—on a whim, but, except for the windsurfing junkies and her slew of servants, she was alone most of the time. She was quite content, particularly now that being alone meant being with her child. Achieving one's fantasies can be a tragedy for some, but motherhood, even more than riches, was all she'd hoped it would be and more.

As soon as she came to shore, her board-groom ran over to take control of her board. Then she rode her private funicular up three hundred feet of sheer cliff to her grand home.

She was excited that Josh was visiting for a few days. Seeing her private jet land a few minutes before, presumably with him on board, was what caused her to come into shore. Yet she knew that a few days was pretty much the outer limit of the time that she would be happy to have him around. She, of course, was ever grateful for the miracle he performed. Their son, Adam, was nothing less than that. However, lately, Josh seemed to believe that he was exactly who Saul said he was.

"It's wonderful to see you," Josh said after a long lingering kiss.

She wholeheartedly missed those kisses. Given the extraordinary effect they had on her, they were minor miracles themselves. She edged him out to the lushly landscaped veranda for some unrestrained lovemaking cooled only by the Atlantic winds. She hoped they would still be at it when the Southern Cross rose, and, if that hello kiss was any indication, he was of a like mind. Physically, they'd always functioned fabulously well together, even from that first afternoon when she seduced him.

Looking back on it now, she was embarrassed that her initial motivation had been to enlist Josh in her plan to bring Saul down and, in the process, to obtain his money. The unrelenting money problems of her youth—which had a painful reprise when Allen stopped working and she left her corporate law job—acting in concert with the hormone rage following her abortion and Allen's suicide had temporarily pushed her over the edge, and she'd lost sight of her basic values. Well, it all worked out.

She smiled, thinking of their *therapy* session when she teasingly spoke of her big plans that evening for Saul, jokingly using double entendres to make it sound as if she planned to have sex with him. God, what a disgusting thought, even kissing him that night had turned her stomach. Thomas's accusations having taken root, she'd suspected that Saul, invisible, was sitting in. For her plan to work, he had to believe she wanted him.

"I've been watching Adam," Josh said. "He's just so wonderful."

"Yes, he is, but let's let him sleep for a while." She pulled him close. God—and she used that term loosely—he felt good.

* * *

It was evening. Her expectations had been fully met. They rested on a king-sized chaise under the stars. Luriel was breastfeeding. Josh was staring with childlike fascination.

"Do you still think I'm a con-man?" he asked.

"I never thought that."

"No, not in quite those words." He snuggled into her side. "You do know that I took the money you gave me only because it makes my work, getting around and all, easier."

"Yes, money makes things easier. That's one of the reasons people like it so much."

"I have no recollection of my life before I came to New York."

"Murdering someone in the belief that you were Azrael, the Moslem angel of death, must've been quite traumatic, particularly given your sensitivities," she said. "Undoubtedly that severe stress interfered with the hormones that form memory."

He smiled, presumably remembering an earlier conversation of theirs on the subject. "That I'm the Vancouver murderer was just Detective Thomas's supposition," he said, managing, as usual, not to sound defensive.

"She showed me a picture of the guy. He bore an uncanny resemblance to you."

"Aren't both Azrael and Jesus manifestations of the same God?"

She looked at him crossly.

"I speak fluent Aramaic and Hebrew; ancient, not modern. Explain that."

She caressed his smooth, firm stomach. "That could prove to be quite useful if Mel Gibson ever makes another movie—a sequel to the one that caused such controversy."

"Why are you always so cynical?"

"Me?" She kissed Adam, who'd drifted off to sleep, a drop of milk hanging from his tiny lips. "I'm completely taken with the miracle of birth, the beauty of this place, the wonders of life. I'm anything but cynical. I'm just agnostic to atheistic on the subject of my lover being Jesus Christ reincarnated."

"I never claimed to be the son of God."

"And you've never denied it either."

"How do you rationalize these scars on my hands?" The moonlight glinted off them.

They were beautiful hands, huge but gentle. "How do *you* explain the absence of scars on your feet? Jesus was flayed with whips, yet your back is unblemished. Indeed, if you're reincarnated and were given a new body, why would you have scars at all?" She tenderly covered his open mouth. "This is the point in the conversation where you accuse me of being a lawyer," she said, smiling.

"Or a sophist." He removed her hand and smiled back. "I've stopped asking you to marry me. You should appreciate that."

"Yes, definite progress. I—"

"I know. You need time to emotionally regroup after—"

"You know I hadn't the slightest idea what Saul had in mind for Allen." Unlike her lover, she frequently sounded defensive. "And, in case you're about to start feeling guilty again, neither did you."

"Do you feel any guilt or doubts about the tricks we played on Saul?"

"He deserved worse than he got. If we hadn't intervened, he might've gotten away with everything *and* killed you in the process."

Josh took a deep breath followed by another, as if he were only now discovering how pure and sweet the air was.

"He's been redeemed by love." He paused. "By *my* love and miracles."

Sometimes she found it difficult to tell when he was joking. He had a subtle sense of humor, when not taking himself too seriously. But, of course, anyone who thought of himself as Jesus Christ was taking himself pretty damn seriously.

"Josh." She stroked his cheek and spoke slowly, enunciating every word. "I, you, and a professional magician playing the role of a lawyer/guest did the water to wine and loaves and fishes tricks," she reminded him. He had an amazingly selective memory. "You hypnotized Saul, then paid…" The woman's name escaped her. It all seemed so long ago.

"Mary Magdalene." He filled in the blank.

"Meri Daniels," she corrected as she remembered.

"Whom we got killed." Josh stood then sat as if he were lifted and pushed down by a huge hand.

"Unknowingly." Yes, sure, that part of it didn't make her feel so good.

"He heard voices. Me calling out to him. I read about it in the *Post*."

"Jesus, Josh." She handed him the sleeping baby. "And I don't mean that literally."

She went inside, still naked. The servants scurried away. She took a microcassette recorder from a drawer and brought it out. "Remember this?"

It was clear from Josh's blank expression that he didn't. A matter of conscious choice, she was certain.

She hit play. Josh's voice, loud with a slight tremble, "Saul, Saul, why are you persecuting me? Saul, Saul, why are you persecuting me?"

"I played the tape for him, then threw one of these recorders with another copy into the cab with him." Finally, she saw recognition in Josh's now melancholy gray eyes. "The guy was on the verge of flipping his lid," she reminded him. "We just pushed him over the edge."

"And you got rich." He stood. "You've never quite understood that the wondrous thing is that hundreds of people, Saul included, have come to know God, and, if he and I have our way, it will eventually be billions of people."

"Not a bad deal all around." In response to a cool wind—one of the few drawbacks to living in one of the world's premier windsurfing locations was that it was windy—she covered her son, threw on an exquisite designer dress as if it were a bathrobe, then tossed Josh his pants. "Are you still planning your…" She struggled to come up with a euphemism that didn't sound euphemistic. "Next step."

"*Our* next step. You promised to help me."

She grimaced but then nodded.

"I plan with your assistance to run into Peter Simonson," he reminded her, "cure his son via hypnosis and get him to throw the money and prestige of his foundation behind us. Peter will be the rock on which I build my church."

She rolled her eyes. "And if your hypnosis and chanting doesn't work?" Her tone indicated that she meant *when* rather than *if*. "He's been to the most renowned specialists in the world."

"It's a matter of historic fact that Jesus, like me, was a Hasid, a term that goes back thousands of years, not to be confused with modern Hassidim." Josh's eyes darkened from blank slate-gray to agenda-driven charcoal. "They worked miracle cures."

It always made her uncomfortable when he did that with his eyes. "That was back when people believed disease was caused by devils and evil spirits," she said. "They were susceptible to the power of suggestion."

"And now they believe in something else. A hundred years hence, current ideas about medicine will seem as quaint and ridiculous as using leeches to bleed people."

She again rolled her eyes. "Josh, scientific experiments show—"

"Experiments in the eighteenth century conducted by some of the greatest minds of the Enlightenment confirmed the salubrious effect of leeches.

Indeed, I understand leeches are making a comeback, something about a chemical they secrete into the blood that affects clotting. Any responsible scientist will tell you that we truly know so little about the way the body really works that it's frightening." He smiled. "Anyway, I've found hypnosis to be more effective than the power of suggestion."

"So you will *return,* thereby fulfilling the *prophecy*?"

"Sure, my plan from the beginning was to come here, find a Saul and a Peter and found a new religion."

Religion sure made for some strange bedfellows.

XXII

On Saul's first day in prison, Jacques and his friends had been just about to enjoy him in the shower when Saul snapped his fingers. Jacques yelled, then collapsed onto the floor, agonizingly curling into a fetal position. As he bucked along the floor, he screamed as if he were giving birth to a rhinoceros.

The men stared fearfully at their fallen comrade. Jacques, making scrotum-tightening sounds, wriggled into the main room. His eyeballs, spiderwebbed with red, oscillated. His head bonked on the floor, and a foamy blood-specked froth bubbled out of his nose and mouth.

The prisoners were on their feet surrounding him, but making sure to keep a sufficient distance just in case he was contagious. Saul stood calmly, like a lion tamer watching one of his charges perform a difficult trick.

"Please make it stop," Jacques wailed.

"In retrospect, I gather, you concur that it was a most grievous error to attempt to violate me." Saul spoke slowly, enunciating each syllable. "Well, it is an eternal truism that hindsight is twenty/twenty. Don't you think?" Saul screwed up his face. "No, on reconsideration, it occurs to me that it is perhaps twenty/forty or even forty/twenty." Saul watched Jacques writhe in agony. "I'd be most curious as to your views on the subject, but I imagine we can all agree that hindsight distorts in its own ineffable way."

"Please make it stop."

The guards were nowhere to be seen.

"My shoes are scuffed," Saul said. "Lick them."

Jacques did the best he could.

"Now, beg some more."

"Please, God, please."

Saul laughed. "If you want to be my slave, you'll have to do better than that."

After more pleading, Saul snapped his fingers, and Jacques sat. He was breathing hard and had a bloody nose and a large bump on his head.

"You haven't changed your mind about being my slave, have you?" Saul raised his hand, putting his thumb and forefinger together as if he were about to snap them again.

Jacques shrank from it. "No, master."

"I'm going to take a shower. Jacques, get me another jumpsuit. Mine seems to have gotten torn." Saul turned to the assembled. "If any of you would like to try what Jacques tried, be my guest." He turned, dropped his jumpsuit to the floor, and strode through the doorway.

* * *

As he had every morning since shortly after Saul's arrival at the prison eight months before, except, of course for the Sabbath, Jacques Baptiste—whom Saul had released from servitude the day after the showers incident—woke just before sunrise. He stood, lifted the tefillin off the little shelf he'd built for them, then took the *shel yad* and placed it upon the bicep of his left arm, adjusting it so it rested against his heart. Before tightening the strap, he recited the *L'ho-niach Tefillin.* He'd gotten better at it. At first his mind would wander, and he'd have to start over. He fastened the strap, winding the two coils over the leather extension to form the Hebrew letter *shin.* He made seven coils on his forearm, then wound the rest of the strap around his palm. He placed the *shel rosh* on his head so the knot was just above his neck, and the box containing the most ancient of prayers was centered midway between his eyes. He then unwound the strap in order to make three coils on his middle finger and wound the remainder around his palm. He recited the *Al Mitz-vas Tefillin* before adjusting the strap, then chanted, "Boruch shem kiv-od malchuso l'olam vo-ed." He followed with the English, "Blessed be the name of God's kingdom forever."

The same words echoed from the other cells.

While waiting for his incarceration, Saul had realized that his comments at the shiva, which had so favorably impressed Josh, were those about the need for religion to require demanding ritual but to avoid both a privileged hierarchy and the doctrine that its ways are the only ones acceptable to God. He then carefully formulated a loving and tolerant creed that Josh would have found pleasing.

Converting Jacques had been easy, as he was already in Saul's thrall. That Jacques had a commanding position within the prison social hierarchy gave Saul's movement instant credibility when the two of them began proselytizing. Saul was proud that not only had they so successfully transformed the spiritual life of the prison, but that they had done it, not by hypnosis or bullying, but with supreme confidence, simple homilies and setting the right example—much like Jesus himself had done. He regretted that he'd caused Jacques pain on his first day there, but at the time, and even in retrospect, it seemed that it couldn't have been helped.

At sunrise, the cell doors slid open, the majority of the prisoners lined up silently against the far wall while the single guard benignly looked on. Then they marched down to the cafeteria.

Saul stood in front of the room as the men got their ritual breakfast of berries, yogurt and granola. Not that there was anything magic about the choice of foods. They were healthy and tasty and the most exotic fare Saul could negotiate with the warden. But Saul believed that a daily ritual was essential to keep the faithful faithful. That and the desire to follow Josh's ways was why Saul had introduced Josh's morning tefillin ritual, complete with Hebrew prayers, to the prisoners. It took the intercession of the Manhattan Legal Foundation and the ACLU to persuade the warden that the men's First Amendment right to free expression of their religion overrode the danger that they would make garrotes out of the leather straps.

Once Saul had converted Jacques and they had converted several other of the prisoners' leaders, the rest was easy. The men, having so little to occupy their minds or souls, and having been disappointed by the flaccid emptiness of the religions of their childhoods, flocked to embrace Saul's love-infused teachings with even more fervor than an earlier generation of inmates had embraced the hate-tinged message of Elijah Mohamed and Malcolm X.

Saul pointed to a heavyset man in his mid-twenties who was in for grand theft auto. The man walked to the front. "My goal for the week is to convert one member of the Aryan Brotherhood," he said. "I had the urge for heroin yesterday, but I fought it successfully. Bruce spat at me. I turned away."

One by one, the men talked about their goals for the coming days and the triumphs and tribulations of the preceding ones. Then an inmate, chosen at random, read from the scripture.

When it was Saul's turn to speak, he said, "Good morning, all. I've been giving thought lately to the historic origins of Christianity."

While he spoke simply, making no effort to impress, he was the focus of enthralled attention. His off-putting awkwardness, all too evident in his past life, had disappeared. Looking into the admiring eyes of his fellow worshipers, he made a mental note to speak on the evils of slavishly following anyone and to develop that thought in the gospel he was drafting. Josh had chosen him in part for his talent with the written word, and, in preparation for his role, Saul had studied St. Paul's letters to the Corinthians, Galatians and Ephesians. He'd been writing several hours a day, and his published articles had already made converts on the outside.

"Early Christianity went wrong when it became a political organization. Roman Emperor Constantine convened the Counsel of Nicaea in 325 A.D. in an effort to unify the Church and thereby the Empire. They decreed that God was, in fact, three Gods in one, a concept that had more in common with Roman pagan gods than the God of the Jews and the early Christians. You see, Christ and his followers were deeply religious Jews, and that fact was a P.R. embarrassment for the leadership who wanted to distinguish themselves from the Hebrews. So, weeding out those Gospels that didn't fit the party line, they codified the malicious fiction that Jews killed Christ, leading to two millennia of vicious persecution."

The inmates, almost to a man, had a ravenous appetite for knowledge. They loved history. If one went into the prison computers that night, he'd see that they each contained multiple searches for Emperor Constantine, Early Christians and Counsel of Nicaea.

"Do you believe what I just said?"

"Yes!" many shouted.

"I don't. It's not true. It's but one of many biased versions of the truth. There is not one story of Jesus or the church, but many. And they belong not to history, but to you. The church hierarchy has always been made up primarily of men trying to do good, and, like all of us, sometimes they did better than at other times. Sometimes they were misguided, but that can be said about anyone. Couldn't it?"

Many of the men looked to the person next to them, smiled, nodded, then bent their heads.

Although he spoke quietly, he fell into the cadence of an evangelist. "Anyway, the sad fact is that for the next sixteen hundred plus years some in the church made unchristian war on so-called heretics—frequently people more pious than themselves. This was a grievous error, and one which we will *never* repeat." He pounded the table in front of him. "It is an insidious and dangerous fiction that one religion has the ear of God. God's will is far too complex for us to understand."

"Yeah," several yelled. Cheers filled the room.

"By the way, doubting and questioning your faith is a good thing." He slipped out of the evangelical tone which he found to be disturbingly showy. "Even Christ had doubts. During a night of doubt, he cried out, 'God, why hast thou forsaken me?' Sounds particularly human to me. What do you think?"

* * *

Detective Thomas's phone rang during her post-coital cuddle with her new girlfriend, the proprietor of a hip downtown restaurant. She checked caller ID. "Fuck." She kissed her companion. "I need to take this." Then she said into the phone, "This better be fucking important."

"Turn on the TV, Channel 10, CNN."

"Juan, are you high again?"

"Wish I was."

She grabbed the remote. "I need to humor my partner," she said to her friend.

Larry King came on the screen. "We're here in Attica, New York, to speak to a remarkable man who over the past weeks has burst onto the national radar, sparking thought and controversy. Saul Stein, an admitted serial killer, has started a new religion, and, in the process, completely transformed this once notorious penitentiary. It is now functioning with a quarter of the guards it previously had. For all intents and purposes, the prisoners run the place. There have been no significant acts of violence in almost a month; previously a day wouldn't go by without one." Larry King wore a black shirt with a solid silver tie and silver braces that were perfectly matched to the color of his combed-back hair.

There was Saul, smiling like a Goddamn Buddha. He wore his orange prison jumpsuit so it looked like relaxed vacation garb.

"So, Saul, you believe that Jesus returned to earth, in the form of a therapist working in a run-down Manhattan office?" King smiled condescendingly. "He made his presence known to you via a series of miracles eerily reminiscent of those mentioned in the Bible, then he directed you to start a new religion. Is that about right?"

"Close enough, Larry, sans the cynical excrescence," Saul said. "And yet more remarkable still, he'll be back within the year, because his job is not yet done."

"And then he will usher in the true Messianic Age?" King asked.

"No, that's our job."

"Your creed has been characterized in *Time* as 'Early Christian,' and in *Newsweek* as 'Judaism with a heavy emphasis on redemption, or Christianity with little emphasis on the afterlife.' And, of course, both publications spoke of your belief that this Josh is the Second Coming and is certain to return in our lifetimes."

"Yes, that's what those magazines said."

"What if this Josh/Jesus doesn't show?"

"Well, then I'm just another fraud, aren't I?"

"Fair enough." King was leaning forward as if about to be won over, even converted to Stein's bizarre creed. "So to what do you attribute your remarkable success at Attica?"

"People need religion, and the existing ones haven't done a very good job of serving those who need them most." Saul looked directly into the camera, his eyes wide, almost innocent, his face open and free of guile. "I'm not referring just to prison inmates but all of us who are troubled and unsatisfied. But back to prisoners. They thrive when given the tools they need to lead a positive God-serving life. Note I said *God-serving,* not *God-fearing*. It is better to love and be loved than to be feared." Saul smiled. "Also, I guess it was easier having a captive audience."

King returned Saul's grin. "And this Joshua/Jesus of yours—"

"He's all of ours," Saul corrected. "He came to New York, for the same reason that he originally came to a corner of the Roman Empire. It's the communications center—the best place to start a worldwide international movement."

"But then he conveniently disappeared after choosing a murderer as his appointed messenger on earth?"

"Not such a bad choice. I've already made it to *Larry King Live*."

King laughed as one would at a bar with a best friend.

"I think he chose me because I'm a good communicator and have a lot of energy and a story likely to get media exposure." Saul paused as if he were accustomed to accepting applause. "If a psychopathic killer can be transformed by love, wouldn't it be even easier for a better adjusted person?"

"So your god is quite media-savvy? King held up one finger as Saul was about to respond. "Your ads for Shredded Wheat featuring you chowing down under the caption 'cereal killer.' Any doubt in your mind that they're in frightfully bad taste?"

"Money for the cause." Saul shrugged. "Even apostles can enjoy themselves."

"Let me see if I've got this right. Your image as a serial killer is helping you market your religion?"

"In a recent survey, both Ted Bundy and David Berkowitz out-polled every United States senator and congressman as someone the respondents would most like to share a beer with. Sure, the president and vice-president of the United States nudged out the killers, but there seems to be a question whether that was because they were perceived to be more or less evil than the killers."

"But—"

"I believe Jesus returned with a goal in mind—to bring God to a humanity sorely in need of Him—and I've chosen to dedicate myself to that goal. I've made a positive contribution to the lives of many of the inmates." Saul's smile was brilliant, yet warm and even modest. "Larry, you're welcome to join us."

"Well, I'll keep an open mind." King sounded as if he were seriously considering it. "I understand you're writing a new gospel."

"I guess that's just one of the reasons I'm being denounced as a heretic from pulpits all over the country."

"Any truth to the story that a group of Southern Baptist churches have put a million dollar price on your head?"

"Several of the inmates tell me they've been approached with some pretty extraordinary offers."

King furrowed his brow. "You don't seem worried."

"I suppose I'd be as good a martyr as the next guy, but so far everyone they've solicited has decided that killing me wouldn't be a very Christian thing to do."

King leaned forward, serious, sincere. "So tell us, Saul, it's time for the truth, are you redeemed, or are you just playing us?"

Saul sat back and stroked his chin thoughtfully. "I'm not completely sure. Maybe time will tell, maybe not."

"Fuck," Thomas said as she smashed her finger into the power button on her remote.

"I read his pieces in *The New Yorker*," said her companion, while she continued staring at the now-dark screen. "He's actually quite remarkable."

"Yeah, maybe even as remarkable as Jeffrey Dahmer and Osama bin Laden combined."

* * *

On visiting day, a guard handed Saul a long list.

He scanned it, making checkmarks next to those whom he had the time and inclination to see. "Please apologize to the rest," he said.

"Anybody interesting today?" the guard asked in the tone he used with close friends and family.

"Possibly."

Saul took his accustomed seat behind the Plexiglas divider. He was free to meet with his visitors in the rec room, but he preferred it this way; made for easier crowd control and helped the guards move people through.

"This is a nice surprise," he said.

"His idea," Thomas pointed to Santos.

"Of course, ever the Doubting Thomas. I was pleased to hear you were reinstated, Juan." He smiled. "There are a number of your fellow officers who've joined us."

"Suckers are born every minute," Thomas said.

"Find out anything on Josh?"

"Disappeared," Santos said.

"Check his fingerprints, DNA, etc.?"

"Dead ends," Santos said, staring at his partner.

Thomas opened her mouth as if to add something, but Santos shook his head, and she closed it.

Saul wondered what they weren't telling him. "I gather you're still investigating the charges that I killed him?"

"That's right." Thomas's eyes became narrow and hard. "If we can prove it, it's beyond your plea agreement, and you get the needle."

"He's not dead," Saul said.

"Be nice if he'd tell us that," she replied.

"He will."

She leaned forward and dropped her voice as if she were about to share a secret. "What's your real play here?"

He shrugged. "What you see."

"Founding a new religion?"

"My comrades are happy."

"Meaning your dupes?"

"Most of them are freer and happier than they've ever been."

"I guess there's something to that," Santos said, more to his partner than to Saul.

Saul noticed that Santos was more clear-eyed then he'd ever seen him. "Join us."

"Actually, I've been thinking about it," he said.

Saul fixed Thomas with a stare.

"My girlfriend has been taken in by you," she said.

"A steady relationship? There's a step up."

"So far."

"I gather in Thomas-speak, you just agreed to consider it, too?"

"I consider a lot of things."

About the Type

This book was set in Qurio, a type face designed by the Greek mystic Apollo Creed during the Fourth Crusade's sack of Constantinople in 1204—two hundred fifty-one years before the printing of the Gutenberg bible. The purchase of more than six books set in this type bestows a state of grace and eternal life on the purchaser.

Printed in the United States
31250LVS00001B/326

9 781413 739312